PROMISES
BOUNTY HUNTERS 3

A.E. VIA

PROMISES PART 3

PROMISES PART 3
Published By: Via Star Wings Books
Copyright © June 2017
Edited By: Ally Editorial Services
http://allyeditorialservices.com/
Cover Art By: Jay Aheer of Simply Defined Art
Proofreading By: Carra Saigh @ Making It Happen Book Blog
Formatting & Illustrations By: Casey Harvell of Fancy Pants Formatting
http://www.fancypantsformatting.com

All rights reserved under the International and Pan-American Copyright
Conventions. No part of this book may be reproduced or transmitted in any form or by any means, electronic or mechanical, including photocopying, recording, or by any information storage and retrieval system, without permission in writing from the author, Adrienne E. Via.
No part of this book may be scanned, uploaded, or distributed via the Internet or any other means, electronic or print, without permission from Adrienne E. Via. The unauthorized reproduction or distribution of this copyrighted work is illegal. Criminal copyright infringement, including infringement without monetary gain, is investigated by the FBI and is punishable by up to 5 years in federal prison and a fine of $250,000 (http://www.fbi.gov/ipr/). Please purchase only authorized electronic or print editions and do not participate in or encourage the electronic piracy of copyrighted material. Your support of the author's rights and livelihood is appreciated.

A.E. VIA

CONTENTS

Chapter One	5
Chapter Two	11
Chapter Three	19
Chapter Four	25
Chapter Five	33
Chapter Six	39
Chapter Seven	47
Chapter Eight	55
Chapter Nine	65
Chapter Ten	81
Chapter Eleven	85
Chapter Twelve	95
Chapter Thirteen	105
Chapter Fourteen	113
Chapter Fifteen	121
Chapter Sixteen	131
Chapter Seventeen	139
Chapter Eighteen	147
Chapter Nineteen	153
Chapter Twenty	159
Chapter Twenty-One	165
Chapter Twenty-Two	171
Chapter Twenty-Three	183
Chapter Twenty-Four	189
Chapter Twenty-Five	193
Chapter Twenty-Six	201
Chapter Twenty-Seven	213

PROMISES PART 3

Chapter Twenty-Eight	223
Chapter Twenty-Nine	231
Chapter Thirty	241
Chapter Thirty-One	251
Chapter Thirty-Two	257
Chapter Thirty-Three	267
Also by A.E. Via	271

CHAPTER ONE

Ford

Ford walked into the busy restaurant with his brother close to him, just a half step behind, like always. Both of them ignored the heads that turned when they moved towards the hostess stand. It wasn't uncommon for people to stare. They weren't drop dead gorgeous, they were just huge. At first glance they could be mistaken for twins, but Ford was two years older than Brian. Both of them stood at six three and a half, with thick upper bodies and solid thighs to match. Courtesy of twenty-two years in the military. Ford would probably still be leading his SEAL team if he hadn't been court-martialed and dishonorably discharged five years ago.

"How many in your party tonight?" The wide-eyed hostess asked when Ford approached. He watched her take in his form before responding.

"Just two," Ford answered.

"Do you mind the bar area? We have a high top ready now." She smiled.

Ford looked back at Brian, who gave a curt nod.

"That's fine," Ford answered.

She scribbled a couple marks on the dry erase board on her podium and picked up two menus before politely asking them to follow her.

His heavy motorcycle boots were loud on the hardwood floor. The thick silver link chain that hung from his belt loop wasn't attached to his wallet, but to the gold bounty hunter's badge in his back pocket. A few men sitting at the bar gave them the side eye as if they needed to watch their backs, but he and Brian weren't the bad guys... they only looked like it. They missed nothing as they took their seats and waited for the hostess to place their menus in front of them. Ford was already scanning the patrons, looking for anything out of the ordinary, while Brian made sure all entries and exits were clear. They weren't paranoid, it was just years of conditioning and training which had made vigilance an ingrained habit.

"What you feel up to tonight, man?" Ford asked Brian.

Brian shrugged, picking up his menu. They'd been here often. It was one of their favorite restaurants. It was a chain establishment, nothing too fancy. On their rare days off he liked to go out and eat with his brother instead of ordering in or microwaving something.

"I'm sure you're ordering a burger." Brian signed to him.

"No, smart ass. I'm getting a steak tonight... I've earned it. This was one shitty week," Ford answered. He didn't have to sign back to Brian, who could hear just fine. His brother wasn't deaf, he suffered from selective mutism.

Brian smirked at him and glanced back down at the menu insert. The waiter came over with a broad smile on his face, his eyes fixed on Brian when he spoke.

"Evening. You men look like you brought your appetites tonight."

It couldn't have been more obvious that their server was gay. His soft features, sweet voice and blond highlights were hard to mistake. Brian looked the waiter up and down, showing that he liked what he saw, and their server definitely noticed it, his delicate cheeks tinging a faint shade of pink. Ford knew the young guy was going for friendly and personable, but Ford wasn't in the mood. He kept his face stoic when he answered. "Yeah, we're ready. Give me whatever ale you got on draft tonight—"

"And for you, sir? Or would you like the special tonight?" The waiter cut Ford off, eager to focus on the more handsome brother.

"He'll have the same," Ford bit off.

Brian looked at him with a slight frown then looked back at the confused waiter. It had to seem odd that Ford was possessively answering for his brother. They looked too much alike to be on a date. It was clear they were related. Usually, Brian didn't care either way. He didn't speak and it was rare he wanted to use his text to speech device when they were out together. Ford noticed that lately his brother had been putting a little distance between them and he couldn't figure out why. He wasn't Brian's keeper, but it'd been his job to look out for him since they were knuckleheads back on the farm in West Virginia.

"Sure. I'll be right back with those." The waiter murmured and walked off.

Brian was glaring at him. Ford barked a hushed, "What?" He could see a slight tick in Brian's jaw. "What, Brian?"

"Nothing, damnit." Brian signed with a couple of jerks of his right hand.

The waiter returned with their brews just when Brian put his hand down. The glint of arousal that had been present in the petite waiter's hazel eyes was now replaced with sorrow. This was what Ford hated, what he wished he could protect his brother from. When people looked at Brian like a man to be pitied. His brother was fierce and brave, not to mention one of the smartest men he knew. But all people thought of him when they saw him signing was "Aww, poor thing can't talk."

"Have you decided what you'd like? A selection of our popular appetizers are half price tonight." The waiter wasn't making eye contact with either of them and he definitely wasn't looking at Brian like he wanted to be chosen as his dessert anymore.

"Bri. The burger, right?" Ford asked.

PROMISES PART 3

Brian nodded, his mouth set in a firm line.

"I'll have the T-bone, medium rare, with a loaded potato and he'll have the mega burger, medium, no onions, with fries." Ford handed the menus back and took a long guzzle of his cold beer, wishing he could enjoy it without his baby brother scowling at him. "Are you trying to piss me off? Because if so, it's working."

Brian's hands started moving in rapid, tight motions, a clear indication he was mad. *"Why do you have to do that? Clearly he was flirting with me and you had to jump in and piss on my fucking leg again, which looks creepy as fuck, by the way."* Brian gulped down half his beer and slammed it back down on the table.

"He was too young," Ford murmured. "He was just being a tease. Or looking for a quick fuck."

"You don't know that. And what is wrong with a quick fuck? Do I look like a goddamn monk to you, Ford?" Brian shook his head tiredly. *"Or you think I can't get laid without using an app and a warning disclaimer."*

Ford turned up his mug to drain the rest of his beer. He knew Brian used hook-up apps. Most of the guys that responded were aware he didn't speak before they met up with him. Ford was the one that recommended he use an app after his brother had found it difficult getting a date. Most men didn't mind a roll in the hay with him, but that's where it would usually end. Brian was deeper than that. The last piece of shit he was in a relationship with ended up walking out on Brian in the middle of the night, claiming he "Couldn't do it anymore." Couldn't handle a man that couldn't communicate without an electronic device. Ford grimaced when he set his glass down. The look on his brother's face ate away at him. He was a good man and he deserved the best. He'd suffered in the worst way for his country. "Stop being dramatic. I always order the food. What's going on? You been in a shit mood for weeks. You need some ass that bad, then do something about it and stop bitching."

Brian's lip twitched before he flicked his brother off and signed for him to order them two more beers. That was their relationship. Ford would be annoyingly overprotective and Brian would bite his head off, then they'd have a drink and it was over. A brotherly relationship didn't get any closer than theirs. Ford had sacrificed his reputation, his career, and his team's lives to save his brother, and there hadn't been a single day he'd regretted it.

When their food arrived, Ford asked, "How's your therapy been going? You haven't mentioned it in a couple weeks."

Brian wiped his big hand over his mouth.

"Brian?"

Brian looked his brother in the eye.

"Goddamn you. That was one of the most sought out speech therapists in the state, Brian. Maybe he can help," Ford argued. "Why'd you quit going to him?"

"I didn't quit. I just need a little time, okay. Lighten up."

"Time for what? You want to speak again, don't you? You said you did. So what's—?" Ford stopped in the middle of his thought when his eyes traveled to the front door and caught on the man staring at him. "What's he doing here?"

Brian turned around and looked towards the front door. *"Maybe he's here to eat, just like everyone else. That girl he's with sure looks like she could use a good meal."* Brian signed.

"I thought he'd dumped her," Ford scoffed.

Brian frowned. *"Why do you care?"*

"I don't," Ford snapped back, making Brian look at him quizzically. Ford didn't underestimate how perceptive his brother was and he could definitely pick up on bullshit. Ford waited for the waiter to put down their plates and quickly distracted himself, loading his potato with butter to ignore the nervous flutter in the pit of his stomach.

PROMISES PART 3

CHAPTER TWO

Dana

He wasn't in the mood to be out tonight. He'd had two bond hearings this morning and a huge recovery today that left him irritable and sore. All he'd wanted was to go back to his place and have a carton of milk and a freshly delivered pizza. So when Jessica called and asked him to take her to happy hour, he'd refused, but she was nothing if not persistent. They'd gotten back together after an amicable break up last month. They'd both decided that he was too busy and she deserved a man who could shower her with the kind of attention she demanded. Imagine his surprise when she called him a couple weeks ago, claiming she'd made a mistake and she still loved him. Even now, Dana didn't know why he'd agreed to give it another shot. He hadn't been able to make her happy before, no matter how hard he'd tried.

His job as a bounty hunter was demanding and time consuming, the hours irregular, but he loved every minute of it. Working for Duke and Quick at Duke's Bail Bonds and Recoveries was a dream come true for a roughneck like him. His father used to tell him he'd never amount to shit, but look at him now. He was a decorated marksman, worked for one of the most respected men in Atlanta's criminal justice community, owned his own condo, and had a team that loved him. More than that fucker ever accomplished. Only thing he'd like to add to his successes was a loving wife… or husband.

Dana could almost feel Ford's commanding presence when he walked into the crowded restaurant. He was sitting in the bar area with his brother, Brian, appearing to be having another one of their heated exchanges. He couldn't help but think: *What has Brian done now?* Ford was always on his younger brother about something. Dana knew this because he was with them so much. When Ford and Brian were first brought on by Judge, one of Duke's business partners, Dana didn't know what to think of the two ex-military men. One *didn't* talk, not *couldn't* talk, and the other was brooding and intimidating. Dana wasn't a small man. He could hold his own. He had broad shoulders, muscular arms, and a fit body, but Ford was in a whole other category. Fucking massive.

"What are you looking at, honey?" Jessica squeezed his hand, looking up at him.

Dana swallowed when he noticed Ford wipe his mouth and sit back in his chair, those midnight eyes boldly glaring at him from across the room. Like he was daring Dana to bring his ass over to him.

What the fuck is his problem now? He'd be damned if he'd let Ford intimidate him. He never had before and he wouldn't now. He started walking, his long legs eating up the distance between him and his coworkers, Jessica's short legs double-timing to keep up. He kept his eyes locked on Ford's. When he got to their high top he saw they were just starting with their meals.

"What's up fellas? Didn't expect you two here. What's going on?" Dana asked, ignoring Jessica's tight clamp on his arm.

"Eating," Ford said drily.

Dana stared at him for a couple tense seconds. "No shit." He liked the way Ford's jaw tightened and his eyes narrowed. Jessica eased back a little when Dana widened his stance. "Um. This is Jessica. Jess, this is Ford and his brother Brian. You may not remember me mentioning them."

"Oh, yes I do," she said, a little too cheerfully. She could sometimes overdo it and come off as fake and insincere. "It's nice to meet you both. Sorry for the intrusion."

Ford didn't say anything, so Dana turned his attention away from him and spoke to Brian. "I'll let y'all go ahead and finish up. I'm trying to get back home soon."

"What happened to the game?" Brian signed.

Ford jumped in to translate his brother's words. "He said 'What—?'"

"I know what he said." Dana cut Ford off and turned back to Brian and signed in not so perfect ASL. *"She got mad."* Dana shrugged. Brian had been teaching him a little sign language during their long days on surveillance duty or waiting at the courthouse for a bond. From the stunned look on Ford's face, it was obvious he didn't know, or maybe he wondered why Dana bothered to learn to communicate with Brian in the first place.

Dana wished he knew more ASL. But he couldn't say what he wanted to out loud and he didn't know how to sign *"My girlfriend whined until I agreed to take her out. Yes, I fully intended to stay home and enjoying the game... alone."*

"I didn't know you knew sign language, honey. Aww. That's great that you can talk to him. Can I speak to him? Can he read lips?" she said innocently, not realizing her words were a bit insulting. Brian was a grown man, not a toddler.

"He can hear you, Jess. But let's go eat, I'm starved," Dana said quickly. He had to get Jessica away from them because Ford looked like he wanted to curse. Dana knew Jess didn't mean anything by it, she simply didn't understand Brian's disability. Dana waved, getting an "It's all good" look from Brian and a pissed off sneer from Ford before he left.

He moved to a table a few up from Ford's and sat down. He picked up the drink menu, needing something to cool him off. He didn't know why Ford got under his skin sometimes. He jerked his head up when he heard Jessica loudly clear her throat.

PROMISES PART 3

She stood there in front of her chair with her arms folded across her chest. "Do I have to pull out my own chair, Dana? Geez. Be more rude."

Dana got up and walked around to the other side and pulled her chair out, trying to ignore Ford's eyes that were still on him. Jessica sat daintily in the seat and placed her expensive bag on the chair next to her. He scooted the chair in and looked up at the amused smirk on Ford's face. Dana mouthed, "Fuck you" and sat back down.

Dana ordered the largest burger on the menu regardless of Jessica's comments about how gross and fatty the selection was. After she ordered a glass of Chardonnay and a grilled chicken Caesar salad, she immediately started in about how stressful her day had been at the upscale boutique she managed. Dana fought off his urge to yawn, remembering how much that pissed her off. He threw in the occasional "Mm hmm… yeah… right… oh really… ya don't say" at all the right places while he waited for their food. He refused to look behind him to see if Ford and Brian were still there, but he hadn't seen them leave. He didn't hear Ford's voice, although neither he nor his brother were strong conversationalists. They were most likely watching the pre-game show that was showing on one of the many flat screens positioned around the bar. Damn, he wished he could be sitting with them. He looked up just in time to see that the Mets were already on the field warming up. He was about to divert his eyes back to Jessica when an update flashed across the bottom of the screen that one of his favorite players was still on the injured list and wouldn't be playing in the game tonight.

"Dana! Are you even listening to me? That's so rude of you to watch television while I'm speaking." She batted her long lashes, looking like her feelings were truly hurt.

"I just noticed something. No big deal. I heard what you said." Dana rubbed his forehead, wondering why he'd gotten back together with Jessica. He didn't like rejecting anyone and he especially hated to see her upset. His father always told him he didn't have a backbone and would constantly get run over. Maybe that's why he couldn't tell her no.

"Oh yeah? Then what did I say?"

Um. Something about wanting to—

"Here's your Caesar, ma'am." The waiter interrupted just in the nick of time.

Dana took a large gulp of his Miller draft. He wouldn't mind something stronger, but he was driving. And hard liquor after a bust made him restless at night.

He ate his burger quickly, wanting to get home by at least the fourth inning. He wiped his mouth and signaled the waiter for another beer while Jessica daintily ate her salad. He cut his eyes to the television and back to her while she talked non-stop. When they first started dating, he thought it was cute the way she rambled on, thinking she was nervous around him. But he soon found out that she was simply in love with her own voice. He groaned internally. He and Jessica had very little in common. He admitted that he'd gone out with her because she was gorgeous, educated, and came from a cultured family. He never thought a woman like her would be interested in a simple man like him. A man who knew more about the new A22 long rifle by Savage that was coming out in 2018 than he did about the recent presidential election. He could talk all day about rimfire cartridges and the shoo-ins for the American Marksman competition next month but he was clueless about pop culture, which happened to be Jessica's current topic of conversation.

"I can't believe she would let Brad go. I mean, her standards are a tad high if you ask me. I guess you reap what you sow. She did steal him from Jennifer." She elegantly wiped the invisible dressing from the corners of her mouth and sipped her wine. "You're sexier than Brad, honey. I love it when you wear that leather coat and those boots. Makes me feel like I'm dating a bad boy."

PROMISES PART 3

"I'm not wearing it as a fashion statement, Jess."

"Obviously. Otherwise, it'd be name brand." She pushed her half-eaten salad away and quickly pulled out a compact mirror from her purse.

Dana ran his fingers through the long hair on top of his head and looked down at his worn jacket. It'd seen better days, especially after this afternoon's recovery.

She spoke to him between applying a fresh coat of lip gloss. "We have some new Varvatos leather jackets coming in next week. They're only six fifty. I could put one to the side for you. You could even use my twenty percent discount."

"You're shittin' me, right?" Dana said, feeling even more exasperated and tired. "Six hundred and fifty dollars. For a coat?"

"That's on sale. It's a great price. No need to thank me on the discount." She smiled like she'd really done him a favor.

"I appreciate it, but no thank you, Jess." Dana tossed his napkin into his empty plate. He waved to the server for the check since Jessica appeared to be finished with her food.

"Oh, wait. I wanted another glass of wine. It's been a day, sweetie."

"I'm ready to go, Jess. It's been a fucked-up day for me too, ya know." *Not that you asked.* "I wrestled with a three-hundred-pound man today. I'm really tired." Dana turned his mug up to down his last gulp when he was hit hard in the center of his back by a hand heavy enough to leave a bruise. Most of his beer flew out his mouth from the surprise impact, jerking him forward so hard the table rattled. Jessica gasped, her eyes lurching upwards at the hulking figure behind him. Dana knew who the fuck it was.

"My fault. Just wanted to say bye," Ford grumbled. He clamped his thick hand down on Dana's shoulder and squeezed, but Dana didn't give him the satisfaction of the pained grunt that threatened to escape his clenched mouth. "You two have a good night."

Ford walked away, Brian right behind him. Brian gave Dana a quick nod and kept moving. The few people gathered near the door hurried out of their path. One guy even stopped to hold open the door for them.

"Well that was childish and uncalled for," Jessica said, looking repulsed and offended. "Are you okay, sweetie?"

"Of course, I'm fine." Dana kept his growl low. He wiped the beer off his chin with the back of his hand, glaring at Ford's broad back. *Motherfucker.*

PROMISES PART 3

CHAPTER THREE

Ford

"Brian," Ford called out before his brother could get out of his truck. He saw the look of exasperation cross his face, but Ford didn't care. "I want you to go back to the therapist. I'm calling tomorrow to schedule you another appointment, don't—"

"I can make it myself." Brian signed angrily.

"Fine," Ford snapped. "I'll be here at seven."

"I'll drive myself or ride with Dana." Brian got out of the truck and jogged up to his small duplex. He watched his brother wave to his nosy neighbor before unlocking his door and going inside.

Ford scrubbed his hand over his short hair. He knew he was being rough on Brian but he also knew his brother had the mental strength to beat this disability. It was going on five years since he'd spoken. They'd had countless tests and evaluations done by some of the best doctors in the country and all of them said the same thing. Without using their complex medical jargon – in nutshell – Brian would speak again when he put his mind to it. Ford drove the eight minutes to his own one-story home just a few blocks from Brian's. When his brother forced him to move out two years after they were back stateside, he probably wasn't expecting his big brother to move right around the corner from him. Ford couldn't help it. Even at forty-six years old, he still had a familial urge to stay close to his baby brother, just in case he needed him again.

His brother was ex-Special Warfare, just like him. He didn't need anyone to fight for him. But Ford had always been the big brother and carried himself as such. When Brian joined the Navy, Ford was able to pull back and let his brother stretch his wings. Give him the freedom and space he needed to become his own man. But when Brian was captured by extremists in a foreign land, those overprotective feelings within Ford surged back to the surface and burned through him with a vengeance.

Ford killed the powerful diesel engine in his RAM 2500 and strolled up the dark driveway. He didn't like security lights or a bright porch. His senses were finely tuned enough to sense anyone's presence. He could move easily in the dark and he knew his property. When he went inside he didn't bother turning on the living room light. He went straight to his bedroom and began removing his clothes. He tossed his black jeans into the pile with the rest of his laundry. Most of his wardrobe consisted of black shirts, dark jeans, or fatigues. He'd been on surveillance for the past couple weeks, and Duke typically preferred that they be ready at all times to blend into the shadows.

The steaming shower was exactly what he needed and he let the hot stream massage the knots in the back of his neck. Lately his brother hadn't been the only one short on patience. Ford didn't know why seeing Dana at the restaurant irked his nerves. Damn, couldn't he get away from him? He was always there. Yes, he worked with him. But for some reason, Duke thought they complimented each other. Dana was a marksman. Ford was a scout and specialist in close quarter combat… that wasn't a compliment. In the Navy, scouts and snipers worked hand in hand, but that kind of discipline wasn't ingrained in Dana. Ford was about his business and his brother. Dana was about chasing the next skirt first, then work. Seeing him with that silly woman again really got under his skin. Ford had heard Dana talking with Duke's partner, Vaughan, about the way she'd treated him before their last breakup. What kind of man would tolerate that? Ford didn't consider Dana weak, he'd proven himself many times over the few years he'd been employed by Duke, but he had a hard time understanding why men put up with some of the antics their rude girlfriends dished out… just for some ass at night.

Ford stepped out of the shower, drying off with a scratchy towel that was too small to fit around his waist. He looked around at the untouched space on his way to his one dresser. His home was bare and desolate. He didn't have a partner to make his room nice for and he was fine with that. He had plenty to deal with without that kind of distraction. His brother barking at him every five minutes was enough. Relationships required a type of work and dedication that Ford couldn't fulfill at this stage in his life.

He'd had some damn good times, tapping asses with his team back in his enlisted days, but those years were gone. Ford dropped down on the edge of his full-sized bed and reclined back on the firm mattress. He didn't think about his days as a Special Warfare Scout anymore. Couldn't reflect long on the experiences and battles if he wanted to protect his sanity. He still missed it. Bounty hunting was as close as he'd get to quenching the thirst of his need to hunt.

It was too quiet. He turned on the television to stop the random thoughts playing out in his head, the station already tuned into the game he'd been watching at Bennigan's. He smirked when he remembered how Dana tried to steal glances at the ball game while eating with his girl. Ford watched her bite his head off the moment she caught him. *Idiot*. He was probably back at his place right now receiving his compensation for playing the ever-attentive boyfriend.

Ford abandoned the thought of Dana fucking his woman. He didn't need the visual. He pulled on a pair of boxers and got in bed, tucking his .45 under the extra pillow beside him. Looking at his high-tech watch – which was synced and exactly like those worn by his entire team – on the side of the bed, he noticed it was almost eleven. Early for most people, but Ford figured he might as well go ahead and try to get some sleep. They had training early tomorrow. Duke and Quick made sure they stayed conditioned for suspect takedowns and didn't allow their submission techniques to get rusty. Ford liked Quick as an instructor, and the martial arts expert he hired was knowledgeable in his field. Ford knew plenty about subduing suspects but he was never cocky in thinking he knew it all. He prided himself on always being prepared, and that required regular training. He hoped he was partnered with Duke tomorrow, because after slapping Dana on his back when he walked by him in the restaurant, the man was undoubtedly eager to get a retaliatory cheap hit in on him when they sparred. Sure, the slap was probably uncalled for, but Dana needed some sense knocked into him. Ford felt the need to be the one to do it.

Dana

"I really don't like the guys you work with, Dana. I mean, what was that? He assaulted you right there in front of everyone," Jessica complained from inside the bathroom. She'd just gotten out of the shower and was rubbing a heavily floral-scented lotion over her arms and legs while he watched the highlights of the game. He didn't pay much attention to her, she always had something negative to say about everyone he associated with. But he didn't like her talking shit about Ford or Brian. They were good men. Men he respected.

"*Those* men fought for this country, Jess. They've been through things you couldn't imagine," Dana retorted. When she huffed a sigh, he took a long gulp of his beer, happy he could drink freely now that he was back home.

"I don't care what they did. That doesn't mean they can go around putting their hands on people." She came out of the bathroom wearing a pale pink sheer nightgown that stopped just above her smooth thighs. "I don't like them. And they were rude to me, interrupting the conversation when I was talking."

Dana didn't grit his teeth, but he wanted to. She was so privileged and sheltered, he knew it'd be pointless to try to get her to understand.

"I wish you'd leave that job. I think you can do so much better," she said softly, straddling his lap. He saw the sexy gesture for what it was. A way to distract him.

"I love my job. I keep people safe, Jess. *We* keep people safe."

"Oh yeah? How?" she purred, stroking his bare chest.

"What do you mean, how? You know what we do. We take dangerous criminals off the street and make sure they appear in court or serve their time. You'd be amazed how many fugitives walk around you every day. Some of them are—" Dana moved her hands away. "Never mind."

"I didn't mean to offend you. I simply recognize your potential, honey." Jessica began to work her lean hips on him, her soft blonde hair falling over his face like a sweet-scented waterfall. "There's nothing wrong with a lady wanting her man to succeed."

"I am a success." Dana's voice was betraying him along with his cock. She was winding on top of him while she degraded him. "Maybe not by *your* friends' standards."

"Shh. We don't have to talk about that right now. I'd rather you stop scowling at me like that and put your hands on me." Jessica bent down and peppered kisses on his neck, trying to get him in the mood. Honestly, it didn't take much for him. She smelled of expensive bath oil, the one that left her ivory skin soft and supple. He closed his eyes and dropped his head back against the thick cushion. If only Jessica would like him for him, but lately all she seemed to do was tell him what he could be… what she wanted him to be. "Go brush your teeth so you can kiss me."

PROMISES PART 3

"What?" Dana opened his eyes and gripped her shoulders, pulling her back so he could look at her face.

"You know I hate the taste of beer. You've had like four already." She shrugged, leaning back in to his neck. "Maybe a shower, too."

"Get up," Dana snapped under his breath. He kept his voice calm. He was too tired to argue. He waited for her to climb off him, trying not to take it personally that she didn't want to kiss him or touch him unless he was fresh from the shower. Didn't matter he'd already showered before he picked her up, the thought of him smelling like the public and beer was too much of a turn-off for her. He went in the bathroom and closed the door. *What the fuck am I doing?* He turned on the shower and rinsed himself again. When he finished, he brushed and flossed just in case and came out wearing nothing but a towel. When he pulled his cover back he noticed she'd changed the sheets while he'd been in the bathroom. They weren't his, either. This wasn't the first time she'd come over with her own expensive sheets and towels. Like his shit wasn't good enough. She didn't say anything, just remained focused on the text she was typing on her phone. He pressed power on the remote, plunging them into darkness. He wasn't even in the mood anymore. From the way she turned over, still conversing with whomever she was this late at night, she obviously wasn't either.

CHAPTER FOUR

Dana

Dana pulled up to the gym and put his classic Chevy Nova in park. He rubbed his tired eyes, wishing he'd gotten more sleep than he did. Jessica ended up texting and talking on the phone with numerous friends until early in the morning. He asked her repeatedly to keep it down but all she did was rub her manicured feet up and down his legs, never breaking stride in her conversation. He looked over when Brian tapped his arm. He understood when Brian signed, asking if he was okay.

"Yeah. Just didn't sleep well."

Brian leered, raising his eyebrows. He signed very slowly and dramatically so Dana could recognize it. *"Long night with girlfriend?"*

"Not in the way you're thinking, hound dog. I wish that was it."

"Shot down?"

"Not really. I'm jumping through fuckin' hoops again, man. It's embarrassing to even say that. I got to let her go. We're not gonna go the distance, so why am I even kidding myself. Hell, we're not even going to make it another month."

"Why?"

"Because she can barely stand anything about me. Or anything about me outside the bedroom, and now even that room is having problems." Dana looked up when Brian motioned a few words he couldn't put together. "I have no idea what you just said, Brian, but it's probably not good, anyway."

PROMISES PART 3

Brian pulled out his phone and pulled up his text to speech app. He tapped a few keys before Dana heard the male computerized voice through the speaker. *"Why did you even take her back? Last I remember, you said she could be mean and demanding."*

"She is demanding and a bit naïve. But mostly, she's gotten even more stuck up than before. It's like I'm a project to her, man. Someone she can mold into the perfect man she can bring home to Daddy Warbucks. Then she'd have her bad boy in bed and a proper one with impeccable manners on her arm at her society functions. I shouldn't've taken her back. But she promised things would be different. I guess it was wishful thinking on my part. Besides, I been feeling… about. Oh never mind. I'm gonna break it off before things get too far, ya know."

Brian clamped him on his shoulder and nodded his head for them to go inside. Being late wouldn't be overlooked by Duke. He was never in a good mood when Vaughan was out of town.

"Hey, why'd you want me to pick you up, anyway?" Dana hefted his bag onto his shoulder and held open one of the wooden doors to the gym.

"My car's been having problems and I haven't had time to get it to a shop and I didn't want to ride with Ford. He's been in a worse mood than Duke lately, and frankly it's pissing me off."

Dana laughed as Brian continued to type and walk to the locker room.

"He needs a life… and a rough fuck, if you ask me."

Dana's smile fell slowly. Even the computerized voice couldn't extinguish the fire he felt from hearing those words. The thought of Ford's strong hips hammering into some woman was too much for him to visualize and walk upright at the same time. He stumbled behind Brian, but thank goodness Brian didn't hear the shuffling. When they walked into the locker room, Quick was there leaning against the lockers, talking on the phone. He wore a black track suit and his long hair was pulled back into a ponytail and braided down his back. He gave them a brief acknowledgement when they walked past mouthing "ten minutes."

Dana turned at his row of lockers and just barely kept himself from tripping again when he saw Ford standing there shirtless in nothing but a pair of long, black nylon gym pants. It wasn't often he got to see Ford's chest, but goddamn, when he did, he appraised it with his eyes as inconspicuously as possible. Jet black hair that laid beautifully across firm, bulging pecs. So big you could pour water in the valley between them. Dana's eyes flicked downward for the briefest of seconds, to the slick trail of hair that disappeared into Ford's waistband. He wished he knew how much hair was down there, covering his abdomen, around the base of his dick. He was sure his thighs had a vast amount on them too. Ford was a bear in its most gorgeous form. Dana's mouth watered, his skin flushing with heat. Had it been that long for him? That long since Fisher walked away from him?

Ford's coal-colored eyes glanced up at him, his thick brows going down into a slight frown before he turned back to pull a black wife beater out of his bag. He didn't know why Ford looked at him the way he did, like he hated him and valued him all at the same time.

"What's up, Ford. Ready for this training?"

"You're paired with me today. Question is, are *you* ready?" Ford answered. His voice was rough, as though it was the first time he'd spoken all morning. His dark beard, coupled with that penetrating glare made him appear menacing. Eyes that were wise and mature spoke words that Ford's mouth didn't have to. Dana continued to look at him, refusing to avert his eyes. Ford didn't intimidate him. He knew what the man was capable of, and all it did was intrigue him rather than scare him. He felt sometimes that Ford considered him a lesser man. He was sick of people doing that to him – underestimating him. He had his own unique talents that he contributed to their team, he deserved respect and he was damn sure going to demand it from Ford.

"Hell yeah, I am. Don't think I'm going to hold back on you, old man." Dana winked. He meant it as a joke, but the way Ford straightened, the muscles in his neck tightening, Dana knew he didn't catch the humor. But he'd be damned if he was going to back pedal.

Ford walked up to him, putting them nose to forehead. Dana tilted his head up a fraction, squaring his own sculpted shoulders as he waited to see what Ford had to say. He was shocked when the back of his bicep was gripped and a thick forearm crashed over his chest, slamming him back against the lockers. Dana gritted his teeth at the force of the blow and grabbed onto Ford's biceps, feeling them flex under his palms. They were huge, solid. Dana knew he wasn't going anywhere until Ford released him… and he secretly liked that feeling. He looked up into Ford's eyes, a slight smile appearing, to show he wasn't scared.

"Grin all you want, you cocky little shit, but I'll show you what this old man can do when I get you on that mat." Ford ripped his arms away and walked up the row, turning the corner without a backwards glance.

Dana pulled in a breath of air and ran his hand over his chest where Ford's arm had been. He felt hot and mildly embarrassed. He thought he'd played it off well, though. He should've known Ford wouldn't take the joke for what it was. The man had no sense of humor… when it came to him, anyway. Dana had seen Ford laugh with his brother and smile when he was going over the latest military gadget he was able to get on the underground web, but lately the man refused to humor *him*. Dana dropped down on the small bench between the lockers. His big mouth had just written a check that his body was going to have to cash. Ford would be more than happy to teach his thirty-three-year-old ass a lesson in respecting his elders.

"Your bounty will not expect you to wrestle with him. Getting him on the ground is the best way to subdue him. Rush him, catch him off guard." Quick walked back and forth across the mat, his muscular arms clasped behind his back while he instructed. Quick was an eighth degree black belt. He'd been studying martial arts since he was a boy. Hell, even Ford and Brian together couldn't take him down. He was fast and a master at counter-maneuvers. You had to be able to get your hands on him first to do anything to him, and that was pretty much impossible. So Dana could respect Quick as a teacher. "Don't second guess yourself. There's no time for that. If you have an opportunity, take it. Got it?"

Everyone nodded their understanding. Duke stepped up. His black and gray hair was thick and disordered. He looked confident as always, but his eyes couldn't hide his concern. "I called the extra training session this month because I've been contracted to go after a couple pretty big fish. These two brothers – Raymond and John Grossman – are well-known meth dealers here in Atlanta. They were bonded out on a five hundred thousand-dollar bond each but failed to appear a month ago. These men are dangerous. They have security, armed guards. They have money and lots of contacts, meaning plenty of places to hide. We're going to have extensive hours of surveillance and scouting ahead of us. We're going to finish training here then reconvene at the office for a strategy meeting later today. We gotta bring our A-game, like always. We were brought on because we know how to do this shit, so let's get ready." Duke looked back at his business partner. "Alright, Quick. Let's get started."

Ford moved back, letting him catch his breath. Dana was panting and sweating all over the place. They'd moved on from counter attacks to take-downs and submissions. Quick was giving them pointers while he demonstrated on the other martial arts instructor employed by the gym. Ford kept dumping Dana on his back every time he came at him. Although Ford never cracked a smile, it still looked like he enjoyed seeing Dana down there in pain, his face a mask of frustration as he tried to gain the upper hand.

"Dana, stop letting him get his arms around your thighs, goddamnit! You're overthinking it!" Quick barked.

"Pair me with Duke or something. How the hell am I going to take Ford's big ass down?" Dana fussed back, slowly getting back up on one knee.

"Are you saying you can only take down smaller men? If you are, then you are useless to me." Quick was in Dana's face, his forehead bumping into him while he pushed him back. "What's size have to do with skill? You've seen me take down Brian and Ford. Both of them are bigger than me. You've seen Duke take down men twice his size. Defeating your opponent only takes skill and confidence, Dana, and you've got both of those in spades, so use them. Now get your ass back in position and stop bitching or I'll have you riding a goddamn desk while the real men do the work."

When Dana got back in front of Ford, the bastard couldn't resist returning the wink Dana had given him in the locker room. "Now you be sure to take it easy on this old man."

"Fuck you," Dana grumbled, crouching down again.

"No. I'll leave that to your prima donna girlfriend."

Dana stood up, wondering what the hell business that was of Ford's. "Jealous?"

Ford grunted an angry breath. "Of what? Being a fool just to get some bougie ass from a stuck-up bitch?"

Dana rushed at Ford like an idiot, shoving his shoulder into his midsection, trying to take him down. Ford folded his heavy body over Dana's back and dropped all his weight, slamming him down face first to the mat. The air rushed out of him and he struggled to breathe with the massive man pinning him down. Ford's reverse bear-hug had Dana's arms wrapped so tight, he felt like he was in the grip of an anaconda. The crazy part was, Dana didn't hear or see anyone coming to his aid. Obviously, this wasn't a technique they were learning.

Ford's mouth was by his ear, his hot breath fanning over his heated skin. "Pretty shitty sneak attack, boy."

"Boy?" Dana hissed, his face flat to the mat. "Why are you always talking shit about her, huh?"

Ford's hold around his entire upper body kept him from being able to do anything but snarl his frustrated words. "Why, Ford? You've been an ass ever since I got back with her." Dana struggled, getting more pissed off by the second. "Answer me. Why don't you want me with her?"

"Because you deserve better than that," Ford said too quietly for the other guys to hear, and let Dana go.

When Dana rose up, he saw Ford's broad back heading towards the locker rooms. Quick stood with the other guys, a confused expression crossing his face before he turned away, shaking his head in disgust. When Dana walked by, Duke grabbed his arm. "Whatever's going on between you two, you better fix it, and fast. I need the two of you working together, not against each other."

"It's all good," Dana said with little conviction and headed to the back of the gym.

Dana was coming through the locker room doors just as Ford was coming out with his bag slung over his shoulder. He hadn't even bothered to change out of his sweaty clothes. Dana frowned, hoping they could talk this shit out. He refused to let Duke pull him off the streets because he and his partner had personal beef. Ford might be okay with that, but he sure wasn't. Dana grabbed Ford's bicep when he tried to brush by him. "Hey."

Ford looked down where Dana's hand held him. It took a few tense seconds before Ford's eyes traveled up Dana's upper body to his face. When they finally locked eyes Dana thought he saw something in Ford's hard glare, but it was gone before he could process it. "Did you mean what you said?"

"I never say anything I don't mean." Ford's voice was gritty and harsh but his words weren't. "You deserve better than her."

Dana couldn't help staring at Ford's firm lips and the sexy, dark hair surrounding them. He wasn't sure when they'd inched in closer, but somehow they were face-to-face. "Did you have someone *better* in mind, Bradford?"

Ford's mouth parted a fraction but nothing came out. When it looked like he was about to answer, the locker room door burst open – a maintenance man – breaking whatever link was building between them. Ford pulled his arm away and turned back to the door, never answering Dana's question. If only they hadn't been interrupted. Dana growled in annoyance. All he'd needed was ten more seconds to confirm his crazy, but hopeful, suspicion. Did Ford find him attractive? He'd assumed Ford was straight, but he'd also never seen him date anyone, never heard him speak of any hookups. Dana was bisexual, but very few people knew that. It'd been many years since he'd hooked up with a man. Even longer since he'd had a relationship with one.

CHAPTER FIVE

Ford

Stupid, stupid, stupid. Ford drove to his house so he could shower and groom his beard before it was time to get back to the office for their meeting. He would've done it at the gym but he had to get some air. What the hell had he been thinking falling onto Dana like that, his mouth on his ear, commanding him? Dana was involved. Ford just couldn't believe he'd said what he said. What did he care if Dana wasted time on a woman who was so utterly wrong for him? He didn't want to give Dana the wrong idea. He liked him well enough as a co-worker. He was a good shooter, he'd give him that. Ford just wished his priorities were in order. He was young and overconfident. That girl took him off his game, that's why Ford thought someone should say something, and since he wasn't a man that held his tongue, he spoke up. But the way Dana looked at him. Those seeking brown eyes pleading with Ford to talk to him. Thank god that maintenance man came into the locker room when he did, because Ford was two seconds away from grabbing a handful of all that messy, un-styled hair and yanking Dana's head up so he could look him in his eyes and yell at him to grow up! Grow up so Ford didn't feel like a goddamn predator when he got hard from thinking about him.

If he could, he'd probably sit this meeting out but instead, he got dressed in his black jeans and a black t-shirt with Duke's Bail Bonds on the chest. He put on his gun holster, tucking a few other weapons inside his leather coat. They weren't expected to make any moves tonight but he was always prepared. The streets of Atlanta were an unsafe place to be, especially when you were on the hunt. He sent Brian a quick text letting him know he was on his way and got back in his truck.

When he walked into the office, Brian was already at his desk looking over some files. His brother's eyes – so much like his own – asked if he was cool. Ford gave him a quick nod and walked towards his own desk, ignoring Dana's eyes tracking him as he moved across the open floor plan that was their office. Duke was the only one with a closed off space. Quick's large desk was in the far corner, next to the outdated water cooler. There were only two other doors besides the back and front ones: the break room and an extra-large supply closet that held their gear. Duke had an open-door policy, but as of right now it was closed and Ford assumed Quick was inside. The two bosses probably discussing if he and Dana should be paired together on this dangerous bounty after what they'd just witnessed at the gym. Ford needed to get things under control. He'd never in his life been a risk or hazard on the job and he wasn't about to start now. He walked towards the break room and called over his shoulder, "Dana. A word."

He heard Dana close his laptop then the loud sound of his footsteps as his boots thudded on the hardwood floor. Ford turned around, waiting for Dana to come in, when he recognized the fluttering of nerves in the pit of his stomach. It was insane. He was never nervous. He'd dodged bullets on the battlefield, jumped from planes, boats, led missions with nerves of steel, but the thought of telling Dana he didn't mean to put the man's sex life in the open or imply anything inappropriate between the two of them was making him apprehensive. He went to the coffee pot and got started with brewing a strong pot to busy himself. There wasn't very much in the room besides empty cabinets and a mounted flat screen television that stayed on CNN at all times. A refrigerator, coffee maker, and two four-top tables. It was a room rarely used.

"You wanted to talk," Dana said. He sounded different. Breathy.

Oh Jesus. "Yeah. Look. About today. It was unprofessional and I'm sorry. There's no reason for me to bring your personal shit into work. I distracted you during an important training session and that was fucked up. It won't happen again."

Dana ran his hand through the long hairs on top of his head, making them fall messily in various directions. Ford watched the movement, noticed every detailed tattoo that made up the intricate sleeves on Dana's arms. "I think I was already distracted. I've had a lot on my mind and all you did was voice what I was already thinking."

Ford wasn't expecting that response so he stayed quiet, wanting Dana to keep talking.

"I, um. I just don't wanna be a dick to her, ya know. She really is good people, she's just from the other side of the tracks. But we're together for the wrong reasons." Dana's voice was back to its usual smooth, deep tone. He propped his lean hips up on the table, one boot on the chair, getting comfortable.

"The wrong reasons?" Ford sagged back against the counter with his arms crossed over his chest while he waited on the coffee. He hoped it brewed slowly. He was no Dr. Phil, but he'd listen to his partner and let him get whatever he needed to off his chest.

Dana's mouth quirked up on one side and he shrugged his shoulders. "Yeah, I guess. She's defying Daddy by dating the bad boy with a GED and working-class lineage, and I was... I was surprised she gave me the time of day at—"

"Seriously? That's why you're with her?" Ford didn't want to sound like an asshole. But Dana had never come off as a man with low self-esteem. When he was around them he was all cockiness and certainty. He was an awarded marksman for shit's sake. Had competed against some of the world's finest shooters and won. What did he have to be self-conscious about? This girl was really doing a number on him and Ford only disliked her that much more.

"No it's not the *only* reason I'm with her. I did like her in—"

"Did?"

Dana smiled at him. "Stop cutting me off."

Ford felt the effects of that incredible smile all the way to the pit of his stomach.

"Yeah, I like her, but we'd be better off friends is all."

Ford hummed, not wanting to reveal his relief at hearing that. He told himself he was only happy because it meant Dana would be fully focused on work again, but in the back of his mind there was a little voice saying, "You just want him single again."

"So thank you for knocking some sense into me. Literally." Dana rubbed his hand over his chest.

Ford shook his head and turned back around towards the coffee pot before Dana could see the slight smile tugging at his own lips.

"Hey! I saw that. Was that a smile?" Dana came down off the table and was next to him, peering around so he could see his face better. "Your neck's a little red, too. Holy shit, are you blushing?"

Ford shouldered him away. He worked hard to school his features, but Dana's humor and excitement were contagious. "Go on, brat, you're annoying me now."

"Mm hmm." Dana's smile spread across his handsome face. He stood close to him and reached for the coffee pot and a disposable cup. Their bare forearms brushed against each other and Ford had to be careful of his reaction to Dana's warm skin. "It's been a while since you smiled, Ford."

"I smile," Ford grumbled, reaching for his own cup.

"I mean, at me," Dana said a little softer.

Ford turned and looked down, but Dana wasn't looking up at him. There were several responses on the tip of his tongue but he held in each one. They were veering back into that inappropriate territory and Ford just couldn't go there. Dana was off limits. A man Ford's age shouldn't be lusting after a man thirteen years younger than him, no matter how much said man might be lusting right back.

"Let's get started!" Duke yelled from his office, his booming voice loud enough to reach them, even if they'd been standing outside.

"We better get in there," Ford said, glad for the interruption.

Dana grabbed his arm – just like before – when he went to walk by him. "We cool, Ford?"

Ford kept his eyes on Dana's nose, refusing to get lost in that pleading look again. "Yeah, we are." Dana looked like he wanted Ford to say more, but when Ford didn't, his arm was released. He walked out of the break room swearing at the heat he felt from Dana's touch.

PROMISES PART 3

CHAPTER SIX

Dana

He thought his eyes were going to catch fire and melt in his skull. That's how badly his eyes burned from staring at his computer monitor all day every day for two weeks. Duke told them it wasn't going to be easy to find the Grossman brothers, not with all the connections and family they had. Thank heavens most of their trusted entourage was right here in Atlanta, but this wasn't a small city. They'd reviewed the case files thoroughly to pick out names of likely people to start watching and put together a pattern. Dana did most of the computer searches and after another eleven hours today, he was exhausted. Duke could be overzealous when he had such a high-profile bounty. His company was considered one of the best and he'd do anything to keep that title. But when Vaughan – Duke's life partner – was out of town on business, Duke had nothing but time and a drive to let work keep him distracted from missing his lover.

Dana went into his kitchen and took out a couple things to make a ham and cheese quesadilla. He wasn't a great cook by any stretch of the imagination, but he didn't have to live on frozen meals or order in every night, either. While the butter sizzled in the skillet his thoughts went back to Ford. The private conversation they'd had helped ease the tension they'd caused in the gym but Dana still had an unsettled feeling in his gut. He and Ford had unresolved issues, and he found himself still thinking back to Ford's admission when they were on the mat… with that massive body on top of him.

PROMISES PART 3

Why did Ford care if he was being treated well by his girlfriend? Men – who weren't even technically friends with each other – didn't worry about those types of things. Dana could only hope that Ford actually did respect him. However, the next thought that entered his mind was: what if Ford cared for him in the same way he cared for Brian. Saw Dana as a little brother. *Ugh. Shit.* He certainly hoped not. Ford didn't exactly reciprocate Dana's touches to his arm.

Dana propped his hip against the counter with the spatula dangling in his hand. He didn't usually take time to reflect back on his life, but the way he'd been feeling lately was causing him to do that more and more.

"Have you been with a man before?" His coach asked. He was so handsome. Maybe not in the conventional, model kind of way, but Dana was so enamored with his skill and knowledge that he'd morphed from a teacher and mentor to someone he had a craving to be around, to smell, to listen to. But his marksman training coach was nine years older than he was. Dana was of legal age, but barely. He'd just turned twenty-one a few months before. Any type of relationship between them was strictly forbidden. He'd been taking a rifle training course through the NRA while working at a gun range in Buckhead. His goal had always been to enter into marksmanship competitions and as soon as he turned legal age, he sought to reach that goal with every ounce of determination he could muster. He heard opposition and discouragement from all directions, especially his old man, but not Fisher. Fisher believed in him. Enough that when his classes were over and he'd far surpassed any other student, Fisher began to train him privately. The heat between them sparked, sizzled and combusted until neither could fight it anymore.

"I've had boyfriends, Fish. I'm not a virgin." Dana tried to deepen his voice and sound more confident than he felt, but his body still backed up as his coach advanced on him. He didn't

know why he was running, God knows he'd wanted this for so long.

"I asked if you've been with a man." Fisher put his large hand up on the door when Dana's back hit it and he couldn't go any farther. "Not boyfriends."

Dana swallowed a mouthful of nerves and saw when Fisher's dark brown eyes dropped to his throat. Damn, Dana wanted him to touch him so bad, his cock was pulsing and jerking in his jeans.

"Once we start this, we ain't stopping, gorgeous." Fisher stroked his hand over his thick beard. One Dana had fantasized about burying his mouth in to let the bristly hairs tickle his lips. He loved hair, always had. When Fisher took his chin in a strong grip, his other hand holding him in place, he covered Dana's mouth with his own and dominated his body, his mind, and his heart all within seconds. He was in love for the first time in his life. Fisher had promised he wouldn't stop, but obviously he'd been talking about the kiss and not the love.

Dana flinched when the pungent smell of burning cheese flooded his nose. "Damnit." He yanked the skillet off the burner and hurried to take his singed quesadilla from the pan, but it was too late. One side was golden brown and the other was dark and crispy. Unfortunately, it was his last tortilla, so he'd have to eat it. He scraped as much of the charred flakes off as he could and took what was left to the couch in front of the television. He turned it on fast, needing the distraction from where his mind was stuck. Thinking about Fisher reminded him why he was hesitant to date men. He wasn't against it, just cautious. He loved women and adored men, but Dana knew he was capable of falling hard for either. If only Ford was open to his advances, he could be a true and faithful partner to him.

His phone buzzed with an incoming text on the small ottoman that was positioned as his coffee table. Looking at the screen, he released a soft gust of frustration.

PROMISES PART 3

Jess: *Hey honey. I'm coming over in about ten.*

He knew what needed to be done, and soon, but he wasn't in the mood to do it now, he was exhausted. He hit reply.

Dana: *Been a long day. Already in bed. I'll call you tomorrow. Night.*

It was gonna be a gruesome day tomorrow, too. Actually, the next couple weeks would be just like the previous ones. Duke believed in being prepared. Dana shut off the game show he wasn't really watching and went back to his bedroom. His condo was small, but it was his and he loved it. He'd done a few renovations over the past couple years and he must admit he thought it was looking great. He was proud of it. He hurried and ditched his clothes and tossed his bath towel over his shoulder. He had a full bath in his bedroom and another in the hallway for the guest room that he had converted into a workout room. He didn't have the time to go to a LA Fitness.

He'd just finished rinsing his hair, was about to turn off the taps when he heard his front door slam shut. *What the hell?* Dana wasn't in a bad neighborhood, but as a bounty hunter he'd made plenty of enemies. Leaving the water running, he eased out the shower and quickly opened the bottom drawer under his sink. He pulled out his chrome Kimber Pro, releasing the safety and cocking the stainless steel chamber. He'd been taught to always have a weapon accessible, so yes, he even had one in his bathroom. He listened for a few seconds, his hand inching towards the knob. Right before he opened it, he heard the sound of high heels click-clacking on the hardwood floor in his hallway. *Jessica.* Dana dropped his forehead to the door, sadly shaking his head. His text couldn't have been clearer. He put the safety back on and tucked his firearm away. After he turned off the water, he wrapped the towel low on his hips and walked into his bedroom.

Jessica was already undressed and pulling out her nightgown. She flung her hair over her left shoulder, turning to look at him with a sweet but sultry grin. "Oh, I'm just in time."

Dana walked to his dresser on the opposite side of the room. "Did you get my text? I responded to you."

"No. I sure didn't." She smiled, picking up her purse, which looked brand new and very expensive, setting it on the nightstand.

He knew she was lying. Instead of arguing, he pulled out a pair of cotton shorts and slid them over his bare ass before he took the towel off. "I said I was tired tonight. I'm going to bed, Jess. Make sure you keep it down tonight, please."

Jessica climbed into bed as soon as he turned off the light. She'd left his closet light on but he didn't bother with that. He stretched out on his back, wanting to spread his legs a little wider, but he wouldn't be rude.

"I'm so sorry about last night. We're trying to organize a fundraiser for the boutique to raise money for new window treatments that just aren't in the budget this month. It's been insane. Never realized how much work is required to put on a charity event." She had her leg draped over his, her silky nightgown rubbing against his rib cage while she cuddled in close to his side.

"Charity? Isn't the money for y'all?"

"Of course, it is. But we are offering some outrageous discounts. That's charity," she answered, rubbing her hand over his stomach.

"How is it…? Never mind. Let's just get some sleep. I gotta get up early."

"I'm off tomorrow. Why don't you stay home with me? Take the day off and let's skip like we're two high school kids."

"Have you lost your mind? Duke will kick my ass. I'd better be either in my grave or in the hospital five seconds from my grave if I don't show up. We're on a big case. We're going after two really big—"

"Your job is way too stressful, honey. You're tense all the time." She stopped him.

"Look, don't start, alright. I love my work. I don't say your work isn't important."

"Oh, honey. I would never say that. Your work is important. Extremely. I'm just being selfish and wanting you all to myself for one day." She climbed on top of him and Dana lightly gripped her hips to stop her from grinding on him. "Promise me you'll give me a day to ourselves real soon. In the meantime… let me see what I can do for my man to help him relax from such a long day."

Dana moved his hands and dramatically draped his arms over his eyes. She always did this and it was confusing as hell. Sometimes she respected him and gave him the care he wanted in a partner and sometimes she was so damn rude. He thought himself a compassionate lover and considerate boyfriend, so he knew he deserved the same treatment from her. Every now and then Jessica would show him what it was like having a thoughtful girlfriend. Like now. Lost in his head, he let her straddle his hips and slowly drag her nightgown up her body, teasingly revealing glimpses of her soft, naked flesh. She didn't have on any panties, and before he could put up any kind of protest, his cock was hard.

"Let me take care of my man the way he should be taken care of." She looked like she really meant that. Maybe she did feel bad about last night and the snide comments she'd made about his home and job recently. When he felt her inching down and pulling his shorts with her, his body reacted to her beautiful face right there at his groin, her hot breath caressing his shaft. His cock bounced up and smacked his abs when she tugged his shorts all the way off. She lingered around his pelvis for a second, only to sit up and reach for a condom in his nightstand.

"Why don't you try it just once, for me?" Dana asked, kissing her perfumed neck, letting his voice drop to that rumbling purr she said made her so hot. "Just a little try."

"Try what?" She giggled.

"You know what. Come on," he encouraged softly.

"Eww. No, that's gross. You know I don't do that."

"Why not? You embarrassed?" Dana caressed the baby smooth skin on her back. "You know you don't have to be. It's only me and you here."

"Oh god." She scrunched her face up like he'd just asked her to suck on a rotten frog leg. "Even the thought of *that* in my mouth... no way."

"I'll pull out before it's time. You sure don't mind me doing it to you."

"Well don't do it to me anymore." She shrugged. "Besides, I'd probably gag. My mouth is too petite."

Dana didn't roll his eyes, but he knew how ridiculous this debate sounded, so he cut it off. She'd never sucked his dick and never would, no matter how many showers he took or how much he begged. He didn't give her shit about it, but damn if he didn't want it, miss it. There were still a few women out there that balked at the idea of a mouth full of dick and balls, and he would be the man to wind up dating one of *those* women.

She winked at him and slid the condom on him. "I got something that feels so much better than a blowjob, lover." She positioned her wetness over the head of his dick and sat down on his lap with very little finesse.

She was slick and snug as always, but he'd lost the heat he'd held felt from her words earlier. She didn't give him a chance to savor the feeling before she started bouncing up and down, setting a hurried rhythm.

"Fuck. Slow down, Jess," Dana hissed, the sensations flooding him fast. "You in a hurry?" He was caught off guard by her wild passion. But this wasn't the first time she'd jumped on him and ridden him like a stallion. She loved to be on top, it was her favorite position, said it made her feel naughty, like she was taming her bad boy.

"Don't curse at me." She playfully slapped him on his chest. She hated dirty talk, said the vulgarity took her out of the mood. "Just touch me. Touch me here, I'm almost ready."

Dana let her position his hand between her legs and he rubbed her pearl while she rapidly rocked back and forth on him. After the conversations he'd had with Brian and Ford earlier and the way she was taking what she wanted with no regard for him, was making him feel like a used piece of meat. As a so-called tough guy, he'd never tell a soul his girl made him feel that way, like she'd emasculated him. He fought to even keep his erection while she wailed and moaned that she was there, never saying the word "coming."

She orgasmed loudly, dropping her head down, letting that long golden mane fall down over her breasts. Dana thrust up into her a couple more times but his desire was fading fast, along with his erection, especially since she'd stopped moving. After she calmed down, she looked down between her legs before climbing off. "That was just what I needed. Did you get there too?"

"Yeah," he lied.

CHAPTER SEVEN

Ford

Ford was in the office earlier than scheduled. He'd woken up with another hard-on after one of the most erotic dreams he'd ever had. And it was about a person whose name he didn't want to voice out loud or even in his head. This was doing a number on him. It'd irritated him when Dana used to complain about how his girlfriend didn't understand him and no matter what he did he couldn't please her selfish ass, but they'd broken up and everyone – not just him – was relieved to have the old, light-hearted Dana back. Then, like all good things, it came to an end when she popped back up with tears and a sob story. That she'd made a big mistake.

Ford stirred his coffee so hard, part of it sloshed over the edge of the cup. He felt pissed when spineless Dana had reared his ugly head again and taken her back. Too decent to turn her down. Gritting his teeth, Ford demanded Dana act like the man he truly was. Strong, determined, spirited, and a ton of other great qualities Ford had taken for granted until someone else started stealing them.

He just wished he was sure that he could go the relationship route with a man. Ford wasn't scared of dating the opposite sex, he was too old, too damn grown to worry about what anyone would think. He'd had experiences with men and women in the past. Had had his fun. He'd eyed a few guys when he was in the service, even patted a few bottoms, but nothing had stirred him this hard in years. He thought he was content in his life. He had his brother, his work, he was good now. He'd lived complications before, wasn't interested in them again. Relationships, lust, pining, dates, romantic expectations, sex, all equaled the same thing to him... complications.

Ford heard the door open and close. He knew it was Duke and didn't bother leaving the break room. When Duke peeked in, he gave Ford an amused, kind of knowing look, and walked inside. "You're here before me?"

Ford didn't think that required an answer. Wasn't he standing there?

Duke chuckled deeply. "You must have a lot on your mind. Wanna talk about it?"

"Nope," Ford answered curtly.

"Oh, come on. I'm not only your boss." Duke spoke in a passé psychiatrist's tone. "I want you to think of me as a friend and contemporary you can confide in."

Ford grumbled and pushed off the counter, shoulder checking Duke when he walked by him and out the room. "Fuck you, Duke." Ford sat down at his desk and began opening up the files they'd gone over yesterday. He might as well get lost in his work. He'd concentrate on finding these fuckers. Yeah, that's right. Hunt. That's what he'd do. *Not* worry about his budding feelings. They were bound to dissipate the more Dana stayed with his girlfriend.

"Okay, okay. Chill out. I get it, buddy. I do, seriously." Duke grabbed an empty chair and pushed it closer to Ford's desk. His firm thighs straddled the seat cushion, his bare forearms resting on the back. "Maybe you should tell him what's up, man. Be honest."

Ford gave Duke a pointed look. "There's nothing to tell."

"I see." Duke nodded like he was contemplating. "So you're not attracted to him?"

"Duke! What the hell? No, okay?" Ford took a large gulp of his coffee, needing something to do to distract from his embarrassment. Not because he was hot for another man, but because everyone wanted to be involved or input their few cents on what he should do. As his throat screamed from the scalding hot coffee he'd just foolishly downed, he continued to try to ignore his meddlesome boss.

"Because, just in case you were wondering, you won't get fired or bullied working here for being gay. We like to consider this a LGBTQ-friendly work environment," Duke said with all seriousness.

Ford looked at Duke like he was a jerk.

Duke paused. "What? Did I miss a letter in there?"

Ford glared while Duke laughed at his own unsolicited comedy.

He was finished with this conversation. His thoughts had continued to get the best of him the past few days and he needed to get back to being focused. Soon, he'd have to put in some long hours with Dana, in a truck cab, late at night, or in a hideout house doing surveillance. Either way, he needed to get his recently reawakened libido under control.

Duke finally got the message when Ford remained quiet. "Fine. But I'm here to talk, bro, if you need to. I been there is all I'm saying. I fought my attraction to Vaughan, too. I wasn't sure if he was serious or old enough to be the kind of serious I wanted."

Ford swiveled his chair around and stared at Duke like he was an idiot. "The man who anonymously saved your life by donating one of his kidneys to you? You mean him? Damn, your standards for proving sincerity are a tad high, don't you think, Duke?"

"This was before I knew he was the donor, asshole," Duke grumbled. "It's cool. You can keep fighting it, but trust me, it only gets worse. Dana will dump that scandalous broad, and when he does, he's coming for you. I know him. I've known him a long time."

PROMISES PART 3

Ford swallowed thickly at Duke's words. If only he really believed them to be true. Oh god, if Dana truly wanted him, what the hell would he do? He'd completely lose himself if he allowed it. Why would a man like that want an argumentative, controlling alpha male like him when he could have anyone he wanted? And goddamn, was he gorgeous. Ford could spend hours running his hands through that thick, dark hair on top of his head, then down his—

Duke chuckled and slapped Ford on his back when he walked by, breaking Ford's daydream. "I can see how *not* attracted to him you are."

Dana came in right behind Quick, looking like hell froze over. He'd clearly run his fingers through his hair this morning instead of opting to use a brush. His eyes were red-tinged and drooping. Despite the fact that he hadn't bothered to shave either, he still looked incredible. Tired, but incredible. What had kept him up, Ford wondered. When *he* went home last night, he'd eaten, showered, and gone to bed. Obviously, Dana must've had other plans. A man like him had to have a pretty full social calendar. Regardless of the considerable hours they spent at work, a man could always find time to play, especially in the wee hours of the night. Ford clenched his jaw when Dana walked by his desk smelling like women's perfume. No wonder he was so tired.

Ford decided against going to lunch with the guys, fabricating an excuse that he needed to make some important calls. He hated to miss a lunch where the bosses were treating, but he couldn't risk having to sit so close to Dana and smell the evidence of sex on him.

"Alright, let's break for lunch. Two hours, since we'll be here late again tonight." Duke spoke while he put on his dark blue bomber jacket and shades. Quick was standing beside him, waiting for Dana and Brian to join them. Ford tried not to watch as his coworkers left, not wanting to look Dana in his eyes at the moment. Ford was chickening out, not even putting up a fight to win Dana over. Why should he? He loved the chase, he'd stalk and capture just about anything or anyone, but he refused to chase after love. Love was never high on his list of things he wanted to accomplish. He'd had such a fulfilling military career – for the time it lasted – and he had his brother, so he was good.

Ford tilted back in his chair wondering if he truly meant what he was thinking. He was about to get up and get himself something cold to drink and order in a sandwich when the front door to their office opened and Dana strolled back inside. Ford didn't say anything as Dana solemnly walked to his desk and sat down.

"No longer hungry?" Ford finally asked, after Dana refused to acknowledge his curious stare.

"Nope. I guess you aren't, either. Or you declined a free lunch because you didn't like the company attending. Well, you don't have to anymore, I've decided to stay and make some… important calls." Dana's knowing sneer and reasoning was an obvious jab at the lame excuse Ford had given earlier.

Ford smirked and shook his head, continuing back into the kitchen murmuring under his breath. "Fuckin'… grow up." Ford thought he'd have a couple hours of peace, but Dana had ruined that—

"Fuck you, Ford. You got one more goddamn time to tell me to grow up and I'm going to give you a glimpse of the man that I am… the man you keep fuckin' insulting," Dana snarled from close behind Ford.

Ford heard Dana's heavy steps, realizing he didn't voice his insult as quietly as he thought. Regardless, he wasn't in the mood to soothe Dana's fragile ego. Instead of responding, Ford kept his back to Dana and concentrated on topping off his cup of coffee. He could feel Dana's heat, his anger and frustration. Ford widened his stance and brought his cup up to his lips.

PROMISES PART 3

"Damn you are hot and cold, man. I thought we were straight, Ford. What's up? You're acting like you can't stand to be around me. What have I done now, huh? I show up for work and you won't look at me for two seconds, or speak to me... at least without being a dick."

Ford set his mug down and spun around, leveling Dana with a hard scowl. "Why are you keeping tabs on me, kid?"

"I'm not a goddamn kid—"

"The hell you're not!" Ford barked.

Dana looked infuriated. He tightened his stubbled jaw and Ford had to keep his focus trained on Dana's eyes and not his plump mouth. "I want to get this shit resolved, once and for all. I don't even understand what the hell is happening here. All I do know is you can't stand the sight of me right now. We start surveillance next week, Ford. Duke has us working together – should I tell him to reassign you?"

Ford narrowed his eyes. He was good at reading people, and right now the man in front of him struggled with his thoughts. Ford watched Dana gulp down a massive lump of nothing as his Adam's apple bobbed and his throat worked to swallow his stress. Ford eased his large body away from the counter, creeping closer to Dana with his mouth set in a stubborn line. "You can tell Duke anything you want to, just keep my name out of it."

Dana grunted when Ford brushed past him, hitting him hard in the shoulder when he did. He had to get out of that small kitchen before he revealed his latest frustration regarding his coworker. That overbearing smell of women's perfume clinging to Dana like funk on a skunk. What if Ford had sensitive allergies or something? Dana was the one being rude if you asked him. There was no way he was going to tell anyone what had his fists clenching at his sides all day. He'd let it slide for now. But when he and Dana started working in closer quarters, he wouldn't be afraid to kick Dana out of his truck at the first hint of fragrance that didn't belong specifically to Dana.

PROMISES PART 3

CHAPTER EIGHT

Dana

"Man, what a day," Dana sighed. He eased his classic Nova onto 10th Street and settled back for the brief commute to Brian's house.

"Thanks for driving me." Brian signed slowly for Dana.

"No problem, man. It's all good. I saw Ford hurry out of the office as soon as Duke gave the go ahead."

Dana saw Brian pull his phone out of his pants pocket and type some words into his text to voice app. The computerized male began to speak as Brian's fingers flew over the keyboard. *"He's been a cranky bastard all day. First, I thought it was because you came in smelling like you were attacked by the fragrance lady at Bloomingdale's, but when he never mentioned it, I figured maybe not. Then he declined lunch. When we came back, you all looked like you had exchanged words again."*

Dana ignored the other stuff and instead went back to the part that stood out the most. "Smell like what?"

Brian released a gusty laugh. *"Yeah... smell."*

Dana pulled the neck of his t-shirt out and dipped his nose inside to get a whiff of himself. He didn't smell anything... then the faint hint of Jessica's perfume hit him. Had he gotten used to it and didn't smell it anymore? "She hugged me on her way out this morning." *Fuck.* That couldn't have been what got Ford so upset.

"I don't know what's going on with him lately. He's driving everyone insane. Especially me. He needs to back off a little and

focus on himself for once. At my age it's rather insulting to have your big brother calling to make your doctor's appointments."

"I guess it is," Dana said distractedly. Still wondering if Ford really was pissed that he smelled like his girlfriend. "So, what are you doing tonight?"

"I'm thinking of logging on and having a little fun tonight before we really get going on this bust." Brian looked up at him before moving his thick fingers across the communication app's keyboard. *"You want to come?"*

Dana chuckled lightly. He knew Brian was gay and knew exactly what type of hookup he was referring to. Did he want someone else... another man? Did he want to take Brian up on his offer? No to both. Brian was into a little more roughness and kink than he was comfortable with. The fact that Brian didn't talk made his hookups rather interesting and erotic. Brian occasionally told him some minor details about his conquests, but even those were a little TMI. His friend already had another window open on his huge smart phone, his thumb pushing past the various pages of men that were available and horny tonight. Dana suspected that Brian didn't have a hard time attracting men. He was the spitting image of his big brother. Over six feet of muscle and brawn. Large, dominant personality – regardless of his lack of speech – Brian's entire demeanor, his build, and especially his dark eyes screamed it. He could easily make you feel some type of way by just looking at you. If Dana wasn't fascinated with the *other* brother, he'd probably have had some fun with Brian.

"Naw. I'm good, buddy. You go on and enjoy." Dana smiled, pulling into Brian's driveway. "I'm thinking of meeting up with a friend downtown tonight."

Brian nodded and went for the door handle. *"No Jessica tonight?"*

Dana wiped his hand over his jaw, scratching at the rough hairs there. "Not if I can help it."

"Grow some balls." Brian signed with a smug shrug of his thick shoulders.

"Fuck you." Dana laughed for the first time all day. "I'm gonna tell her, alright. Give me some time, dude. I'm trying not to piss her off again. I need to do it in a way that makes her think it was her idea to end it."

Brian stared at Dana for several long seconds. Those expressive eyes making him feel like he was two feet tall. He knew what Brian was thinking. He'd already signed it for him, too. Dana needed to grow a pair. Not only was he ducking and dodging his girl, but he was getting the business from a guy he was too chicken-shit to put in his place... on top of him.

Dana made a left off of Brian's street and headed towards the front of the small neighborhood. Ford's house was just around the block. Dana needed to drive past it to get to Brian's. When they'd come in, Ford wasn't there yet. But as he drove back out, he saw Ford's truck in the driveway. He was at the tailgate pulling out a couple bags that looked like they were from a few different stores. Dana slowed down and pulled up to the curb at the end of Ford's driveway. Ford looked over, his brow furrowing when he noticed him. He didn't speak or wave, simply took a handful of plastic bags from Home Depot and walked up the porch to his front door. Ford's lawn needed to be cut and his azalea bushes were overgrown.

Dana saw there were a few more bags in the truck bed. He turned his ignition to accessory mode and got out of his car. He didn't like the way Ford looked at him, like his presence wasn't welcome, but he pressed forward. Ford was going to respect him, if not as a coworker, then definitely as a man.

He heard Ford come back out, the screen door slamming shut behind him. Dana tried not to be nosy and look inside Ford's lone grocery store bag, but he couldn't help but notice the sad-looking frozen dinners. The small six-pack of beer, one tomato, an onion, and a couple cans of tuna. From the looks of it, Ford wasn't planning to have company for dinner any time soon.

"What are you doing here, Dana?" Ford grumbled, reaching around him to pick up the two bags remaining in the truck bed.

"I just dropped your brother off at home and was leaving and saw you could use some help." Dana followed Ford into the house and set the bags down on the two-person dinette set in the eat-in kitchen. It was especially quiet and clean… and empty. But what Dana noticed the most was that the place smelled like Ford. Strong and masculine with a touch of spice and disdain.

"I didn't need help. I've always *managed* to bring in my own shit." Ford gave Dana an exasperated look that he returned ten-fold. Ford mumbled, "But thanks anyway."

"No problem." Dana looked around uncomfortably and shoved his hands into his leather coat's pockets. "Look, um, Ford. I'm sorry about the attitude today, alright. I know you didn't go to the lunch because of me and—"

"You don't *know* anything." Ford leaned against the wall beside his still-open door, his huge arms crossed over his chest.

"Then enlighten me, Bradford. You seem to have all the answers. I don't know shit and you know it all, right?" Dana fussed.

Ford mumbled what sounded like, "Damn, grow up, already," and turned towards his front door. A clear sign that Ford was done with Dana's unexpected, unwanted visit.

Fuck. What the hell am I doing so wrong? Dana pulled at his long hair on top of his head – feeling off-kilter – knowing it was probably sticking up all over the place. He felt like hell and he probably looked like it, too. He was tired and upset, but he recognized that was quickly becoming the norm when he was around Ford.

Ford opened his front door and turned to face Dana, nonverbally cuing him to leave.

"Really? Damn, Ford, it's like that?" Dana took slow steps toward the door, trying to think of what he could say or do that would revive their once amicable friendship.

"Yeah, it's like that when you're stinking up my place." Ford propped one boot up on the door frame waiting for Dana to move his ass.

Stinking? Shit. The perfume. He really didn't smell it, but obviously, Ford and everyone else did. Was that why he was getting this shitty treatment? All the other guys hadn't seemed to mind his scent today, or were able to ignore it... all except Ford. It felt like a lightbulb switched on in Dana's head. Ford had to feel something for him, and even if it was confusion he was feeling, it was better than nothing or repulsion. Now he had to work out how to get on Ford's good side. Needed to figure out how to let him know that Dana was interested but nervous also. He hadn't been with a man in so long and he admitted to himself that he missed it terribly. Missed the warmth, the strength, the familiarity of being with a man. One thing he remembered when dealing with men was that they preferred action over lip-service. Dana could *tell* Ford all day long that he was burning a short fuse with his girl and soon they would no longer be an item, but talk was cheap. Dana had class, he wasn't a bastard. He'd try his best not to hurt Jessica. For now, though, his focus was the man standing a few feet from him wearing an amazingly sexy and annoyed expression.

Dana held his head down and said a quick prayer that he was about to do the right thing, a safe thing. Looking up through his lashes, Dana slowly began to peel off his worn, black leather coat.

"That looks like the opposite of leaving," Ford ground out, giving Dana's chest a cold once over, but Dana could see heat behind that guarded look. Dana still had on his scented white t-shirt, and made a show of smelling the collar. Ford's jaw clenched and his lip turned up into a fraction of a snarl.

Dana's stomach dropped but he wasn't going to turn back now. He walked closer until he was standing toe-to-toe with Ford. With both hands, he gripped the hem of his t-shirt and pulled it up and over his head, leaving on only his thin wife beater. He heard Ford's sharp inhale before he barked, "What are you doing, kid?"

"Am *I* stinking up your place, Ford? Or is it this?" Dana gripped the offending shirt in his hand and tossed it out the front door. He didn't see where it landed on Ford's porch, choosing to keep his eyes on Ford's uninterested expression. Dana inched in as close as he dared, still careful of Ford's quick hands, and rumbled tiredly, "Now how do I smell?"

Ford stared at Dana like he was trying to gauge if he was serious. He saw those coal-dark eyes drift over his face, felt them easing over his features. Dana fought not to close his eyes and burrow into Ford's masculinity, because damn, did he have it drifting off him, hot and visible, like steam rising off the Florida asphalt in June.

"I think you need to leave."

"Whatever you say, Bradford. I'll go. I just thought." Dana was losing his bravado fast. He stepped back a couple feet and put his jacket back on, realizing he'd lost this round as well. "I thought maybe we could have a drink and talk about the surveillance we're about to start."

"We can talk about *that* at the office, kid."

Dana bared his teeth like an insulted animal. "Enough with the 'kid' bullshit."

Ford stepped aside and gripped the edge of his front door. "Then stop the kid bullshit."

"How do I…? Damnit… I give up," Dana mumbled on his way out the door. He held his head high until he got in his Chevy and fought not to peel rubber pulling away from the curb. He thought he'd rip his steering wheel off, he was fisting it so hard.

On his way home, which was only a ten-minute drive – all of the guys lived close to the office for emergencies – he got a call from his best friend and it almost immediately reversed his sour mood.

Dana pushed the speaker on his phone. "Sway, you little shit. It's about time you returned my calls."

Dana heard a soft chuckle before Sway spoke. "It was only a couple days, D. I'm just coming off of a thirty-one hour shift. I slept for six hours and then I called your sorry ass."

"I'm messing with you. I know you practically run the nursing department. It's all good."

"Yeah, I practically run it, but I don't get paid like I do. The chief nurse sits back and lets me handle everything, while she gets the big check."

"You love it. That's all you wanna do is take care of people. Since we were kids and you made me and Stanton play doctor all the time. So you could heal us." Dana laughed along with his friend before it tapered off with a sigh like always. Remembering Sway's twin brother, Stanton, always left a pang of longing in both their chests. The once notorious trio became a duo when Stanton was killed in college.

"I do love it. I'm just… tired, ya know. There's so much going on and I can hardly keep up anymore, D." Sway sighed heavily across the line and Dana could imagine his friend's dirty-blond eyebrows angled downward with his sad, big, brown puppy dog eyes that always got him his way.

"Sounds like something's heavy on your mind," Dana responded.

"And you too," Sway added.

They knew each other too well. "You too tired for a rendezvous at our spot?"

Sway laughed again. "Will we ever be too tired for Applebee's?"

PROMISES PART 3

"Beers and Bacon Burger!" They both blurted out at the same time, laughing at their usual order.

"Shit, yeah. The triple B." Dana genuinely smiled for the first time all day. When they were kids the first B had stood for root beer and they couldn't wait to make it real beer as soon as they got old enough. "I'm down. I'm getting ready to turn onto my street now. I just have to take a quick shit, shower and shave."

"That's more information than I needed to know, bro. But okay. I'll meet you there in an hour."

"Sounds good, I'll be— Oh no," Dana whispered like someone was suddenly in the car with him and could hear his concern.

"What, D? What is it?" Sway asked just as quietly.

"Damnit. Jess is here." Dana almost had a mind to make a quick U-turn, but his old muscle car was way too loud for that. He was sure she'd already heard him, if not seen him. "She didn't call or text me she was coming by."

"Wow. She can do the pop-up thing now? Does she have a key too, D?" Sway asked. Dana could hear the annoyance in his voice. Was everyone tired of Jess, including his best friend? "So, I guess Applebee's is out."

Dana frowned. "The hell it is. I'm still coming. I need to talk with you, it's important."

"I'll be at the spot in an hour." Sway hung up to let Dana take care of his impromptu situation.

Dana pulled into his other designated parking space and killed the engine. Jess was leaning against her pristine white BMW laughing with someone on her cell. She reached into her back seat and pulled out her overnight bag and without a word held it out for Dana to carry for her. When he took it and put it back in her car, she scowled at him and told whoever she was speaking to that she'd call them back later.

"What's going on, handsome? How was your day?" She smiled and moved into his chest, before cringing and backing away. "Goodness, you need to shower."

Usually, he'd be annoyed at her distaste, but he was glad she'd backed away, especially when the smell of her strong perfume hit his nose. She had on an expensive-looking, pink ruffled blouse tucked into her size two, pin-striped pencil skirt. Her black high heels with the bright red bottoms clicked across the concrete as she moved back towards his house.

"Jess. I wish you would've called. I have to go right back out. I have important plans tonight."

She swirled around, her long hair landing over her shoulder with flare. Everything she did seemed so rehearsed. With one perfectly arched brow raised, she sauntered back to him. "More important than me?" she purred. "Can't be."

Dana hated when she did this. "It has nothing to do with you. A friend needs me."

"And I don't? I need you too. So badly."

She was using her sneaky tactics, but they weren't working. Dana had a lot on his mind, mainly a big, brooding, ex-Special Warfare officer. "Jess. I'm not going to stand my friend up."

"Fine." She crossed her thin arms over her chest. "Well, I guess we won't see each other for a while. I have to go out of town for a business trip. I won't be back for a couple weeks."

He didn't know if this was another one of her tricks. He'd never known her to go out of town for anything but pleasure. Dana opened her driver's side door. "I understand. Where are you going, anyway?"

She sucked her teeth, cocking her hip to the side. "You're really making me leave? Unbelievable."

"Jess, come on, don't over dramatize. I'm only—"

"Don't tell me how to act, Dana. I come over to try to take care of my man after he's had a full day of work and all he can think about is going out to see someone else." She slid easily onto the butter-soft leather seat. The immaculate tan interior still had that new car smell even though she'd bought it seven months ago.

"Travel safely and call me when you can. We have some things to discuss." He briefly made eye contact with her before she yanked the door away from him.

"Yes, we certainly do. I won't be treated like this, Dana. I'm your woman. I deserve respect and to come before anyone else. Anyone," she stressed.

Dana didn't respond. Instead, he stepped back and let her drive off. There was nothing he could say right now. Clearly, she was going to be outraged that someone as common as him would have the audacity to break up with someone as classy as her, but he'd let her know it was him… not her. Shaking his head at that weak line, he unlocked his door and hurried inside. Excited to see his friend and get some of this craziness off his chest.

CHAPTER NINE

Ford

Ford: *Come over and we'll watch the game.* Ford texted to Brian. He took out a pizza from his freezer and set it on the stove. He set his oven to four hundred, not needing to look at the instructions on the box. He and Brian loved this brand. He thought of inviting him over and possibly trying to work in a conversation about Dana to see what his brother thought. He knew he wouldn't be pissed about him taking interest in a man, but he had to get his opinion, regardless.

Brian: *I got plans bro.*

Ford: *Doing what?* Ford could almost hear his little brother's scoff of irritation.

Brian: *Grown man shit. You should try it sometime.*

Ford read the text and hostilely punched in his reply. Why did it seem every time he tried to spend time with Brian, he got attitude?

Ford: *Then come over after, asshole.*

Brian: *I think I'd rather bask in the after-sex ambiance alone. See you tomorrow.*

Ford dropped his phone back on the counter. He'd been dismissed. He aggressively shoved the pizza back into the box, not interested in throwing half of it away. No way could he eat it all, and he didn't do leftover pizza. Maybe he shouldn't have gotten rid of Dana so fast; at least he acted like he wanted to be around Ford. He put the pizza back in his freezer and instead grabbed a XXL Hungry Man meal. *Looks like it's a rib and chicken night for one.*

While his oven was still on preheat, he opened a water and thought about checking out one of those hookup apps himself. He must be crazy to even think it. It was way outside of his comfort zone. He wasn't a trusting enough person to let a stranger have at his body. God, what would he say? Where would he take them? Do they just fuck and walk away with a cheeky grin and an "It was fun, lover" thrown over their shoulder? It sounded so absurd to him. If his brother didn't mind faceless fucks, then good for him, but Ford wasn't built that way. In the Navy he'd stayed clear of relationships for the most part, happy to have a career with goals and ambitions. To finally be able to pave his own way. And he'd done that. But living as a civilian now – even with a job as demanding as Duke's – he found himself with time that often left him alone with his own thoughts.

Both his bosses had significant others, lovers they enjoyed when they left the strenuousness of the job. Duke was cuddled up with his business partner's son and Quick was in love with the doctor that saved his business partner's life. Duke and Quick did the double-date thing a lot, which made it so they all could have some sort of social life. It was a nice sentiment for the bosses, but it didn't help a man like Ford, who would've preferred to be consumed with the job instead of being home alone.

He sat at the small dinette table and fingered through the mail while he waited on his dinner. It was too quiet. As he mindlessly flipped through a local grocery paper, his mind went to Dana. The way Dana looked at him made him feel like a king. Made him feel like he looked handsome or something. No one had ever looked at him like they wanted to put him on a serving dish and have him for dessert. He covertly loved it. Too bad he didn't trust the man. Not with his personal life. He could work with Dana and believe he'd back him up in the field, but the man was too much of a player outside of work and Ford couldn't respect *that*. He wouldn't be another victim Dana captured with his sexiness and charm.

Ford got an ink pen and notepad out of the kitchen drawer and started to make a small grocery list to distract himself. He'd neglected his bare refrigerator the past couple weeks, eating more takeout than usual, which he hated. He wasn't the greatest cook, having lived on military food all his adult life, but he could work the hell out of his oven and microwave. After tomorrow, he had the entire weekend off since surveillance started first thing Monday. He had court duty tomorrow from eight to two and then a long evening in his truck with Dana… alone. He was going to need two days off to recover from that.

God help him if he smells like that stinking perfume… he'll do his surveillance from the truck bed.

Dana couldn't stop the wide grin that split his face when he saw his friend sitting at one of the high-tops around the bar, waving him over. When Dana reached him, Sway rose on his toes and threw his arms around Dana's neck, holding him close. Dana did the same, with his arms secured around Sway's back. His friend looked even shorter than he had last month.

"Have you shrunk, Squirt?" Dana pulled back, looking down at his best friend. He loved to tease him.

"Fuck off. You're just freakishly big." Sway got back on his stool and took another sip of his water.

"I'm not big. I've seen big," Dana added, waving their waitress over.

"I bet you have." Sway nodded. "Anyway. You look amazing… worn-out… but amazing."

"Thanks, man. You know you're always the cutest in the room." Dana ordered the seasonal ale on tap for both of them, grateful the waitress didn't try to make small talk. He propped his elbows on the table and watched as his friend perused the menu that he had to know by heart. Even the promotional items. Sway had on a light brown sweater with the sleeves pulled up and a pair of threadbare jeans. His outfit didn't look glamorous, only his face did. Soft ivory skin, big doe eyes with long, brown lashes that most women had to pay for, and pouty pink lips. He'd pass for androgynous if he didn't have a groomed goatee outlining a sharp jaw. His chestnut hair was combed back and held in place with a little product, but a few strands still fell and curled by his ears.

"Don't try to sweet talk me. What's up with you looking so bummed? I'm sure it has to do with Jess."

The waitress brought their beers and they both ordered the burgers with some chips and salsa to snack on while they waited. Dana took a long gulp and wiped his mouth with the back of his hand. Jess hated when he did that. He frowned before he asked, "What do you think of Jessica?"

Sway flicked those big browns up to his face, looking slightly uneasy. "Do you really want me to tell you what I think of your girlfriend, D?"

"She won't be my girl much longer, so yes, let it rip." He was comfortable saying that, because, like him, Sway respected women a lot. He'd never say anything blatantly disrespectful.

"I think she's a user… a spoiled user." Sway wiped his hands on his napkin and thought for a moment. Dana didn't interrupt. "You seem so much happier when you two *aren't* together. You both break up to make up and when the honeymoon period ends quickly, you're back to being consumed by her neediness."

Dana sighed when his friend confirmed his own thoughts and probably those of the guys he worked with, too. "I'm gonna break it off."

"For real this time or for a few months?" Sway chuckled.

"Well, at least I have had a lover in this millennium." Dana threw a chip at Sway's lithe chest.

"Hey!"

"You know I'm telling the truth. I think you dumped Jonathan in ninety-nine. Dude, that was—" Dana tried to do the math in his head.

"Seventeen years, jerk. If you're gonna make fun of someone, at least have your facts in order. Besides, I was turning nineteen. I was heading to college, I had other things to focus on besides getting laid, my horny friend." Sway drank the last of his beer and motioned for two more since the waitress seemed to be hovering close by. "Wow. It really doesn't feel like that long. After Stanton died you know how hard it was, dude. I had to help my mom. Priorities, brother."

"I know." Dana didn't mean for the conversation to get so heavy. But Stanton was always mentioned when they got together. The two of them being at Applebee's sparked nostalgia for when all three of them used to come together. He was gone but he would never be forgotten. "How's your mom doing? Is she ready to disown me?"

"Almost. You haven't seen her in a while. I told her you were on a big case. She has a new chair she's dying to show you." Sway inched back when the server brought their entrees. The burger was smoking hot and it smelled heavenly. "It's a new power wheelchair. She's all over the place now. She goes to the market up the street, to Walmart. All by herself, now. She's so proud, Dana."

Dana smiled. That was good news. Sway's mom had rheumatoid arthritis, so she could no longer walk, and the joints in her hands were so bad it was becoming more difficult to push the wheels in her non-electric chair. "She still doing her therapy?"

"Every Monday, Wednesday and Thursday. She's trying to keep as much strength as she can, but it's a hard battle," Sway said around a mouthful of burger, juice dripping down his chin that he didn't bother to wipe away. He may be pretty but his eating habits were all manly. "I'll tell my mom you're coming to see her real soon. Now, moving on. What's got those dark spots under your eyes and your forehead crinkled?"

"A man."

Sway's big eyes widened comically. "A man! Oh wait… wait… don't say another word." Sway ordered two shots of Patrón and their third beers.

"Damn, man. I'm not depressed about it." Dana smiled, thanking the waitress for the fresh glasses she placed in front of their half-eaten dinners.

"These are celebration shots!" Sway laughed and held up his shot glass. "If you're even *considering* dating a guy again, I'm celebrating."

While they drank top shelf tequila and ate their burgers Dana told his best friend all about his new crush. And yes, that's exactly what it was… a crazy crush. He admitted to the nervousness in his stomach when he knew he was about to see Ford. The sparring match that had ended with him pinned and completely submissive to Ford's control. He told him how Ford insisted he deserved better than Jessica. Even described Ford's look from his cropped cut, to how big his boots were. He confessed to the way he infuriated Dana by calling him kid and telling him to grow up.

"Sounds like he's flirting back to me." Sway chuckled around a deep belch. He hit his fist against his chest and let another go. "So, you gonna go for it?"

"I don't know, man. He's pretty wound up."

"What do you mean? You said he's military, does he have some PTSD issues?"

Dana shook his head. "No, not that I know of. He works fine around the crazy shit we have to deal with. Even his brother, who's mute, does fine. They seem to be okay, compared to how a lot of those guys come back. He's so driven and professional. Ford was like the shit when he was enlisted, too. He had rank and he saved lives. Maybe I'm overshooting, here. He's kinda awesome." Dana stopped and hid his blush around taking a large drink of water when he realized he was gushing over Ford, and his friend was looking quite amused as he did.

"You're kinda awesome too, D. That's why I don't like Jess, because she makes you feel like you aren't. You pulled yourself up by your bootstraps despite how your dad constantly came down on you. You can shoot like no one's business and you're recognized for it. Has Ford seen your marksman awards?" Sway waved his hand in the air, continuing his point, not looking for a response. "You save lives too, every day. Keeping those batshits off the streets. I think Ford probably recognizes that. The issue is not if you're equally matched, like you questioned with you and Jess. The question is can you really have something with him? Can this actually go the distance? You've had quite a bit of fun in the sex department, if you know what I mean, no shortage of bunnies over the last couple years. This guy could think you're too much of a good-time Charlie. You're thirty-four, Dana, and you said he's forty…?"

Dana cleared his throat. "Um, forty-six, something like that."

Sway jerked his head back. "He's a little long in the tooth, huh."

"No, he's not! He especially doesn't look like he's in his forties."

"That's because he's almost in his fifties." Sway laughed, the alcohol making him find everything hilarious.

"You're hammered." Dana laughed too, enjoying himself. He'd missed his friend. He always knew what to do and say. "Besides, I'm not a slut. I think I'm ready for a real relationship again, if it's with someone who respects me. And, honestly, I don't think Ford has any for me."

"I doubt that. He wouldn't even bother if he didn't. You said he's always getting on you. It's because he likes you too, or at least finds you hot." Sway leaned back, rubbing his flat stomach. "And look at you over there, in your leather and white t-shirt. You look like a modern day Fonzie."

Dana shook his head at his friend's silliness. He took both hands and smooth them over the sides of his hair and gave him the classic Fonzie thumbs up and rumbled, "Eyyyyyyyy."

Sway almost spit out his beer when he doubled over laughing.

"Enough about me. What about you, man? Any hot doctors tried to get your attention?" Dana drank some more water. He needed to dilute some of that tequila or else he'd be waking up at seven in the morning with a pounding headache, giving Ford something else to complain about.

"Nope. It's still just me and mom."

"You know I love your mom. But don't you think she'd want you to live a little? Have a social life?"

Sway groaned. "God, you sound just like her. And who says Saturdays at the flea market and watching Golden Girls every night with your mom isn't a social life?"

"Um, whoever came up with the term social life says so." Dana and Sway smiled and made light of it, but he knew his friend was a romantic and probably craved some in his life, but his mom would always come first. She'd lost one son, so Sway did any and everything he could to keep his mom smiling and happy with the son she had left.

Sway was talking about this new underground gay club an orderly told him about and how Sway could definitely get lucky there when Dana noticed two dark SUVs pull into the Applebee's parking lot. He kept his eyes on his friend but watched the vehicles in his peripheral. Four men got out the first one and three got out the second one. They were no good and Dana knew somehow they were there for him. Thugs didn't usually frequent this place or this neighborhood. Dana recognized one of the guys as one of the Grossman brothers' top goons from the pictures they'd gone through during the last weeks. Ray and John Grossman had clout and eyes everywhere, surely they knew Duke was on the case by now. Dana discreetly hit the alarm/panic button on his watch to alert his team. There were seven of them… he needed Duke, Quick and the King brothers.

"What's wrong? Your jaw looks like you just sucked on a lemon," Sway said, looking around at the other patrons to see what had Dana so upset.

Dana sobered almost immediately at the thought of sweet Sway in danger, the fierce bounty hunter in him roared to the surface, his mind focused on getting his friend out safely. Surely, the sudden seriousness could be seen in his tense expression. "Sway, listen to me. I need you to be Polo. I want you to go through the kitchen and out the back door. Don't try to come around to the front, they'll see you. You hide in that alley until I call for you. Don't look back, and ignore the staff, just go and hide. I'll call for you."

Sway looked scared, and so did Dana. He wouldn't be able to handle his approaching problem until he knew Sway was safe. The guys were walking across the parking lot and Sway finally saw them, turning back to Dana shaking his head. "I won't leave you."

"You know the drill. We've been through this. My guys are coming. Go now, before they see you," Dana growled. "Now. Go, Sway."

Dana watched Sway hurry from the table and across the restaurant – never turning around – and through the double doors the staff used. Hopefully, no one gave him a hard time and he could get to the alley. Dana had the waitress quickly take Sway's plate, in hopes it would appear he was eating alone. Dana didn't turn around, instead using the mirror behind the bar to see that one of the men stayed outside, one sat down in the waiting area by the front door, three went to the bar, while the other two approached him.

Dana kept his composure even as the leader took Sway's seat, the other one making his big body comfortable on the other stool. "Have we met?" Dana said drily.

The man simply looked at Dana with a "Don't bullshit me" expression and waved over the waitress. She looked uncomfortable when she stood next to the table, her smile long gone, like she knew something wasn't right. Sway's charming presence was missing, replaced with ugly hoodlums.

"Hey, sweetheart. I'll have a double of your best whisky." The man ordered in a rough voice, his sinister smile making an unwanted appearance. Beady green eyes surveyed the shot glasses on the table and the three or four empty beer mugs. The thug looked up at Dana with a skeptical expression. "Did you drink all this yourself or am I *really* interrupting?"

"Nope. Just a night alone. I might have a slight drinking problem," Dana answered, hoping the waitress caught on.

"Sad." The guy sneered. "Make it a triple, beautiful. And put it on *his* tab."

The server looked at Dana but he didn't contradict, just nodded his head once. He didn't want her at the table longer than she needed to be. "Sorry to interrupt your sad party for one, but I'm here to deliver a message."

"Figured as much." Dana looked unaffected. "May I ask who you are, or can I just call you errand boy?"

A flash of anger shone in the man's eyes before he curved just the edges of his mouth. "I'd be careful if I were you. My name is Mack and my leniency only extends so far. Now, John said don't hurt you… yet. Just to relay the message, so I'm going to try to do that, but don't think I won't drag your ass out of this cheap restaurant and pound you into the fucking concrete. We usually don't like to make a public spectacle of ourselves, but don't make the mistake of thinking that you're safe just because there are others around."

"We wouldn't want that, now would we, Mack?" Dana said the man's name like it tasted disgusting… it did. "So, what's the message?"

"The Grossmans know Duke has been hired to bring them in. From my boss man to yours. Tell Duke to drop the case." Mack held up his hand like Dana had opened his mouth to say something, but he hadn't moved. "We don't want to hurt you guys. My bosses know of Duke's reputation. He always gets his man… some say he's practically indestructible, but does he really want to test that myth? I doubt it. Our beef isn't with you. All you guys gotta do is stay out of our way and big John is willing to generously compensate Duke."

Dana could feel the heat of a powerful glare on him. He had to fight the urge to rub the back of his neck where the hair stood up. A feeling of bravery and brotherhood washed over him as he looked up into the eyes of Bradford King across the room, tucked behind the server's station. The eye contact was brief but there. The alarms on their watches were silent but alerted the entire team to his location. They were used in emergencies, military ops team watches, which Ford was able to get through one of his many contacts. It didn't typically take long for one of them to reach the other. But it felt amazing that Ford had gotten to him first, and in only six minutes.

"Stay out of the way of what?" Dana asked like he could care less.

"Our business," Mack snarled.

The waitress brought his triple and Mack had it in his mouth and down his throat before she even left. Dana asked her for the check so Mack couldn't order another and prolong this bullshit meeting.

"You got it?" Mack bit out.

"You didn't say much, but the little that you did say... yeah, I got it." Dana shrugged. Mack looked pissed but he smiled and stood, his silent goon next to him doing the same.

"Let us know." Mack moved to Dana's side of the table and slammed a card down in front of him. It was white card stock with ten digits on it. No name, no email, or other identifiers. "You got forty-eight hours."

"That's sure generous of you."

Mack bent closer, inches from Dana's face, and out of the corner of his eye Dana saw Ford push off the wall, ready to strike. Dana gave him a subtle signal letting him know he had this.

"You talk a good game, bounty hunter, but y'all are severely outnumbered and you know it. Your boss knows it. Do the right thing. No one wants this to get ugly. Take the money and walk." Mack actually sounded like he wanted nothing but peace. Dana knew those kinds of men. Played you to make you trust them, then they stabbed you in the back... literally.

As they filed out the door and back into their vehicles, Ford finally came to the table. "You good?" were his only words.

"Yeah, man. I wasn't sure what they were up to but they only had a message," Dana responded, throwing a few bills on the table, including a considerable tip and standing to leave.

Ford followed him outside after they were sure the Grossmans' men were gone. "I told the guys we had it under control, so no one else is coming. What was the message?"

"Hold on." Dana had jogged to the end of the block and around the corner when Ford finally stopped him.

"Where are you going? Why are we running?" Ford frowned.

"I had someone with me when they showed up. I told him to run and hide." Dana made his way back up the alley.

"And he did? He left you alone against seven men?! Not only do you have bad taste in women, but obviously men too," Ford growled.

"I wasn't on a fuckin' date, Ford." Dana couldn't even look at his partner. Nor was he interested in justifying himself again. He had to get to Sway. He stood and listened but didn't hear anything. Dana called out, "Marco!"

After a second he heard a soft "Polo."

It was one of the only games they'd played when they were boys. Marco Polo and doctor. Dana released a gust of air and ran a few more feet to where Sway was crawling out from behind a dumpster. His knees had dark stains and there was some grime on the hem of his sweater. His face was flushed and his eyes were red, but Dana knew it had little to do with the brisk temperature. Sway ran towards him and threw his arms around his neck.

"I was scared. I thought you weren't coming."

"You know I wouldn't leave you." Dana buried his face in the top of Sway's head, holding him tight until his friend stopped shaking. If anything had happened to him, he'd never survive it. Criminals, thugs, didn't fight fair. It was a common tactic to use your enemies' loved ones to gain the upper hand. Sway was his brother, he'd been there from the beginning. Ever since his father moved them into the neighborhood when he was six, the three of them had been inseparable. He couldn't lose his family.

"I can see you're fine. I'll leave you two alone." Ford turned his back, completely misreading their brotherly affection.

"Ford, wait," Dana called out.

"Ford? That's him?" Sway tried to whisper, but when Ford slowed and turned his head, Dana knew he'd heard him.

"Yes. And thank you, Sway, for pointing that out right now," Dana murmured, releasing his friend.

"Ford, this is my best friend, Sway Hamilton. We grew up in the same neighborhood. Sway, this is Bradford King."

Sway quickly threw his hand out, waiting for Ford to drop the skepticism and accept the gesture. When he finally did, Sway continued, "I've heard a lot about you. Thank you for coming so quickly. I'd only be a distraction to Dana if I didn't go. He's always made me hide. Even when we were younger. I had to run and he and my brother would fight. It was a rough neighborhood."

"It's the cards you were dealt, Squirt. You're a healer not a fighter." Dana tried to lighten the mood but no one was smiling just yet. The situation was still too fresh on their minds, all of them realizing that the ambush could've gone very differently.

"Your name's not Marco?" Ford asked.

Sway and Dana both laughed before Sway explained. "No. It's the old kid's game, that's why I answered 'Polo.'"

"Why not just call his name?" Ford grumbled at Dana, folding his big arms over his chest.

"Because. I was tricked before. Someone called my name to come out of hiding – said my brother sent them to get me – it was bull. So later, I only came out when one of them called Marco. I know it's kind of elementary now, but I knew he was serious when he told me to be Polo. I don't question him anymore." Sway looked back over his shoulder at Dana. "But, like I said. Thank you for coming."

"Of course, I came," Ford answered, looking over Sway's head at Dana. "He knew I would."

"Yeah, I did know," Dana almost whispered, staring into Ford's midnight eyes.

Ford could only stare back.

Dana finally broke eye contact. Sway was looking back and forth between them with a perceptive smile on his lips.

"Come on. You better get home. I'm sure your mom is wondering why you're late for Golden Girls."

"Piss off." Sway blushed, covering his face. They made their way back to the parking lot and Dana closed Sway inside his late model Impala. "You know what to do."

"I know, I know. I'll text when I'm home, D." Sway started his car and powered down the window as he was leaving the space. "You be sure to text *me* when you dump that witch."

Dana couldn't even retort because he was too busy balking at Ford's response, which was a grunt and a squint of his eyes.

Sway whispered successfully, "Oh yeah. He likes you, alright."

Dana waved Sway away. "Go home, Squirt."

PROMISES PART 3

CHAPTER TEN

Ford

Ford wasn't sure he was buying the friend crap, but the more the smaller man talked, the more Ford realized that their relationship had to be brotherly. He spoke of Dana like he was an over-protective older brother. Ford could relate.

When that alarm sounded right after he'd finished working out, his heart practically leaped out of his chest seeing that it was Dana who had activated it. He hadn't felt such an overwhelming urge to attack since Brian had pushed the alarm when he was held captive at the office. Now that he knew Dana was alright, he felt a crushing sense of relief.

Ford walked with Dana to his car and the tension felt as frigid as the fall, night air. He had so much he wanted to say to Dana, but everything seemed wrong for the moment.

"What was the message?" Ford asked.

"The usual. Back off." Dana leaned against his driver's side door.

"What do you think Duke will do?" Ford asked. He and his brother hadn't been with Duke as long as Dana. He hadn't been around for the last threat so he didn't know how Duke and Quick handled them.

"He's going to do what he always does... catch them."

Ford nodded, liking the sound of that. With his military background, he didn't know the meaning of cowering from a threat. Ford waited for Dana to keep going, but all he did was stare at him. Those sharp brown eyes roaming over his face and chest. Why did he have to look at him like that? Make Ford think things that weren't true and want things that were out of his reach. Wish for things that would never exist. Like the idea of him and Dana together.

Ford's phone rang, breaking their connection. "It's Duke." Ford hit the speaker phone and moved in closer to Dana on the pretense that he wanted him to be able to hear everything. But he just needed to be close to him.

"Talk to us. Quick's on three-way," Duke said instead of hello.

"He's good. We're in the parking lot. They had a message," Ford responded.

"Let me guess," Duke hissed. "Don't keep after them."

"You got it."

Duke and Quick's laughter filtered through the line. They all loved this part of the chase. The Grossmans were terrified. Like Mack said: Duke always gets his man.

"Let's meet at the office at seven. I think these boys are about to jump ship. The threat is a stall tactic. They have to know I won't back down, but they probably suspect we'll take time to reassess. Big John's getting his affairs in order, collecting on debts, and then he's making a run for it. Our time table just shrunk significantly." Duke continued, "Ford, I still want you at the courts by eight, but make sure you and Dana are ready to get me some intel tomorrow night. I'll have Judge send over a couple guys to cover court duty for the next few weeks. This case is top priority."

"Roger that," Ford answered for them, ending the call.

Dana met his eyes again. He looked so unsure and Ford hated it because he knew it was his fault. Dana couldn't have a clue where he stood with Ford right now. He'd treated him like shit earlier at his house because he was pissed at himself for wanting something forbidden and had taken it out on him. If he'd only known that mere hours later Dana's life might be in danger, he may not have acted like such a jerk. Dana was his partner at work, he needed to do better with their communication, or this complete lack thereof could put them at risk in the field.

"So much for our weekend off. I guess I'll see you in the morning." Dana opened his car door and Ford could see his window of opportunity fleeting before his eyes.

"No problem." Ford cleared his throat. Anxiety once again kicking in. "I just want you to know, I got your back." *Damnit.* That wasn't what he wanted to say. He wanted to say, "I'm sorry for giving you such a hard time but I want you in *my* bed, not in hers."

"I know, Ford. See you tomorrow." Dana drove away, leaving Ford standing there with his regrets.

PROMISES PART 3

CHAPTER ELEVEN

Ford

Court was boring, as usual. They only had one bond hearing on the docket and their jumper actually showed up. As soon as Ford saw him, he left, he didn't worry about securing anymore bonds. Duke said the Grossman brothers were priority, so he wouldn't worry about obtaining more business for now. Ford texted his brother as soon as he got back in his truck.

Ford: *Bri. Got some addresses?*
Brian: *Yep. Dana has them already.*
Ford: *He at the office?*
Brian: *Waiting on you.*

Ford's stomach flipped over. *Waiting on me.* How could he spend all evening and most of the night with Dana with all this shit lingering between them? Ford drove through the busy streets of Atlanta, taking the scenic route westbound on Memorial Drive. He knew he needed to get to work but he wanted a plan together. He may even have to eat a little crow. Ford had no right to tell a grown man who to date or give him shit for who he laid down with. Ford wasn't even a close friend, not like Dana was with Brian. Ford was merely a co-worker. *And whose fault is that?*

Ford kept thinking while he transitioned onto Whitehall Street. There wasn't much to look at on the desolate road. A few eateries, mom and pop businesses, automotive shops, but mostly empty fields with either dead grass or concrete slabs where businesses once sat and flourished. Homeless men and women made their way around the backs of buildings, either looking for supper or shelter from the cold. A man in a camouflage jacket held a cardboard sign in his scarred hands at the corner of Northside and Whitehall. Bold dark letters read: RETIRED VET HOMELESS WILL WORK FOR FOOD. Ford stopped at the light, regardless that it was green, and ignored the angry blares of car horns behind him as he fished out his wallet and gestured for the man to hurry over and get the three twenty-dollar bills Ford held out the window. He was tempted to flick off the jerk behind him that was still laying on his horn, but instead he gave the old vet the money, a sharp nod and drove off. He glanced in the rear-view mirror, watching the vet amble back over to the median to tuck his bills in his pack. Ford hoped he used it to get a room and a hot meal for the night. He knew many veterans developed alcohol and drug problems when their country turned its back on them after they'd served and lost everything: their families, homes, money... even their minds. But Ford couldn't worry about what the ex-soldier would buy with the money, he just wanted to help. He understood that he or Brian could've been in that man's shoes. Although Ford accepted the dishonorable discharge, he hired a JAG Officer to sue for his benefits. He'd fought too hard for the United States – served for over twenty years – to just be dumped on the streets like trash. He used every trick he knew to save himself and all his brothers. The ones who'd disobeyed direct orders and followed him to that dangerous cave in Afghanistan. Ford had dirty information on high-ranking military officials. It was in their best interest to give him his demands. All he'd wanted was his pension for him and the men that had followed him and for Brian to have full medical benefits when they got back stateside. Ford had kept them all from being just another homeless military statistic but he'd always carry the shame of being dishonorable.

"The United States doesn't negotiate with terrorists. My brother and his team will all be dead by the end of next week. I'm afraid this is going to be my last act as your Lieutenant... as

a SEAL." Ford looked his men in the eye. He struggled not to show his emotions, because at that very moment he knew his brother was being tortured by the Taliban.

Ford and his team had been holed up on a Marine base called Delaram when Ford heard of the ambush in Kandahar. He knew Brian was there with his team, waiting for their General to arrive so they could transport him to Camp Leatherneck. That's where he and Brian were supposed to meet tomorrow. It wasn't often they were close enough to each other for a face-to-face. Ford was usually on one side of the desert and Brian on the other. As soon as he heard he'd be in Delaram for three days, he'd emailed Brian, anxious to see his baby brother after another long nine months of deployment.

"We're going with you, LT." Master Chief Johnson – Ford's closest friend – was first to stand and object to Ford going alone.

"I'm with you, King." Chief Petty Officer Roland stood next. "There's no way you're going to that sand trap without me."

"We fight and die together," said their Special Demolitions Master.

Ford didn't try to stop the tears. Some of these men had fought beside him for over fifteen years, some only a few months, but none of them were willing to let him go alone. All of them understood the term "brotherhood."

Ford's phone rang, yanking him out of his memory. He hit the Bluetooth on his steering wheel and connected the call.

"What's your twenty, Ford?"

"Be there in ten," Ford answered Duke.

His boss was ready to get some much-needed information on the Grossmans' whereabouts. Ford pulled into the small parking lot in front of Duke's Bail Bonds and Recovery and hurried inside. Brian was at his desk, doing what he was amazing at. Dana looked dressed and ready to hit the streets, his head lifting up from behind his own computer. Quick was nowhere to be found, but Ford could hear raised voices coming from behind Duke's closed door.

"What's going on?" Ford asked both of them, tossing his knee-length leather coat onto the back of his chair.

Brian rolled his eyes and went back to his work. Dana nodded towards the door. "Vaughan's in there. Duke wants him out of town until he catches the Grossmans, but you know Vaughan's a badass, so he's refusing. Duke doesn't want John to get the upper hand by snagging anyone's partner. Quick went to take Dr. Chauncey to some doctor's cabin in east Atlanta. Trust the doc wasn't happy about having to commute an extra forty-five minutes to work."

Duke's door flew open and an immaculately dressed Vaughan stormed out with Duke right behind him.

"This isn't a request, Vaughan. You'll go and that's it," Duke argued.

Vaughan whirled around to face his lover. His purple and cream designer suit jacket flying open as he did. "Is that an order? Because I don't take them from you or anybody. I have a job to do too, Duke. You think I can up and leave my clients whenever you take on the city's most wanted. I won't run and hide. If they come for me, they better be ready for a fight."

Duke rubbed his forehead. "It's only for the weekend, maybe a couple days after that. I need you safe, Vaughan. Can't you understand that? These men won't hesitate to exploit my one and only weakness. If they get to *you*, that's it. I'd submit to all of their demands if it meant saving you."

Vaughan sighed. Even Ford felt sorry for him. It wasn't easy to choose. Your loved one or your career. Hopefully, Vaughan could understand. Ford didn't turn away when Vaughan enfolded Duke in his arms and kissed his neck, his whiskery jaw, then his firm lips. "I have my watch, I'll be fine."

"Vaughan, please baby," Duke whispered, but his begging was still heard by all of them.

Vaughan pulled back and looked into Duke's dark eyes, his black and gray hair was sticking up like he'd been pulling at it while he tried to get his boyfriend to see his point.

"Okay," Vaughan murmured. "I'll take a few days leave and go see my mom."

Duke's breath of relief mimicked all of theirs.

Dana

"It must be nice *and* frustrating to love someone that much, huh?" Dana said almost to himself while they pulled out of the parking lot heading towards the first address Brian had given them, which was the Grossman brothers' last known address. It was unlikely anyone would be there, but it was a starting point. They'd sit on it a while and then look inside for a sneak peek.

Ford rubbed the thick hairs on his full beard. "I wouldn't know."

Dana chanced a look at Ford, but he was looking straight ahead as he took DeKalb towards Edgewood. It was a run-down neighborhood with old townhomes. There were tons of side streets and forest to provide coverage or a quick getaway.

They were quiet the rest of the way, only speaking if it was about the case. They hadn't even mentioned last night or the lingering elephant in the backseat. Were they interested in each other or not? Was Ford bisexual or gay? The man lived a private, isolated life, so it wasn't common knowledge which way he swung, but Dana could read body language and Ford was giving him crazy rhythm.

The GPS announced that their destination was on the left. The home looked like it had been abandoned or was the victim of a drive by, more than likely, both. The Grossmans had enemies and rival gang leaders everywhere. The windows were boarded up, a couple of the ones downstairs had graffiti spray-painted on them. The foundation was unstable and unlivable. There was no one there and hadn't been for a while. "This is a bust," Dana huffed.

"Let's take a quick look when the sun goes down," Ford answered, his dark eyes taking in the surroundings of the empty house. "We can probably pop that board off on the side and get in that way."

"Whatever you say," Dana sighed, leaning back and getting comfortable. He didn't expect to see much activity and they still had some time before it was dark enough for them to sneak inside.

Ford cut his eyes over to him but didn't let them linger long. It was at least thirty minutes before Ford spoke up, his deep voice staggering even in the large cab. "You wanna talk about… you know. Just so we're on the same page?"

Dana swallowed a thick lump of air, his heart accelerating at the possibility of getting some answers. "Sure. If you want to."

Dana decided to let Ford start. He'd initiated this, so Dana would let him get what he needed off his chest first. "Um. I think we should just start over. Squash all that old stuff."

Dana acknowledged that he was listening. He wasn't making eye contact, but neither was Ford. Instead, his sharp eyes were still directed at the run-down house. *Squash it?* "When you say start over, do you mean—?"

"Before we clamped onto each other's throats. That's what I mean." Ford finally looked at him. "Fact is, we have a job to do and petty bullshit can't get in the way."

"I agree. I think we can drop it, then." Dana chuckled humorlessly. "Although, I'm not quite sure what exactly it is that we're dropping. Are we dropping the cold shoulder you keep giving me? Are we dropping the constant bickering over nothing? Are we dropping the façade that we're not—?"

"Who is that?" Ford interrupted, his hand quickly fumbling in the center console for his camera.

Dana turned and looked where Ford was aiming the long scope. A man was cautiously making his way to the side of the same house they were watching. He looked Hispanic with olive skin and jet-black hair that was slicked straight back like an old fifties gangster. He had to be around thirty or thirty-five years old at the most. It was the Adidas track suit with the pristine white tennis shoes that made him stick out like a sore thumb and Dana hadn't even noticed him. *Fuck.* Hadn't even seen what direction he came from. This thing between him and Ford was absolutely a distraction. "I don't recognize him."

"He came from around the back, through the cut there." Ford pointed his meaty hand at the house two doors down. "He's looking for something or someone and he's being obvious as hell about it. He has to know whose place this is. I wonder what he's looking for."

Ford unlocked the doors. "Let's go ask him."

They both pulled their bounty hunter stars from beneath their shirts and let them show, suspended around their necks. It was almost dark now. The sky was a deep purple and the couple of streetlights that were still operational on the street had come on, casting an eerie glow on the cracked asphalt. Glad that the lights above them were out, Dana got out first, quickly crossing the street and closing the distance between him and the curious man who was still looking for a piece of board to work loose. Ford took up the rear, watching Dana's back just like he'd promised. Usually, it was Dana's job to be the watchman, but he and Ford could unconsciously read what the other needed.

"Looking for something?" Dana asked, making the man startle and drop from where he was standing on a milk crate, prying a board loose.

"Who are—?" Before the man could finish his question, his eyes traveled down Dana's chest to the gold star with engraved black lettering: BOUNTY HUNTER. The only warning Dana had that the man was about to bolt was the widening of his deep brown eyes and the determination in his glare. He took off in the opposite direction, towards the back of the house. He had a good jump off but he was no match for Dana's agility or speed. In a few steps he'd walked the guy down, practically running right up beside him when he swept his feet from under him and sent him crashing – back first – to the filthy pavement.

"For a man wearing a track suit, you're exceptionally slow." Dana smirked, looking down at the man he'd just sent feet first into the air. He was still groaning about his back, but it didn't stop him from reaching in his pants pocket and pulling out a switchblade, a quick flip of his finger had the blade snapping open with an intimidating click.

Dana lifted the hem of his shirt, showing off one of his Glocks tucked securely in his waistband, shaking his head in annoyance. "Please. You've brought a knife to a gun fight. Put that thing away and get up. You tell us why you were snooping around over there and I might let you stay up."

"I thought you were about to tell me I had a warrant." The guy frowned, wiping off his pants leg as he made his way up off the ground.

"Maybe you do have warrants, but I'm not in the mood to check. You cooperate and my mood will stay that way." Dana flicked his head toward the house. "Now what were you looking for?"

"I was just wondering what the hell was going on… that's all. I heard they'd moved out."

"Who's they?" Ford growled from behind the man.

"Jesus, man! Don't do that." Track Suit had to be wondering how a man as huge as Ford had snuck up on him without a sound. Not even the faint crunch of gravel under his large boots could be heard if he didn't choose.

"Grossmans' men. There was a ton of activity around here about a week ago. My sister and little niece stay a few doors down. They were scared. There was a shooting and those two criminals were part of it. Next thing she tells me is the house was gutted and boarded up. I just wanted to see for myself that they weren't coming back. Are y'all close to catching them? If you're not looking for me then you must be here looking for them."

Track Suit wasn't lying. He looked nervous for his sister. Dana understood what it was like having loved ones that were subjected to rough environments. This man was just trying to get some answers for his sister. "Stop poking your nose in business that's not yours. The Grossmans could have men sitting on this house, too. And you weren't even trying to be slick about it."

"I ain't afraid of them... none of 'em."

"Maybe they'll put that on your gravestone. Go on. Go. Stay out of this business," Ford ordered gruffly, turning back towards the house.

The man mumbled something in Spanish and walked off in the opposite direction. He and Ford headed back towards the house. This time, Dana a couple steps behind Ford. Ford stopped at the window and ripped off the loose board with one hand, shining a bright flashlight inside with the other. Nothing. Trash, beer bottles, paraphernalia, a few busted-up tables, milk crates and a vast amount of trash littered the entire first floor. There was nothing here they could use. Back in the truck, Dana had a regretful feeling they weren't about to resume the conversation they'd been having prior to the interruption.

"I'm gonna send this photo to Brian anyway to make sure that guy's face doesn't pop up again later." Ford pushed a few buttons on the high-tech camera then set it back inside the console before leaving the dark neighborhood.

"I don't think he was playing us. If so, he's wasting his talents here, he should be acting in Hollywood." Dana fastened his seatbelt and pulled up the next address.

PROMISES PART 3

"No, I don't think he was lying, I'm just being cautious. I'm pretty good at spotting deception," Ford said confidently.

"Are you really?" Dana responded roughly. As soon as Ford came to a full stop at the intersection, Dana turned and gave Ford a look he hoped he could see and decipher. It was an open and honest confession. *I really like you.*

CHAPTER TWELVE

Ford

It was after two in the morning. Ford dropped down in bed, his body still flushed and damp from his hot shower. What he should've done was taken a cold one. He felt unsettled and warm all over. He still felt like things were tense between him and his partner. It sounded like they'd agreed to let it go, though it felt like anything but.

After two-and-a-half weeks of surveillance, nothing had turned up. At least Duke finally gave them a Saturday off. He'd put out word through his street contacts that he was gonna lay low and maybe back off the Grossmans to see if they could be flushed out. Ford needed Saturday to get his head straight.

He and Dana hadn't had another opportunity to discuss anything private between them, but the tension hung over their heads like a dreary storm cloud. Both of them figured it was best to leave their personal shit out of the field since it was far too distracting. When they talked, when he looked into Dana's soft, bedroom brown eyes, everything else around him seemed to fade away. That wasn't the way a man hunted – by taking his eyes off his targets. But he knew the day was coming, and soon. He'd tell Dana how he felt and hoped he wouldn't completely embarrass himself.

For now he'd make the best of his one day off. He had a million errands he had to run. Despite the hour, he texted Brian.

Ford: *Going to the grocery store and to run errands. You coming?*

Brian responded almost immediately. Of course his brother would check his messages, no matter the hour. *Sure, bro. I'll be ready at 9. How'd the surveillance go? Dana isn't walking on the side of the road again is he?*

Ford murmured a few curses under his breath. The guys were never gonna let him forget the day he kicked Dana out of his truck, during another one of their heated arguments, and made him walk all the way from Kirkwoods for almost thirty minutes before Brian got there to pick him up. That wasn't one of his finer moments. Just another instance of him fighting his wants. He needed to talk to Brian soon about his predicament. He had no one else and his therapist told him it wasn't good to let everything stay bottled up all the time. Ford trusted his brother completely, so he'd confide in him and seek his advice. Brian didn't speak out loud, and he had a lot of trauma within his soul, but one thing those fucking Talibans couldn't fuck with was his brilliance. He'd help Ford get this straightened out.

Stop fighting me. You want me, Ford. Look at me, look at my need for you," Dana purred, rubbing his talented hands up and down Ford's hairy chest while he hovered over him. He looked gorgeous. Ford pried his eyes open and feasted on the man's striking face, he looked like he was glowing, floating above him. Then Ford suddenly felt the weight of Dana's body on him.

"Unnnh," Ford moaned loudly. He couldn't fight it any longer. Yes, he did want him. "Don't, brat," Ford whispered painfully.

"Don't what?" Dana was writhing all over him, his hard body a work of perfection, and Ford didn't know where to put his hands first. God, he'd been wanting a feel for so long.

"Don't stop," Ford hissed when his cock was gripped tightly. "Dana. Oh, you bastard."

Dana was still radiating that beautiful light and Ford wanted to bask in it forever. This was the first time he'd thought of forever. For the first time, the idea of Dana's face being there when he thought of his future didn't give him a stomach ache.

Dana lay beside him staring back at him. His brown eyes the color of a rich, smoky quartz, pleading so sweetly. "Let me in, Ford... let me in... Ford... let me in."

Ford bolted upright in bed. The pounding on his front door stopped, then he heard a key turning in the knob. His brother letting himself in. Had to be Brian, because he was the only one with a key to his place. Shit, what time was it? Had he overslept? Thinking of what he was just dreaming about, no wonder his dick was making his underwear stick out like a teepee. He was so hard it hurt. He heard Brian making his way down the short hallway to his bedroom. Ford jumped out of the bed and hurried into the bathroom and closed the door. He hollered to his brother to make a pot of coffee and give him ten minutes.

Ford dressed in a pair of comfortable jeans and a white t-shirt under his blue and grey flannel shirt. He wasn't a fashion guy by any means. He pulled on his five-year-old, broken in boots and tucked his badge in his back pocket along with a brand-new chrome and black 9mm weapon secured at the small of his back. Dana loved that weapon. Ford sighed and shook his head. *Oh no, it's already starting.* Ford walked into his kitchen to a cup of coffee *not* waiting for him. He looked at his brother expectantly. "What happened?"

Brian held up Ford's empty coffee jar. Damn, he really needed to get to the store now. A quick stop at a 7-Eleven for some coffee with two breakfast bites and he'd be good to go for a few hours. "The Orioles are on tonight. You coming over?"

Brian nodded his head while he threw the empty container in the trash and picked up his jean jacket off the chair. On the way to Ford's truck Brian began signing. *"It's not like you to sleep so late. Something wrong, Ford?"* Brian didn't finger-spell the letters of Ford's name as was common in ASL. He signed the word "brother" but instead of using an L-shaped hand like you're supposed to, he used an F. Ford liked that a lot.

Ford was quiet until he felt a comforting heavy hand on his shoulder. He turned his head to face his brother. He looked so much like him it was almost like looking in a mirror. Except Brian's beard wasn't as thick as his, opting for the dark stubble. His hair had grown quite a bit longer on the top, just enough to put in a tiny man bun, which was what Brian had done today. The sides, he kept shaved close. It wasn't a style Ford could pull off, but it wasn't bad on his brother. A jagged scar ran from his brow to his temple, some were hidden under his dark beard, and several marred his neck where his captors had threatened to yank out his tongue through his throat if he didn't talk. Ford moved his eyes from them, his heart clenching every time he thought of that period in their life.

"Let me get some coffee in me. And I'll talk, though I'm sure you probably already know what it's about."

Brian's grin was irritating, but he faced front and didn't press him. After scarfing down their breakfast sausages and coffee in the car, Ford balled up the trash and tucked it back in the 7-Eleven bag. He stared at the already full Save-A-Lot parking lot. It was a brisk forty-two degrees and the sun was out, but dark storm clouds were approaching fast from the south. Regardless, that didn't stop the people from coming out in droves this Saturday. He knew Brian was waiting patiently on him to start talking, but he had no clue *how* to start it.

"You going to taxi this thing to death or you going to bring it in, brother?" Brian finally signed.

"Yeah. Things are crazy in my head, Brian. He's driving me insane," Ford started out, letting his worries flood to the surface and drown him. "I'm dreaming about him, thinking about him, pissed about him, and everything else in between. It's all his fault, too," Ford growled, then murmured, "Needs to grow the hell up."

"He's great and you know it. If he knew you were even slightly interested, he never would've gotten back with that deceiver." Brian had to finger spell the last word.

"So you would be good with that, if me and him, ya know?" Ford always looked his brother in the eye, but he was struggling today. He was embarrassed.

"Why wouldn't I be? He's Dana. And I know he likes you. And you obviously like him. Or else y'all wouldn't fight like Ike and Tina." Brian cocked his brow when Ford gave him a dirty look. *"Just being honest."*

"He's young," Ford contended.

"Age is a state of mind."

"Not when you're almost fifty," Ford scoffed.

"But you look like a thirty-year-old, and you're probably healthier than one, too. Do you feel forty-six?"

Ford shook his head. Sometimes he forgot his real age. Duke's and Quick's, as well. Teenagers couldn't outrun them. Ford ran five miles, three, sometimes four times a week. Worked out more than that. He was extremely fit and he felt it.

"State of mind, brother."

"He shouldn't've gotten back with that girl any-damn-way. That's not exactly a way to earn someone's trust."

"He already has your trust. You would never go in the field with anyone that wasn't up to your standards. He was lonely, that's all. He doesn't love her. But he's the type of man that needs companionship, and that's not a bad thing. It's a human thing, Ford. Most people – men too, bro – don't want to be alone." Brian tapped Ford's thigh so he'd turn and look at him. *"If I can put myself out there… so can you. I don't want you to be alone."*

"I'm not alone. I have—"

Brian threw both hands up, cutting him off, his hands moving so fast, Ford had to squint to keep up. *"Oh no. You have me and the guys, but not in that way. You need 'that way' in your*

PROMISES PART 3

life, Ford. You're not ready to hang up your coat and hat. You've got a lot of years left, a lot of nights. Do you want to spend them watching the sports channel and eating oven dinners alone, or do you trust your watchman to take you on one helluva ride?"

"Shit, Brian," Ford huffed, then signed the rest of what he had to say, because speaking the words out loud would be too devastating to his macho pride. *"I'm afraid of him."*

Dana

Dana grabbed a small hand cart, then checked his list. It wasn't too bad, he should be able to get in and get out of the crowded store in, oh, about two hours. Shopping and running errands wasn't his favorite thing to do, but at least it kept his mind occupied. He'd had a peaceful night's sleep with Jess being out of town, but it'd taken him a while to finally *fall* asleep. His thoughts were filled with Ford.

Dana walked towards the produce section first, then decided he'd work his way over to the frozen food. After two repeats down the same freaking aisle, being practically fondled in the meat department, and his hip almost dislocated by a lady operating a scooter, he was finally able to say he was almost done. Last was his deli meat. When all else failed and he was too tired to cook –or even go through a drive-thru – a turkey and cheese sandwich worked in a pinch. Dana was standing in the lengthy line – four people was too long – waiting on his number to be called. He tried to think of what else he needed to do before he went home, but his thoughts kept straying. *Of course. It's either zero or a hundred for me.* He'd accepted his attraction to his partner, no longer able to fight it, now he was all the way in left field. Ford consuming his thoughts every free moment.

Dana wasn't a man who was easy to sneak up on, even at his worst, and with the current bounty they were working on, they were all supposed to be on high alert. So when his bicep was clasped from behind and a strong presence towered over his back, Dana barely flinched, his hand automatically whipping back under his jean coat.

"Easy, shooter. You gonna draw in a store full of people?"

Dana's eyes widened, then slid half closed as he felt Ford lean in closer to his ear. His dark, voice superseding any and everyone around them. "How did I get the drop on you?"

"You didn't," Dana grunted through his slightly parted lips. He turned around to look at Ford and almost swallowed his tongue. It was rare he saw him outside of work hours. He and Brian hung out, but Ford consistently declined. He looked different without all the black and leather. Dana wanted to inch in closer and engulf himself in the obscenely masculine scent coming from the big SEAL. He didn't smell like cologne, he just smelled like man. Ford looked open, despite the hard look on his handsome face. Dana loved that look. A look of seriousness, maturity and focus at all times.

"What are you doing here?" Ford asked.

"I'm playing a scavenger hunt." Dana barked a quick laugh when Ford tightened his jaw. "What do you think I'm doing here?"

Ford leaned in, his intense eyes blazing. "Is everything a joke to you?"

Dana glared right back. "No."

The line had moved on but they were still standing there staring hard when Brian came up looking incredulously between the two of them.

"For real? Here. Now?" Brian shook his head at them, then walked away, his hand-basket still practically empty. But Dana saw the economy size pack of Magnums in there.

"I wasn't trying to goad you, man. Looks like we're both getting chores done before we have to go in tomorrow."

Ford was looking all over Dana's face like he'd never seen him before. Those hot eyes smoldering all over his skin. *What is he doing?* Choosing not to piss Ford off more by asking if he had an eye problem, instead he asked, "So what else is on the agenda for today?"

"A couple more things. Then I'm watching the game with Brian tonight."

Dana raised his brows, like he'd just remembered. "Shit, the game. I forgot. I'm definitely watching that. I might go to a sports bar or something… or just stay at the crib and watch it alone."

Ford looked like he was waging an internal battle in his head. His forehead creased with concentration and his mouth opened, but nothing came out. Luckily for him Dana's number was called and he turned to quickly place his order. When he was finished, he thought he'd turn around and find Ford gone, but he was still there, looking… fixated.

Dana didn't speak anymore. He'd thrown a line out there but didn't get a bite. The deli clerk gave him his order, terminating his reason to stand there in Ford's company any longer. "I'll, umm. I guess, I'll see you tomorrow." Dana forced a smile and started to walk away when he heard Ford clear his throat.

"You can come over and watch it with us if you want," Ford said as quietly as his powerful bass-filled voice would let him. The sound still rattled Dana's chest. That voice could be the death of him.

Dana walked the few steps back, needing to see if Ford was extending the invite out of pity or if he genuinely wanted Dana there. Last time he'd been in the man's space it hadn't gone well. He did see uncertainty, but he didn't see pity. "That sounds good."

"What sounds good?" Brian gestured, appearing back beside his brother with ease. One would think those big men would have a time moving their bulk through the throngs of people, but they didn't, they moved with quiet precision... scarily.

"Watching the game with you guys tonight. I'll bring some nachos." Dana smiled, feeling so lightheaded it was funny. It was crazy how even the smallest, most platonic invitation from his partner could make him high. *It's just a ballgame.*

Brian didn't let his shock show, but Dana imagined there was surprise somewhere in the man's calculating mind that his brother had invited someone to hang with them on *their* night. Ford's time with his brother was sacred. They all knew that.

"Actually. I forgot that I do have other plans tonight." Brian signed with mock seriousness, having a hard time hiding his classic smirk.

"Fuck you." Ford turned and glared at his not-little-at-all brother.

Dana had to admit that Brian *was* being pretty obvious. This was clearly a lame attempt to get them alone.

"Really, I do." Brian's charming grin was contagious and Dana began to join in while Ford stood there looking really uncomfortable. *"But you guys still chill out and watch. Make sure to text me the score."*

"Yeah, whatever, Brian," Ford hissed.

"Starts at eight." Ford turned and walked away, leaving Dana beaming behind his back.

"He likes DiGiornos on game night." Brian signed hastily. Dana didn't catch it the first time, and Brian signed it slower.

It took a second for Dana to piece it together but he got enough to interpret what Brian said. "I'll bring the pizzas!" Dana yelled at Ford's hastily retreating back as he smoothly maneuvered his huge body through the aisle, but not before earning himself the finger over Ford's broad shoulder. This was getting more fun now.

There's no way the looks he just received from his partner could be interpreted as simply casual perusal. No, Ford was sizing him up and liking what he saw. Dana knew that look, especially on a man. He looked over at Brian and thanked him for the backup. He was going to need every ally he could muster if he was going to snag Ford's stubborn ass.

"Ball's in your court."

Dana gave Brian a one-armed hug and walked off.

Chapter Thirteen

Ford

Ford got up from his chair again – fifth time in twenty minutes – he couldn't sit still. He alternated between wanting to choke his brother for ditching him and making him look stupid, not to mention desperate, and wanting to text Dana and tell him a lie that they'd turned off his cable. His eyes were usually glued to Sports Center before it was time for the game to start – him and Brian arguing stats – but he couldn't find it in himself to care about them right now. He checked his watch again. It was four minutes past the last time he'd checked it. He looked around at the meager furnishings in his home, grimacing at the lack of hominess. Decorating was never his strong suit. On the mantle he had a couple pictures of him and Brian as boys on the farm and one with him and his SEAL team. That was the only thing of value in there. He kept his high-end gadgets in the vault at the office. Then of course, he had a few weapons in his home. Ford could care less about the tiny dinette set he'd got from a thrift store or the loveseat and mismatched recliner, Dana would probably hate it.

Ford tightened his jaw and fisted his hands. This was exactly what he'd been referring to when he said he was worried about complications. Already he was questioning if his place was good enough. *If he doesn't like it, then screw him.* Ford dropped back down in his chair, determined not to get up again. The game would be starting in fifteen minutes and Dana better not be—

A sharp knock at the door cut off his thoughts. "It's open," Ford barked from across the room.

Dana peeked around the door before he stepped fully inside. He had a twelve pack under one arm and two DiGiorno pizzas in the other.

How much does he think we're going to eat and drink?

"Hey. What's up?" Dana automatically headed towards the kitchen, looking at home in only five seconds flat. "You want me to put these in the oven?"

Ford stopped staring long enough to close his mouth and get up to be somewhat hospitable. He was raised in West Virginia, he knew better. "I'll get it preheated. You can put the beer in the fridge."

"Nice place. You got a lot of room to work with," Dana said, looking around, already turning a beer up to his lips. He took off his leather coat and tossed it over one of the small chairs in the eat-in kitchen.

"Thanks. I don't have time to do much with it. Maybe I will soon," Ford said unconvincingly.

"Yeah, if we ever get a long enough break, huh?"

Ford didn't answer. Instead, he let Dana walk around his home and make himself comfortable while he readied the pizzas. Ford hated to admit it but he already liked that Dana's scent was quickly filling the small space. He smelled good enough to eat, better than his DiGiorno was going to smell. He'd obviously gone home and gotten spiffy, freshly showered and shaved. He had on a gray collared shirt with black jeans and black Jordans while Ford had on the same thing he'd worn all day. Then he got a sick feeling like he and Dana were on a date.

"Hey. Stop thinking so hard. You're making me nervous." Dana chuckled. But his smile faded when Ford failed to see the humor. Then he realized that he'd been staring at Dana too long with a tight scowl over his brow. Dana squeezed his eyes closed and touched his hand to his forehead. "Do you… do you want me to go, Ford? Maybe… yeah, maybe I should go."

Ford's chest constricted at the hurt look in Dana's eyes. His smile had been sexy and open when he first came in Ford's door, and Ford had only said a couple words and already Dana was thinking he should leave. Leaving was the last thing he wanted Dana to do. Ford stood there with his hands braced on the counter, his jaw firmly locked.

Dana picked his coat back up and began to walk towards the door. "Look. I'll see you at work tomorrow. I'm sorry I jumped in on your time. Enjoy the pizzas." Dana moved solemnly but he kept his spine straight and his shoulders back. Next thing Ford knew, his feet were moving and he was there, slamming the door back shut as soon as Dana cracked it open. His partner didn't turn around, just stood frozen there with his hand still on the doorknob, facing the door, his chin dropped to his chest.

"I'm not trying to upset you. I'll go if that's what you need." Dana's voice sounded broken to Ford's ears.

His chest was just touching Dana's back while he kept his palm pressed firmly to the thick wood. He didn't know how to voice his wants, but his actions had to say that he didn't want to be left alone. "I apologize." Ford saw the shiver in Dana when he spoke and god did that do things to him. "This is… I'm not sure what… I mean—"

Dana turned around and Ford realized how impossibly close they were. His eyes dropped down to Dana's mouth all on their own. "It's fine, Ford. I'm just gonna watch the game with you, man."

Ford swallowed thickly, fighting the compulsion to lean forward and sneak a taste of Dana's soft-looking lips, his curiosity nearly getting the better of him. And it didn't help that now Ford's erotic dream last night was right at the forefront of his mind. His cock thickened and he felt his cheeks heat like Dana all of sudden knew his secret. Knew he'd beat off to thoughts of him, the smell of him, the sheer magnificence of him.

"Sure. Let's watch the game, okay. I'll loosen up." Ford finally put a string of words together that made sense.

"Yeah, loosen up, partner. I'm not gonna bite you." Dana slowly licked his lips – on purpose – and watched Ford's eyes as he did.

Ford groaned and rolled his eyes. "Grow up, brat," he said softly, surprised by how husky his voice was.

"Whatever, you say, old man." For the first time, Dana didn't look offended when Ford said that to him, and Ford saw too much admiration coupled with heat in Dana's eyes for him to take offense, either. Somehow, they'd turned those phrases into flirty innuendo. Dana casually touched Ford's waist and eased him from blocking his path. "I'm gonna get the pizzas in the oven, the game is already on."

Dana

Dana was stuffed with too many slices of oven pizza and beer. The game was over, the Orioles having won by two runs. It'd started out quiet between them, but once they'd sat down and gotten into it, the conversation flowed easily. They talked about all kinds of things, like they were making up for lost time. Sports was first. They both liked similar teams, but Ford was a Dallas fan and Dana liked the Redskins. They both gave a sly grin, realizing football season was going to be intriguing. When commercials came on, they'd face each other and talk. They didn't talk much about the case they were on, thank heavens. That's the last thing Dana wanted to talk about.

He wanted to get to know Ford the man. Not just Ford, his work partner. He found out more about the crop and livestock farm Ford grew up on, that he claimed was nothing more than daily, depressing monotony. He didn't get much information on Ford's duties as a SEAL either, finding that was a sensitive subject, especially the details about him rescuing Brian. Maybe one day soon Dana would be trusted enough to hear that story. Dana answered a lot of questions about him and Sway, but Ford didn't go too far into detail about his teenage years, just that his father pushed a lot of responsibility on him at a very young age. It appeared they had that in common, too.

"My mom left my dad when I was nine and Brian was seven." Ford drank from his fourth beer, becoming more and more talkative with each one. It was good to know that Ford was a chatty drinker. He'd remember that. Ford shrugged indifferently. "I barely remember her, but I knew she was a bad mother."

"You mean like how Shaft was a 'bad mutha'?" Dana laughed hard at his own joke while Ford sat there staring at him, desperately trying to hold in his own laughter.

"God, brat," Ford retorted.

Dana's laughter dwindled when he noticed the rich look of lust on Ford's face. He'd never *ever* seen that look on him. He kept his eyes on Ford's, wanting that look all to himself. Craving that look. He released the air he'd been holding and sucked in a much-needed breath. The temperature in the room spiked thirty degrees as they stared unashamedly at each other. If he weren't such a gentleman he'd be up off that small loveseat and straddling Ford's lap before he could erase that look from his face. But first, he had a girlfriend to break up with. Dana was not a cheater. And second, this was all new territory for Ford and he wouldn't be a jerk and push him into something he wasn't ready for.

"I better go. It's late," Dana said, breaking the tension. As soon as he stood up, he pulled at the hem of his shirt to try to cover his half-hard erection. "I had a good time, Ford." Dana turned around and groaned under his breath. *Why'd I say that?* He'd just made it sound like he'd been on a date.

"Me too," Ford said from close behind him. Dana was relieved Ford didn't read too much into his choice of words.

Dana put on his coat and slowly made his way to the door, hesitant to leave Ford's company after only a measly four hours. He could enjoy being around him – especially when he wasn't so uptight – for much longer. Before he opened the door, Dana turned, desperate for even a few more seconds. "Have a good night."

Ford looked so serious again, like he was debating with himself. The bad guy on his shoulder winning over the good guy on the other. Then everything seemed to move in slow-motion. Ford braced his palm flat on the door beside Dana's head, mimicking what he'd done earlier, preventing him from leaving. While some might find the action a bit barbaric, Dana's cock was getting harder and harder. He didn't move, careful to let Ford go at his own pace. Oh so slowly, Ford brought his right hand up and gently caressed the bristles on Dana's cheek. Dana just remembered to breathe before he passed out. Ford was touching him, and not in a hetero kind of way. It's what he'd wanted for so long. Ford leaned in, carefully watching Dana's eyes as he did. Before their lips could touch, Ford whispered gravely, "Stay still."

Jesus Christ. Dana didn't move, barely inhaled. There was no way he was about to ruin this.

Ford's beard brushed his cheek and Dana realized he'd been right. It was soft to the touch, like Ford used conditioner on it. Dana felt his knees go weak but he locked them in place. Was Ford going to kiss him or was he going to just whisper in his ear and tease the hell out of him… what? All he felt was a deliciously solid, rock hard chest against his own and warm breaths behind his ear. But he followed orders and stayed still, didn't dare move. He kept his fists clenched tightly at his sides to keep from pulling Ford even closer to him. When Ford was done inhaling him, he grazed Dana's ear with his lips. Not a kiss… a caress. Dana felt Ford turn his face into the crook of his neck and he fought not to whimper like a love-sick girl.

"Get rid of her. Now," Ford ordered, making Dana almost come in his pants.

PROMISES PART 3

CHAPTER FOURTEEN

Dana

Dana woke up with a smile on his face, still thinking about the intimate contact he'd had with Ford last night. Without sounding like an adolescent, he needed to call and tell his best friend all about it. Dana put on his jogging pants and an Under Armor compression shirt, then laced up his favorite running shoes. He threw a hoodie over his head and tucked his phone in the front pocket. He stretched for a few minutes then took off down his street at a warm-up pace. When he got to the main drag, he pulled out his earbuds and dialed Sway's number.

"What's up, D?"

Dana smiled even wider. "Swish-and-sway. How's it going?"

"You're a clown." His friend laughed tiredly at the horrific nickname Dana had used to irritate him since high school. "At least I don't have a girl's name."

Dana chuckled. "Are you sure about that? And Dana is unisex, Squirt. Thank you."

"Ugh," Sway grunted. "We need new arguments."

"True. But we'll have to think of more later, right now I have something to tell you."

"Well it better be good, it's eight in the morning on a Sunday." Sway yawned in his ear.

"You're not taking your mom to church?"

"No. She had a rough night."

Dana could hear the weariness in his friend. "I'm sorry. She okay, Sway?"

"Yeah. No worries. It happens, D. But anyway, tell me your news."

"Ford invited me over to his place last night to watch the game. Things started out rocky, but once we both chilled out, we had a good time." Dana looked both ways then hurried across the intersection before the light turned green again.

"Ohh, now that *is* nice. Making good headway on your straight crush," Sway teased.

"When I got up to leave, he stopped me at the door." Dana paused for affect. "Then he kissed me."

Dana heard a shout, a loud clunk and a bit of shuffling, before he finally heard Sway's voice. "No-freaking-way. That big, macho motherfucker kissed you? You didn't steal a kiss then called it mutual, did you?"

Dana threw his head back and laughed loudly, drawing the attention of a couple older men walking into a coffee shop. Yep, he was still on cloud nine. "Well he didn't actually lay a deep, tonsil-sucking kiss on me, it was more like a brief but memorable brush of his lips behind my ear." Dana knew he sounded like a Hallmark movie, but there was no other way to describe that hint of heaven. He had to rein in his thoughts. He couldn't pop wood while he was trying to jog. But damn if he hadn't replayed that scene over and over and it still wasn't enough.

"Wow. Behind the ear. That's sexy as shit," Sway said wistfully.

"It was, man. Who knew he'd be so gentle. I was expecting a hand on the throat, forcing me to yield to him." Dana almost tripped when his cock jerked at the thought of Ford handling him. Dana turned at the next block instead of continuing all the way to the freeway ramp like he usually did before turning around. He was too wound up. He had to be in the office at one. Duke had some new information for them and Dana had a feeling it would involve long hours with his partner tonight, so he had to get himself together. God, how should he act with Ford now? *Oh shit, and I have to talk to Jess. ASAP.*

"D, I can hear the excitement in your voice. But I wouldn't be me if I didn't worry." Sway paused then exhaled slowly. "Are you sure you want to put yourself out there with this guy? I mean. I don't know. He looks like a tits kinda guy. I don't want you to get hurt again and then swear off men for another ten years."

"It hasn't been that long," Dana bit off unsurely.

"Doesn't matter. It was a *long* time."

"You don't know him, Sway." Dana was already turning back onto his street while he listened to his best friend's argument. "He's not a good faker, he doesn't sugarcoat, and he definitely doesn't do phony. I've seen the way he looks at me."

"Anyone would look at you like they want to devour you… you're hot. It doesn't mean that he'd want what you want."

"Well. You think I'm hot, Swish-and-sway?"

"Okay, I'm nauseated now."

"You said it." Dana jogged up the steps to his front door.

"No, I said I want you to be careful. Just don't move to fast and show him how huge your heart is before you know if he even has one."

Dana rolled his eyes. "He is a hard ass, but he's not the tin man."

"I'm serious, D. You love nothing more than to fall in love. Be careful and go slow."

"I'll be careful. I swear. I'll let *him* set the pace."

"Okay, then. That's all I ask."

"Man, you really have to stop hanging out with your mom so much, you sound just like her. Stop acting like you're seventy years old and get out and do something grown up… well grown and reckless. Have some fun, Sway, and stop worrying all the time." Dana wasn't even winded when he removed his clothes and got his shower ready.

"I have fun. See how much you know. I'm going out tonight. To a club."

"You're not talking about the Price *Club,* are you?" Dana burst out laughing.

"I should hang up on your ass. But if you must know. It's a hot, exclusive spot another nurse told me about. Invitation only, so *you* can't even get in." Sway tried to project some snootiness into his voice, but all it did was make Dana laugh louder.

"Interesting. You have to have a membership to get into the Price Club, don't you?"

"I'm done with this conversation. I love you, be safe. And I shop at BJs, you dick."

Sway hung up on him and Dana didn't stop smiling the entire time he was getting dressed, up to the moment he walked through the door to their office and saw Ford, his smile going from jovial to predatory.

Ford

Damn, why does he have to look so good? Ford could've easily blamed his demand for Dana to dump his girlfriend on the multiple beers he'd had, but that was pointless because he'd been far from drunk. He'd wanted to put his hands on Dana, but he wouldn't take what belonged to someone else. Dana's response to him had been so heady, so much more than he'd expected. His partner's heavy pants and the scent of desperation flooded Ford's senses, and *that's* what made him drunk. It was as if Dana hadn't been touched in years, like he hadn't received affection. Which couldn't be the case because the man's dance card seemed to stay packed.

"Afternoon," Dana said when he moved past Ford's desk to his own. A sexy soap and water smell drifted to him, followed with a subtle hint of cologne.

"Hey," Ford managed. His dick was horribly restricted in his leather. There were times he was grateful for the unforgiving fabric – like when his body came into contact with the asphalt – and then there were times his dick wanted to burst through it. Dana was just so sexy. He had on black jeans and a black shirt. He rarely wore leather pants like he and Brian did, but he didn't go anywhere without his seven-year-old, worn leather riding jacket. Dana was engrossed and ready for work, his maturity shining through like a beacon; drawing Ford to him as if he were a ship lost at sea. Then there were times that he joked and played too much. Ford remembered him saying that he missed Ford's smile… maybe he joked because he wanted Ford to be happy. Shaking his head at the silly musing, Ford got down to business.

"What's new? Why are we dressed to hunt? Did Duke get a tip on the Grossmans' location?" Dana asked.

Brian looked up from his computer, signing way too fast for Dana to keep up, so Ford translated.

"One of Duke's contacts came through with a tip. Said that Ray Grossman's main girl hangs out at this ritzy bar called The Grove in Buckhead. The have a male review on Sunday nights. From what the guy said, she practically hosts the event. It's for the high-end crowd with money to spend. Duke doesn't think the Grossmans are there, but he wants us to see if you—" Ford pointed at Dana, "can get close enough to her and try to get her car information so I can LoJack it in the parking lot. Maybe she'll lead us to them."

Dana looked doubtful at hearing the plan and Ford knew why. It was risky at best.

"Get close to her. If she's Ray's main squeeze, then no doubt she'll be protected. Watched like a hawk," Dana responded.

"Or not. This is what she's always done and it's not a place that Atlanta's most-wanted hang out at. It's for the upper class," Ford countered.

PROMISES PART 3

"So, we get in how?" Brian signed.

"You're going, too?" Ford frowned.

"Yes. Duke wants all of us there on the off chance a Grossman might rear his ugly head. He and Quick will be on location, waiting for the tracker to be put in place. The guy at the door is doing us a favor – after Duke paid him five hundred to let us in, no questions asked. Hell, we could probably pass for the entertainment for the evening." Brian put his hands down and blew a teasing kiss at Dana.

"Forget that. I told y'all last month. I won't be pimped out again," Dana grumbled. "Assholes."

Ford laughed and Dana's head jerked up in surprise, a slight quirk of his own mouth making a beautiful appearance. They shared a brief look before getting back on topic.

"No one is pimping anyone," Ford assured him. "We'll do what we do. Be subtle."

"We hardly look subtle in black on black on black. You guys look like you're going to stick up the place and I look like I just robbed a liquor store." Dana looked back and forth between them. "Not to mention all the weapons we have on us."

"So what are you trying to say?" Ford smirked.

"We look like thugs, Bradford! We should've dressed like we were going to schmooze with the lifestyles of the rich and famous, not attack them."

Schmooze? Ford loved when Dana got passionate about the job. His big brown eyes danced with each word he spoke and his chest stuck out even farther as he got worked up. Ford stood and went to the vault where he kept his gadgets, he was ready to get out there with his partner. He felt he was being watched as he walked across the room. When he looked back, he saw Dana's ravenous eyes leveled on his ass. Even when he'd stopped walking, Dana was still gawking. Ford cleared his throat and Dana's eyes snapped up, his cheeks turning red so fast Ford thought they might spontaneously combust. Maybe the man really did find him sexy. He hoped so. He wasn't sure how much longer he could hold everything in. He'd had the tiniest taste of Dana's skin, not nearly enough to quench his hunger or curiosity. He needed more.

Brian stood and put on his black trench coat and began checking his Glocks.

Ford came back out with a tracker about the size of a twenty-five-cent pack of gum. "Don't worry. Duke covered everything. We'll get in. And this isn't the type of place with metal detectors and a pat-down before you can enter."

PROMISES PART 3

CHAPTER FIFTEEN

Dana

Like always, Duke came through. They got in with the bouncers barely giving them a second look. When they walked inside, Dana was surprised and put off at the gaudy glitz and glam. Virgin white and gold as far as the eye could see. He immediately wondered how the hell they kept all the white clean. He looked around at tables covered with white tablecloths, gold flakes littering the tops. Even the candles were glittering. The music was good and it flowed from a state of the art sound system while immaculately dressed bodies moved stiffly to the beats. It looked like half of the space was set aside for dancing and mingling while the other side had tables where waiters brought foo-foo food delivered on gold trays. The customers sat at two-, four-, and even eight-top tables, with their noses in the air and Waterford crystal stemware in their hands.

Looking at the grand staircase that led to the second floor, he couldn't see anything of interest up there since there was a large white curtain obstructing his view. A man sat on a stool just outside it. His thick arms were crossed over his chest, daring anyone to approach that shouldn't. "I'm in the Twilight Zone," Dana murmured.

"Agreed." Ford was behind him, his deep voice drifting over the hard bass of the soft rock playing. "Let's find this girl and get out of here. I'm getting a bad feeling."

Already. Oh no. They'd only been there two minutes. Dana didn't like Ford's bad feelings, if his partner felt something wrong in the air, then something was off. He trusted Ford's instincts. He was a SEAL, he could assess and react quickly. They'd hashed out a plan before they left, now they needed to execute and get the hell out of there since they were already sticking out like renegades in the bright white room of model citizens.

Dana felt it the moment Ford left his side. He turned and watched him move through the crowd, earning way too many looks for Dana to be comfortable. He and Brian went to the bar, and from there they discreetly scanned the room looking for the face they had committed to memory.

A bartender in a cute white dress, with a gold-colored pendant pinning her bright auburn hair on top of her head, stopped in front of them, placing two glass coasters on the bar. "I don't think I've seen you two in here before." She had a smile of perfect white teeth a mile wide. "Believe me, I would know."

Brian stood there watching the woman closely, his dark gaze taking her in, not giving anything away but a hint of mysteriousness and a whole lot of danger. Dana spoke up after she flushed under Brian's inspection. Perfect. Now that Brian was working his dark magic, all Dana had to do was order a couple drinks and turn on the charm, then he'd get her to talk.

"Sweetheart, let me get whatever you have dark on draft, and the same for—"

She giggled, stopping Dana mid-sentence. "Now I know you two aren't from around here. Look around, gentlemen. There are no taps here. That would look too tacky… according to management, anyway." She veered closer like she had a secret, showing a tasteful hint of freckled cleavage as she did. "Personally, I love a good slider and a Miller draft, but you won't find either here."

Dana felt slightly embarrassed, but he didn't let it show. "Of course not. Wishful thinking. So what can you recommend, love?"

She stood back up and tapped her shiny, purple fingernail to her chin. "If you like dark, I have an imported Schorschbock 57, it's smoky and nutty. Tastes delicious. Ohh, I also have Carlsberg's. It's barreled for six months and its vanilla and cocoa taste is to die for."

Dana winked. "Alright, babe. I'm sold. Give us two of the Carl's."

"Coming right up."

Dana turned to Brian, who gave him an irritated shrug. Yeah, he had a feeling they both hated this place for the same reasons. It was nice they had a down-to-earth bartender, and it looked like she'd be their best bet to squeeze some information out of.

She brought back two frosted mugs that looked too expensive to drink from. Both bottles were wrapped elegantly in a white cloth. She unveiled one and presented it to them like it was Dom Perignon 85. *It's just beer.* She looked at Brian and he gave her a tight nod, his jaw as stern as a drill sergeant's. She swallowed hard and poured the bottles with grace, leaving exactly a quarter inch of dark foam at the brim. "Enjoy, gentlemen."

Dana and Ford both drank at the same time. Dana frowned in disbelief at the smooth, amber liquid and took another deep gulp, amazed at how delicious it was. *Where the hell was this from, again?* Brian was casually drinking his like his palate wasn't impressed. But Dana knew it was bullshit, because Brian was already three-quarters finished when their bartender made her way back to them, wiping the bar with a thick, soft cloth as she did.

"What do you think, gentlemen?" She was looking at Brian, but Dana spoke up.

"It's amazing. I'll have another when you get a chance."

"And how about you, tall, dark and handsome. Would you like another?"

Brian set his empty glass down and pushed it towards her, silently answering yes.

"Someone's gonna make me work for it, huh?" She threw Brian a sultry look before turning and sashaying away to get their beers.

Dana looked up and saw Ford standing next to one of the bouncers at the edge of the dance floor. The man looked like he wasn't interested in what Ford was saying because he kept trying to inch away. That meant Ford was striking out on the information front. They had to get going. When the sweet server returned with their second round, Dana started up a conversation.

"So how long you been working here?"

She smiled and began to wipe again at the spotless white bar. "Since college. About seven years."

"Seriously? You enjoy it that much?" Dana gave her his undivided attention. What most women wanted.

"I majored in secondary education. But honestly, this pays way more than teachers make in Atlanta's public school system. Once I have enough saved, then I'll do what I love most… teach."

"That's pretty awesome, girl. Beauty and brains to match." Dana gave her a good once over.

She blushed from head to toe, absently waving him off, but her eyes secretly begged for more compliments. Dana kept going. "I bet you'd be an amazing teacher."

"And what makes you say that?"

Dana shrugged. "Just a hunch."

Her eyes cut back to Brian. "Does your friend always play hard to get?"

Dana looked up at Brian, still standing at his six foot three height. "No. Not always. He's actually looking for someone."

She perked up immediately. "Who? I'm sure I can help if they're a regular here."

Bingo.

"We got an invite from Ray's girl, Diamon, to come check out the place." Dana looked around nonchalantly. "But we haven't seen her yet. Do you know her?"

As if someone had flipped their sweet bartender's bipolar switch, her entire demeanor did a one-eighty. Her back went rigid and her inviting smile transformed into a grimace of fear. Dana watched, dumbfounded.

"Diamon?" she whispered.

"Yes. Have you seen her here tonight?"

The woman stepped back, shaking her head at them. "No… I mean… I don't know who you're talking about."

Dana slowly rose from his stool, trying to calm her down. "It's fine. If I knew what car she drives, I could just go look myself."

"I… I don't know. I'm sorry, I have to go now. It's time for my break." She hurried down the bar too fast for Dana to stop her without raising his voice and drawing attention.

"Fuck," Dana hissed, downing the rest of his beer. "These guys got everyone terrified."

Another bartender came over and placed a black billfold in front of them and walked away. It was obvious their lady wasn't coming back. Dana scanned the bar, but she was nowhere to be found. He picked up the jacket and opened it, his fingers fumbling the bill before he steadied it. "Jesus H. What the fuck! Two hundred forty-nine dollars for four beers." Dana looked wide-eyed up at Brian. "Did you know those damn beers were fifty bucks a pop?"

Brian shook his head, his hardened façade dropping for a moment and a mocking grin replacing it.

Dana blew out a hard, frustrated sigh. "Well, going half on it, won't be too—"

Brian began to back away, signing he was going to the bathroom.

"Fuck you, Brian." Dana sneered. "Get back here and pay half."

Brian gestured again, *"I'll be back."*

Dana gritted his teeth as Brian moved through the crowd, farther away from their ridiculous tab. *Son of a bitch. Well, she can forget about a tip, that's for damn sure.* When Dana pulled out his wallet and placed his credit card on the bar, he noticed forty-one dollars of the bill was gratuity, so the joke was on him. *Great.* Now he was going to have to tweak his budget for the rest of month. He was still mumbling obscenities when the other bartender came to run his card.

"Who exactly are you talking too?" Ford was standing next to him. "You look like a lunatic, standing here bitching yourself out."

"If you saw this damn tab, you would too." Dana signed the slip when it was placed back in front of him. Ford peered over and gave a low whistle.

"Why would you buy a drink here?"

"I was blending in, Ford," Dana snapped. "What should I have asked for, huh? Tap water?"

Ford looked like he didn't care. "Yeah, why not?"

"Because there are no fucking taps!" Dana barked, making Ford look around anxiously before he gripped Dana's elbow and dragged him to a dark corner behind the DJ stand.

Ford pushed him up against the wall, the bass from the sound system vibrating his back while Ford pressed his hard chest against his front. "Calm down," Ford growled.

Dana breathed through his nose. It'd been a while since his partner had checked him, and Dana didn't bite back, knowing he'd be striking a heated feud. Things had changed between them. And no matter how ticked off Dana was… Ford was right. He shouldn't be causing a scene. If Duke and Quick had been in there, that would've been his ass. Ford taming him felt different now, after what happened between them last night.

"I'm cool," Dana said, close to Ford's chin.

Ford leaned in, bracing his arm on the wall. He spoke directly into Dana's ear to be heard over the music. "Good. Because as much as I don't want to do this, because you might take this wrong, I have to show you."

Dana wanted to wrap his arms around Ford's waist but he didn't think it was that type of establishment. Instead, he brought his hand up and discreetly brushed it across Ford's thick beard. He heard and felt Ford's sharp breath. "Did you do what I told you to do?"

Dana moaned and closed his eyes, his chest rising and falling rapidly. He knew what Ford was talking about. *Oh god.* All he wanted was one simple touch. He wanted so badly. All that bulk and brawn right there. A big bear playground for his mouth and hands. "I am. I mean, I will. She's out of town. But as soon—"

"Stop right there," Ford bit out, pushing Dana harder against the wall with his massive frame. Dana wasn't a little guy, standing at six foot one, one hundred and eighty pounds of tight muscles, but when Ford loomed over him, he fought the urge to tuck his tail and roll over for him.

"No. I swear, I'm going to do it." Dana looked in Ford's mature eyes, begging for him not to doubt him. "If I have even the smallest chance with you, no one is going to stand in my way. I just don't want to send her a text, Ford. That's foul, ya know. I'm not like that."

"That's not it, Dana. I believe you," Ford whispered. "But look to your left. Nine o'clock. Curved booth in the corner."

Damn. He'd lost focus for a moment, but it only took Dana a split second to get back into hunting mode. He casually turned his head, thinking Ford was pointing out their bounty's girlfriend or even better, one of their bounties, but his mouth dropped when he saw Jessica sitting at the booth with several people. Five to be exact. Dana was surprised to see the woman he was supposed to be dating hugged up with another man… right here *in* town.

He turned and looked back at Ford. He didn't like the cynicism he saw. He hoped Ford didn't mistake his look of shock for anger or hurt. Because he wasn't angry or hurt. It did suck that his girlfriend had obviously been cheating on him, but most of all he felt foolish… played. "Now looks like as good a time as any."

Ford gripped his arm when Dana tried to walk towards the booth. "Not here," Ford demanded. "We're working."

Dana stopped to think. As usual, Ford was right. If Dana went over there and told her it was over, there was no doubt it wouldn't go well and would probably get Dana and his guys thrown out.

Dana looked back over at the booth then turned away. He didn't know when Brian had slid up next to him his huge body there signing something to his brother.

Ford shook his head repeatedly. "Things could get heated, Brian, if she gets mad."

Brian and Ford communicated some more before Ford finally translated. "Brian thinks you should go over there and act like you aren't mad and see if… if she knows anything about Diamon. All we need is a car make. She's got a reserved booth, so she might be a regular. Brian said… use her now… dump her later."

Dana groaned in frustration, pinching the bridge of his nose between his thumb and forefinger. "*Use* her. That's not even my MO, Brian, you know that."

"She's a bitch."

"Whatever. I don't care. She can go on and be happy now," Dana said. "Let's go, fellas. No one will talk to us here. Let's just sit on the place. Maybe we'll spot her coming out."

"They don't close until two. That's three hours from now. Just see what she knows," Ford translated for Brian. "He said he'll go with you."

Dana shook his head in disbelief. He wanted to leave right at that moment. He could if he said the words. Technically, he was the one with field command. Despite Ford and Brian's combined years of experience and sheer military excellence, Dana was the watchman. His job was to identify and eliminate threats in the field. He also had the authority to pull the plug and abort the plan if necessary to protect his team. Wanting to save face with his conniving girlfriend wasn't a reason to abort, because his primary job description was to get his bosses the information they asked for by any means necessary. When no other option came to mind, Dana huffed. "Fine. Let's get this over with."

PROMISES PART 3

CHAPTER SIXTEEN

Dana

Confronting Jessica was the last thing Dana'd been expecting to do when he walked into the overpriced, ostentatious club. But as he stood there gritting his teeth, not liking what his team was suggesting, he knew he had no choice. They were running out of time on this case. The Grossmans would be out of their reach soon if they didn't make some headway. Not only would that be a ton of money lost on the bounty, but Dana desperately wanted those killers off the streets.

Dana walked across the room with Brian on his heels. As he got closer he could hear his soon to be ex-girlfriend's laughter filtering through the continual chatter in the dining area. The man she was nestled close to had his arm draped over her shoulder while he whispered something to her that made her blush and lick her glossed lips. The entire scene made his stomach turn and he had the impulse to turn around and go back. He stopped mid-stride and stared. He felt a gentle nudge in his back that finally got him moving again.

Jessica didn't see him until he was standing over her. A shadow blocking the bright lights that were shining on her. Without even looking up, Jess held her glass up in his direction. "I'll have another."

Seriously. She thought he was the damn server. And even if he had been their waiter, was that how she asked for what she wanted? By not even respecting them enough to look them in the face. When her glass lingered there in the air, a man sitting in her group cleared his throat, finally capturing Jess' attention. "I don't think he's our server, though I wouldn't mind if he was… or you." The man said, eyeing Brian.

Jessica blinked, then turned her head and looked up at him. Dana tried not to have a pissed-off look, but he had a feeling he'd fallen short. Her mouth gaped open like a fish for a couple seconds before she composed herself and smiled affectionately at him. "Dana, what… how'd you… what are you doing here?"

"I could ask you the same thing. May we join you?" Dana was already sliding in, pushing Jessica closer to her date.

"No, um."

"Sure." The man who was still eyeing Brian hurried to say and scooted over, patting the seat beside him. Without taking his eyes off the man, Brian slid his big body into the booth next to him, not making a sound. "Jessica, please introduce us to your friends."

Jessica was looking so confused and mostly humiliated that Dana started to feel glad he'd come over. Jess' image was everything to her. Surely, her pompous group wanted to know how in the world she knew these men. With a toss of her hair, she sat up straighter. "Dana, can I talk to you in private, please?"

Dana looked at Brian and got his subtle no.

"Wow, Jess. Pump your brakes, girl. I actually been wanting to meet some of your friends." Dana looked around the table. "My name is Dana Cadby, and across from me is my colleague, Brian King, I'm an old acquaintance of Jessica's. We *used* to be an item, I guess you can say." Dana turned on his full mega-watt smile and a couple of the ladies at the far end of the booth gushed and turned to give Jessica "that's unbelievable" looks.

Dana had to crowd in closer to Jessica unless he wanted to fall out of the booth. He felt her aggressively squeeze his thigh under the table, but he didn't flinch, still watching the reaction of the table. They looked intrigued, almost fascinated, as their eyes bounced from him to Brian, taking in their dark clothes, leather coats, and ass-kicking boots.

"I don't think I've seen you two here before. Do you have memberships?" Jessica's new man decided to speak up, peering around Jessica to look at Dana. The disdain was all over his face. He looked just like the type that Jessica's rich daddy would approve of. The jacket to his expensive suit was gone, but his shirt and tie were enough to show he had plenty of money. His hair was cut in a style that reeked of corporate America.

"We do now," Dana quipped right back, then averted his eyes to Jessica. "This is just my type of hangout."

"I can tell." New Boyfriend said drily.

"Pipe down, Jameson." The small man sitting beside Brian inserted. "These men are guests. Let me buy you two a drink, please. We hardly ever get to meet friends of Jessica's."

"Ditto," Dana added, still staring at Jessica. She looked like she wanted to crawl under the table and cry until Dana went away. No chance in hell he was leaving now. Right at that moment the waiter came over, one hand tucked behind his back, the other resting in front of him with a crisp white hand towel draped over his forearm.

"I see we have a couple of newcomers. May I get you a menu, sir? Perhaps a drink?" The waiter smiled warmly.

"We do." Brian's admirer answered before Jessica could stop him. "And I would like to buy these important-looking men *whatever* they desire." Dana didn't miss how he stressed that particular word and directed it towards Brian. It was amazing that the man never uttered a word, but just a look from him could have men and women leaking in their pants.

Dana pretended to think about it, then shrugged coolly and asked the waiter for two Schorschbock 57s, like he drank them all the time. That would be impossible even if Duke gave him a considerable raise. Thank god for Brian's new fan, or Dana would've asked for water.

PROMISES PART 3

"My name is Sascha Orlov. I'm a buyer for the boutique with Ms. Jessica." He held out his hand to Brian first, holding on to it for much longer than necessary, then reached over and did the same to Dana. His hand was baby soft and Dana found himself not wanting to grip it too hard. "Pleasure."

"Likewise." Dana smiled.

Sascha introduced the other three ladies at the table as more coworkers.

"And what do you do?" The woman with the largest diamond earrings he'd ever seen in anyone's ear, finally joined in, eyeing them curiously.

Dana leaned back against the booth, showcasing his full swagger. "We're bounty hunters."

There were excited expressions and a few oohhs and ahhhs sounded around the table. Not only from the ladies but from Sascha, too. "That's incredible." The small man preened, inching a little closer to Brian.

Dana thought it was gutsy as hell. But if Brian had been straight, the guy would've picked up on Brian's disinterest and perhaps toned it down. However, the way Brian's sharp, black eyes raked over the man's face and body, it was clear his flirting wasn't offensive. Brian slowly winked down at Sascha and Dana could almost smell the man's arousal kicking into overdrive. Dana had a thought. Since it looked like Jessica would rather stab Dana in his side with her sharp, nude-colored talons than sit there with him another minute, he didn't think he'd get any answers from her – even if he agreed to crawl in a hole and never invade her posh hangout again. That thought didn't hurt him in the least. There was only one person whose opinion mattered. He turned and looked back towards the DJ stand and saw Ford was still there, not even pretending like he wasn't watching. Dana's chest expanded with the thought of the SEAL being his soon.

The waiter brought their beers and tried to present them in the same fashion their lady bartender had but Dana stopped him mid-flourish. "That won't be necessary, buddy." Dana took the beer bottle, not requiring the frosted glass either and turned it up to his mouth, gulping down almost half before he set it back down. Jessica scoffed and turned her body away from him, leaning into her stuffy man. At least he didn't release a loud belch like he wanted to. He did have some class, whether she thought so or not. Brian took his and did the same, licking his full bottom lip, putting on a nice show for Sascha, and the other ladies, as well.

"Would you like to see a menu, sir? Or hear tonight's specials? The forty-day old, aged Wagyu Beef with fingerling potatoes is our best-seller this evening." The waiter suggested, looking between him and Brian.

Dana had no clue what that waiter was talking about. But whatever expired, foreign meat he was trying to sell them… Dana wasn't buying.

"Did you say, Wagyu? Oh, no, thank you. My partner and I prefer the pseudo beef they serve at Taco Bell," Dana chuckled. The waiter laughed along with the entire table – except Jessica and her date – Brian covering his smile behind his fist and a fake cough. Okay, *that* he'd said just to tick Jessica off.

"And to think I almost didn't come out tonight, but I'm so glad I did," Sascha purred in Brian's direction. "So, does he always do the talking and you do the watching… observing."

"He's the watchman. I provide his intel." Brian signed and the table went silent, their eyes wide. Dana had no reaction. He was used to Brian's shock factor. A big man like him, signing with those huge hands. Most were probably surprised how intelligent he looked when he signed, how sexy the quiet power made him.

Dana translated what Brian said. He used words that Dana was used to, that he'd seen Brian use a million times.

"I didn't even realize you were deaf. You read lips well." The lady with the short, black pixie cut gave Brian a considerate smile.

"He's not deaf, he's mute," Dana answered like always.

"A vow of silence?" Sascha quirked his brows.

"Not a voluntary one."

"This visit has been nice, but I'm sure you have better things to do than sit here with us." Jessica finally had the audacity to speak, her sharp tone clipped, cutting through the pleasant ambiance like glass.

"Why in the world are you being so rude, Jessica?" Pixie Cut asked and Sascha was quick to second that.

While they bickered in that arrogant way rich people did, with their heads high in the air and a demeaning superiority in their tone, Dana gave Brian the go ahead to make his move. It was done discreetly, but Dana saw when Brian slid his hand to Sascha's leg under the table and gestured for him to get up with him. And the man did just that, completely ignoring everyone else. His tight little body trailing behind Brian like an eager puppy. Dana was just glad *he* wasn't the one being pimped out for information this time.

The conversation was a little forced after Brian and Sascha left, as Jessica continued to shoot daggers at not only him but her coworkers, too. He'd made her uncomfortable enough. After Dana finished his beer, he turned to the women. "It was nice meeting you, ladies. Please enjoy the rest of your night. I think I've infringed upon your evening long enough."

A couple of the ladies looked like they didn't want him to go, but he still stood, thanking them for the company. Jessica wasn't looking at him, instead staring straight ahead at nothing. Her stuck-up man had removed his arm from around her and was gritting on Dana like he wanted a go at him. He wished he would.

"Jessica, glad you made it *back* from your trip safely. I wish you well, sweetheart. Take care." *Nice knowing ya.* Dana walked away, not bothering to look back. He didn't need to. His future was in front of him.

PROMISES PART 3

CHAPTER SEVENTEEN

Ford

Watching Dana bust his cheating girlfriend wasn't really something Ford wanted to witness, but he couldn't take his eyes away. It felt like Ford hadn't breathed until he saw Dana get up and walk away from her, his beautiful brown eyes and sexy smile for no one other than him. When Dana got to him, Ford moved them back to their secluded corner. He made sure they weren't attracting any negative attention as he pulled Dana deeper into darkness.

"Looks like that was relatively painless," Ford mumbled, not taking his eyes off Dana.

"It was… for me, anyway. She looked mortified." Dana shrugged uncaringly.

"You good?"

Dana gripped the edges of Ford's coat and pulled him against him. "What I am… is single."

"We'll see about that," Ford growled. "But for now, stay focused. Brian has hot-pants outside, behind the building. Let's go."

Dana and Ford slipped out the side door and made their way around the back of the building. Ford watched behind them to make sure they weren't being followed. He'd mentioned the Grossmans' name to one of the security guards and scared him off. Dana had freaked out the bartender, so it was best to hurry and get what they needed and disappear. Ford turned the corner and made his way down the back street. He saw his brother with his head dipped down low, his big arms around the smaller man's waist, holding him close to him. The small man had his head tilted back while his brother made him moan and writhe on his big thigh, which was wedged between his legs.

Ford stopped and leaned against the wall, Dana doing the same, both of them shaking their head at Brian's smoothness. "How much longer?"

"If Sascha has war secrets, I think he'd tell Brian right now. Come on, let's go." Dana took the lead and walked up on Brian and Sascha.

"Sorry to interrupt." Dana coughed to hide his grin, as Sascha's eyes rolled back to the front. He looked stoned.

Brian's chest vibrated with his hushed groan while he thrust his pelvis harder against his willing partner.

Ford huffed. "Do you mind, Brian?"

"Yes. A lot."

Ford ignored his brother. He could get the guy's number if he wanted to continue this, but they were on the clock. Brian tilted Sascha's head up to look at him, and if a human being could be liquefied, then Sascha would've been a puddle at Brian's feet. Brian kissed and touched the short man for a few more seconds before he began to sign, never taking his eyes off Sascha, while his brother interpreted for him.

"You said you're a regular here?"

Sascha turned his head to listen when Ford spoke, but he quickly turned back to Brian and eagerly nodded his head. "Have been for three years. I have a platinum status."

"What does platinum status get you?"

Sascha rubbed his smooth hands up and down Brian's chest as he answered every one of his questions. "Any and everything."

"Access to the male review?"

"Yes. But I'm not interested in those tawdry strippers. You'd think a place like this could afford the best dancers. Diamon should be ashamed."

Ford kept his features schooled just like the rest of them, but this was great. Their informant knew exactly who they were looking for.

"Is she here now? Have you seen her?"

"Yes. She runs the upstairs. It's by exclusive invitation. I would never go to one of her events, though."

"So you've seen her tonight?"

"Yes. She's up there now," Sascha confirmed. "Do you guys want me to take you up there to see her? I can get one of you in with my platinum pass."

"You'd do that for me?" Brian tilted the man's dimpled chin and kissed him there, making him moan unashamedly.

"Anything," Sascha whispered. "I'll take you now."

"Do you know what kind of car she drives?" Ford asked.

Sascha pffted. "Everyone does. It's a white Lexus with god-awful pink leather interior. I'm telling you, the woman has no taste."

Ford checked his watch, it was close to eleven. "Do you know who else may be up there?"

"I've been on the other side most of the evening so I don't know who's come and gone. It's usually ladies and a few men on Sundays. Her man and his entourage are usually up there, too. No one likes Ray."

All three of them bristled at the thought of one of the Grossmans possibly being there now. Ford spoke into his watch. "Duke did you get that? White Lexus with a pink interior… Roger that. Brian's going in… I'll let you know when we're in position."

"Oh my gosh, you're working?! How many bounty hunter guys are here? Are you here to arrest Diamon?" Sascha was absolutely pulsating with enthusiasm as they got their game faces on. "I want to help. Please. I can assist you in any way you need."

"You're doing great already, baby."

PROMISES PART 3

"I'm not fucking translating that. Let's go Romeo, it's time. Duke and Quick are putting the tracker in place now." Ford pulled Brian back from Sascha and ordered the pretty man to lead the way. Brian set his watch up to record video and audio so they could make sure he was safe. When they got back inside, Ford and Dana split off while Brian let Sascha lead him up the long staircase to the upper level. They talked with the bouncer for a couple seconds, Sascha flashing a card at him and tucking it away as the curtain was pulled back for them to enter. Then his brother was out of his sight. Duke and Quick were the ones with visual now.

Ford leaned against one of the small bars off the dance floor, slightly bopping his head to the music while he waited for the signal. After a couple minutes, Ford's watch vibrated and an alert came through.

Ray is here… six men! Move in.

Ford made eye contact with Dana. They could handle six. Actually, they could handle a lot more. With the element of surprise on their side, they'd catch Ray off guard. In sync, he and Dana reached inside their shirts and pulled out their stars at the same time Quick and Duke burst through the front entrance with their weapons drawn and pointed down, the large block letters – BOUNTY HUNTER – across their chests, scaring anyone in their path. They moved beside each other like they'd been partnered for years… they had. As they made their way to the stairs, a few people had already started to hurry towards the exit, panicked at the sight of four men in all black with weapons inside their nice white establishment.

The guard at the door stood when he caught sight of them and reached behind him as if going for a weapon. Dana was behind the three of them, Ford heard Dana loudly identify who they were and yelled an order to the guard to back away. When he ignored the warning and kept reaching, Dana fired two rounds from his SALT, pepper spray pellets hitting the guard in the chest at over 50mph. It hurt and stunned the hell out of him, immediately blinding him and limiting his ability to breathe. The man fell to his knees, gasping and choking. He should be glad Dana was able to eliminate him as a threat without the use of lethal force.

Two more men rushed from behind the curtain at the sound of the guard's pained shout. As soon as their eyes landed on them, before they could react, Dana popped both of them, again, dead center. Ford loved it. This got his blood pumping viciously through his system. His watchman was at his six, taking out any threats before him. A man came flying out between the curtains, landing with a hard thud at Duke's feet. Brian's handiwork. He and Quick darted to the sides of the curtains and Ford went through first, with Dana right behind him, Quick and Duke filing in next. Brian was standing just inside the curtain with Sascha tucked behind him looking two parts terrified and one part excited.

Brian motioned past the closed double doors. That's where Ray was. Club music filtered through the cracks. The party was still going on, everyone upstairs completely oblivious to the fact that the music had stopped below them and people were being quickly ushered out to safety.

Ford double-checked his weapon. He stood next to his partner while Dana added more pepper pellets. Ford had given Dana the new weapon a few months ago, before it even hit the market. He'd never seen his partner look as pleased as when Ford introduced a new weapon to him. No one knew how much he enjoyed watching the man's face as he learned how to use his new toy.

Duke gave a few hand signals. Brian and Ford were to remove any hostiles, Dana backing them up while Duke and Quick went for Ray. They came through the doors like a well-trained black ops team, most of the people in the room not even realizing there was a problem until Quick and Duke were almost to Ray's VIP table in the back corner and Brian had killed the loud music. Women began to scream and run towards the exit as realization set in that they were not five new dancers lurking around to entertain them.

Ford had just caught a guard in the jaw with a devastating right hook and another in the mid-section when he saw Dana leap up onto one of the tables and start firing off pellets like a scene out of a Bruce Willis *Die Hard* movie. And what was so dynamic and sexy about it, was his marksman never missed. The man heading towards Ford with an angry snarl on his face never got close enough to him as he was hit in the throat with a pellet traveling at the speed of a major league fastball. *Damn, that had to sting.*

Dana

Dana's job wasn't an easy one. All four members of his team were in the room and it was his responsibility to keep them safe and prevent any sneak attacks while they executed the bond order. He caught sight of Brian pushing through the crowd, making his way towards the back. He was good, didn't require any assistance from him. Quick and Duke's loud voices boomed over the screams. "Bounty Hunters! We have a warrant! Everyone out! Everyone out, now!" They called out over and over. His bosses were on top of shit, as always.

With Ford still in his peripheral, Dana caught sight of Ray. Quick rushed him and had him pinned on the ground with his knee in his back so quickly that if Dana had turned for a second he would've missed it. Quick expertly secured a set of wires around their bounty's wrists while Duke had his gun pointed at Ray's flunkies, warning them to stay back. Dana could hear the police sirens in the distance. It never failed that the cops were called. No matter how much identification they flashed, even with a warrant, no one ever believed bounty hunters could legally come in and arrest someone.

There were a few people clapping when they made their way downstairs with a handcuffed Ray Grossman. It looked like Ray's presence and scare tactics were never welcomed there. Dana caught the eye of the bartender who had run away from them earlier, her eyes blown in disbelief when Dana gave her a sluggish salute. He looked away, keeping his weapon ready just in case Ray had any other devoted guards willing to try to break him free.

When they got outside, Duke secured Ray inside their transport truck while Quick spoke with the local authorities, letting them review the warrant. Dana and Ford stood there with Brian, waiting for the okay to wrap it up for the night.

With the little Grossman brother down, it would only be a matter of time before big John Grossman got emotional over his brother's capture and made a mistake. Then Duke would get his ass, too. Who knew Ray's weakness was his girl, who he couldn't stay away from? Instead of laying low, he was at a club full of people, regardless that he was a wanted man. Ray's girl was arrested for harboring a fugitive, her banshee screams for her lawyer piercing the cool night air.

"One down, one to go," Dana sighed.

Quick came back and told them to meet up in the office tomorrow so they could strategize. Big Grossman was going to pop up any minute. As he and the King brothers got ready to leave, Sascha called out to them, hurrying through the crowd. He ran right into Brian's arms, looking up at him with sad, green eyes. He was a cute little thing, Dana would give him that. Full of bravery and spunk, just how Brian liked them. The man hadn't even hesitated to help them when everyone else had cowered away.

PROMISES PART 3

"You are something else, Brian King," Sascha said with bated breath. Tenderly stroking the dark stubble on Brian's cheek.

Dana saw a hopeful expression pass over Brian's handsome face as he stared down at the man in his arms.

"I would love to spend some time with you. But you'd have me worried and going gray before my time, bounty hunter. As exciting as all this was… it was also terrifying. And that's not my life. You take care, handsome." With that, Sascha kissed Brian's cheek and walked away.

No one said anything, not even about the hurt expression on Brian's face as he watched the pretty man walk away. Unfortunately, it was something they'd all experienced. Their job was dangerous, reckless, and required crazy hours. Not everyone could handle it. So it left them alone until they found that one person who was crazy enough to stick by them. It's why they all adored Vaughan and Dr. Chauncey. Through the good and dangerous, Duke and Quick had two men in their lives that loved them and would never walk away because the fire got hot. No way. Vaughan and the doc would be the first ones to pick up a fire extinguisher and jump into the flames. Their bosses both had someone they could come home to and leave all the bullshit they endured in the streets behind for the night. Dana didn't have that and neither did Ford or Brian… yet.

Ford clamped Brian on his shoulder to get him moving. "His loss, brother."

Dana agreed.

CHAPTER EIGHTEEN

Dana

It was almost midnight. Brian didn't want to go home, said he'd go with Duke to process their bounty. Dana hoped his friend was okay. Brian might look and act tough and he was able to hide his feelings behind a massive exterior and the unapproachable glare he had perfected, but he was a wounded soul in need of companionship. He signed to his friend he'd call him later, but all he got was a "Don't bother" look in return.

"You got plans?" Ford asked, climbing back into the truck.

"No. Nothing. Why? What's up?" Dana asked, checking their surroundings before fastening his seatbelt.

"It usually takes me a while to settle down after a bust. Thought maybe you'd… if you want to… maybe come over." Ford looked gorgeous when he was flustered. It wasn't a look anyone saw on the big SEAL often. "If you wanna come over and have a beer or something, unwind, or whatever."

Dana barely stopped himself from screaming "Yes, hell yes!" and instead casually answered, "I can do that." Dana just hoped this was what he thought it was. Why else would Ford want him at his house so late? He wouldn't call it a booty call, those were reserved for people you weren't trying to invest any serious time or commitment in. Ford didn't fit that category at all. He wanted a lot with Ford. He wanted it all.

"Cool, so I'll drop you off at your place so you can get your car then you can head over." Ford was already pulling into traffic, leaving behind the mess they'd made. The parking lot was still full of haughty rich folks giving their statements about the night's events to the abundant police personnel. Maybe even a few of them threatening to cancel their expensive memberships. Until the news showed up. Neither he nor Ford cared, they were long gone. Those oblivious space cadets should've been glad they'd removed that virus – Grossman – from their clueless little perfect, white, crime-free world.

He hurried inside his condo to dump his gear and freshen up. He was even presumptuous enough to pack an overnight bag, telling himself he was only being practical and prepared, since they had to be in the office early. Dana was standing on Ford's doorstep twenty-four minutes after he'd dropped him at his place. Taking his car ensured he'd be able to leave if things went south. These were uncharted waters for both of them. It'd been so long since he'd been with a man, he was probably more nervous than Ford. He just didn't want to mess anything up. He also didn't want to move too fast and get hurt like Sway had warned him against.

Dana rapped on the door a couple times and waited.

Ford

The sharp knock made Ford's heart drop down into his nervous stomach. *He's here. Okay, just be cool. Don't overthink. It's just Dana. Hot, young, extremely sexy, goddamn expert marksman, Dana Cadby.* Ford didn't know what he'd been thinking inviting the man back to his home so late. No, he did know what he'd been thinking. He'd been thinking with his dick and of how strongly it'd reacted to Dana's work tonight. The way the man could shoot had always been a turn-on for Ford. What was even more of a turn-on was how his partner liked to shoot the weapons Ford provided for him. And, as if to thank him properly, Dana shot those weapons with particular skill and purpose. Protected him with them. For three years, Ford ignored the signs. Ignored how much Dana tried to please him, make him smile, guard him, be the best partner to him that he could. And how had Ford shown his appreciation? By giving him hell. Pushing him away. Not realizing he was trying to fabricate a reason to dislike Dana because he wanted him… god help him, he did.

Here he was at his front door. Had accepted Ford's invitation without hesitation. He hadn't thought Dana would actually say no. The man had been giving off crazy vibes ever since Ford opened his big mouth and told the man he deserved better… falling just short of saying *he* was the one Dana deserved.

Ford reached for the doorknob and realized his hands were shaking. Fuck. He tightened his fists a couple times before releasing them and reaching for the knob again, this time turning it slowly. Dana stood there in a sweat suit with a big hoodie and no coat. His hair was slightly damp, like he'd taken a shower. When Ford stepped aside for Dana to come in, he meant to speak but his tongue got caught in his throat at the smell that blew in with the crisp breeze. A fragrance of masculine soap and clean cologne. His blood quickly began to head south and Ford had to close his eyes and count to three before he pounced like a dog in heat.

"Want a beer?" Ford asked, clearing his throat when it came out sounding like a frog's croak.

"Nah. I'll have some milk though, if you got it," Dana said, pulling his hoodie over his head, making his undershirt ride up high enough that Ford could see his sweatpants were hanging so low he could see the top of Dana's black briefs, and the slick brown hair that disappeared into them. Ford didn't like baby smooth skin, he loved hair, the more the better. He hoped Dana liked the same, because he sure had enough of it. Enough that it turned most women off. He wasn't usually self-conscious about his body or his body hair, but for some reason he found himself hoping like hell that Dana didn't mind it.

"Milk?" Ford asked skeptically.

"You wanna know how I unwind after a bust, right?" Dana came into the small kitchen with him while Ford poured him a large glass of two percent.

Ford hadn't bothered to turn on the kitchen light because there was enough filtering in from the small lamp in the living room. It was dim and quiet, their bodies taking up most of the confined space.

"I drink milk and I'll exercise after exerting a lot of adrenaline." Dana continued telling Ford about himself. "Usually push-ups, sit-ups. Or, if it's not too late, I'll run."

Ford should've known these things about his partner already. If he'd been half as good a partner as Dana had been to him, he'd know he preferred milk to bring himself down.

"I don't usually drink alcohol." Dana nodded towards Ford's beer. "I'm more of a social drinker."

"Like you did tonight?" Ford said with a tilt at the corner of his mouth.

Dana didn't try to muffle his deep, boisterous laugh. "Fuck you. Two hundred fifty bucks is not social drinking. That's my grocery money for two months."

"I hope that beer was good." Ford continued to tease, secretly loving Dana's smile and how easily he could loosen up.

"It was better than good." Dana drank all of his milk before adding, "It's something I'll have to remember enjoying because I don't think I'll be having it again anytime soon."

"I hear ya," Ford answered, drinking from his beer. They were quiet after that, both of them just watching each other. What was he supposed to do now? He couldn't believe how rusty he was at this. But the more he looked Dana up and down, the more he thought of how he'd moved like a soldier tonight, the more he thought of all the times the man had protected him, the more his body reacted until he was standing there panting like he was going into cardiac arrest.

Dana's flushed cheeks and elevated breathing were just as noticeable, as well as the bulge forming in his sweats. Dana was just as turned on as he was, if not more from the way his hooded eyes were fixated on Ford's chest.

Please take the lead.

As if he'd been able to silently communicate to his partner, Dana set his empty glass down and walked the few feet until he was standing in front of Ford. Neither one of them touched or moved, they just stood there in each other's space, accepting the closeness, simply breathing.

"Ford. Are we really doing this?" Dana whispered. "Are you... are you okay?"

Ford didn't even realize his eyes were closed until he opened them at the hint of concern in Dana's hoarse voice. He wasn't sure if he'd heard that tone before, but he knew he wanted to hear more of it.

"Yeah." He couldn't say any more than that since most of his brain function was restricted at the moment.

"Okay. Because. I want to... can I... can I just... touch you?" Dana asked breathlessly. He looked like he might pass out. His eyes were heavy and full of desire. That toned chest was moving rapidly behind the tight white t-shirt he had on. Ford fought not to groan and close his eyes. He needed to see that look of unbridled need in his partner's eyes and know it was for him. No one, and he meant no one, had ever looked at him like that. In all his years, he'd found no woman or man who'd wanted him as badly as Dana was exhibiting at that moment.

As a young man, Ford had taken responsibility for everything his father placed on him, running the farm and taking care of his younger brother. Then he'd enlisted and had taken on a leadership role from the second he'd left boot camp. He fought and he bled for his country, for his team. Always looking out for the well-being of everyone else and ignoring his most basic human needs. He wasn't a robot, he was a man, a man that never took any pleasure for himself. That ended right now.

"Yes." *Touch me, please.*

Ford was surprised that Dana's hands were shaking too, but he didn't try to hide it. Slowly, his long fingers clasped the bottom of Ford's shirt and instead of lifting the shirt up and off him, Dana closed his eyes and inched his hands underneath. Using his sense of touch to not only feel, but to see. He'd seen Dana do that in the field when his visibility was reduced. He'd close his eyes and listen, feel the movements in the air, then he'd fire and hit his target dead-on. Ford watched every expression imaginable flitter across Dana's face: surprise, lust, appreciation, hope, relief… and then he saw what he'd prayed he would… happiness.

Dana's hands explored his torso like he was the most beautiful sculpture he'd ever seen.

CHAPTER NINETEEN

Dana

Dana swallowed thickly in an effort to quench his thirst. Needless to say, it wasn't working. His mouth was salivating for one reason – he wanted to taste. He felt so fortunate to finally have his hands on his partner, he feared he'd get too greedy and scare him off if he wasn't careful. No matter how badly he wanted to drop to his knees and bury his face in the warm fuzz that covered Ford's strong abs and thick pecs, he would wait for his cue. And so far, Ford had been still.

"I've wanted to touch your body for three years, Bradford King," Dana whispered while still smoothing his hands up and down Ford's chest. "Is this okay?"

Ford jerked beautifully when Dana brushed his thumbs over his erect nipples. Being the greedy bastard he was, Dana did it again, getting the same reaction, but this time Ford moaned and gripped his wrists, stopping him. Dana thought he'd overstepped, but the way Ford was trying to control his breathing suggested to him that he'd been stopped for a whole other reason, which, of course, skyrocketed his lust and boosted his ego.

"I think I'd better sit down if you're going to keep touching me," Ford said slowly, but he didn't let Dana's hands go.

Dana ran his nose down Ford's throat, inhaling the strong scent that was always there. "Yeah. Let's sit down."

Dana tried to walk with confidence but his dick was so hard it ached. Ford sat down on the loveseat, slouching down until his head was resting on the back. With his forearm over his eyes, he confessed, "I'm not good at this, Dana. Matter of fact, I most likely stink at it."

"At what?" Dana asked from beside him, so close that they were touching from shoulder to thigh. "Seems like you're doing pretty good to me." Ford couldn't tell what Dana was referring to, but if he uncovered his face he'd see the massive tent in Dana's sweats.

"Let's just say I'm a bit out of practice," Ford admitted.

"I think I knew that already. But I'm not concerned about it. We're not in a competition over who's the most experienced." Dana paused. "Have you been with a man, Ford... ever?"

"Yeah. But not all the way," Ford grumbled and released a heavy breath. "I sound like a frat boy. I haven't had sex with a man. Fooled around, yes."

Dana wasn't sure how to restore Ford's confidence. Hell, he was way out of practice with men himself. But he figured sex was like riding a bike. With Ford, it'd be like riding in style... luxury. It would all come back to him, he was sure of it. But he had to put his partner at ease or they weren't going to get anywhere. He'd worked with Ford for three years. The man didn't like to be out of control.

"I haven't been with a man in ten years. Last guy I was with, I thought he was the one and he burned me... bad. So I backed off of men for a while. Longer than I wanted to. No one had interested me until I saw you. You ticked off every one of my boxes, man. But I knew I didn't have a chance in hell with you. So I tried to cover up my want for you by being with someone else, anyone else. It hurt that I had to see you every day and wish."

Ford had dropped his hand and was listening intently to Dana's confession. He needed Ford to know that he had even less control over the situation than Ford did.

"I wanted you, too," Ford replied after Dana had stopped. "I probably always did. But I didn't want any problems."

"Problems?" Dana frowned.

"Not like that. You had a lot of options. Meaning… fuck, how do I say this? I'm not good with explaining my feelings." Ford uttered the last three words like they left a bad taste in his mouth, and Dana chuckled at him. He understood that.

"I think I know what you're saying." Dana rubbed the coarse hairs on his chin. "You didn't want a tramp."

Ford reared up at that. "No! I'd never call you that. Not even in my own head. Damnit. You're really going to make me say it, aren't you?" Ford gritted his teeth. "I felt like why would you want to waste time with someone as old as me when you could have anyone you wanted. I think Brian told me you were seeing a model or big movie star last year."

"She wasn't a model or a star." Dana pffted. "Marcia was a non-speaking extra in a movie filmed here six years ago. That doesn't exactly qualify as a big star. And regardless of her or anyone else, if you'd given me any indication that I had a chance, Ford, I would've focused on you and only you."

Ford was quiet for a long time and Dana wondered if he'd said the wrong thing. Was he supposed to wait and be celibate while he pined for his straight work partner? He'd done what any red-blooded male would do, he'd tried to numb the pain of longing and rejection by being with someone else. "Ford, don't go there, okay. Can we just look at the here and now?"

"Can we?" Ford hissed. "Because you literally just broke up with your girlfriend less than two hours ago, now you're here, telling me you've wanted me and only me all along."

"I haven't dated another man," Dana snapped back.

"I don't care!" Ford barked.

Dana bolted up off the couch. *He doesn't care.* He went for his hoodie. He wouldn't do this.

"Where are you going?" Ford yelled, his strong voice sending chills down Dana's spine. He heard Ford following him.

PROMISES PART 3

"Home! Did you really invite me over here to tell me I'm not good enough for you? To insult me? Son of a bitch," Dana fussed, yanking to right his clothes. He felt so foolish and it was the second time tonight. "I'm not gonna let you do this to me. I know I'm a good guy. I wanted you, but you didn't fuckin' want me, man. *You* acted like an ass any time I tried to show interest. Now you thumb your damn nose at me for not staying home night after night alone, wishing you'd suddenly knock on my door."

Ford did what was starting to be a habit and blocked Dana from opening the door.

"That shit's not sexy right now… move, Ford." Dana bared his teeth. He was angry at the pain of another rejection. He was so scared moisture would form in his eyes, and there was no way he could get emotional in front of this man. But he was just so tired of hearing he wasn't good enough, especially from men. Men he looked up to and admired… who never admired him back. It hurt deeply.

"Whoa. You're taking this the wrong way." Ford glared at him.

"There's not too many other ways to take that."

"It's so easy for you to run." Ford gripped Dana's shoulder when he tried to move his arm from holding the door.

"Let go." Dana was quick when he knocked Ford's arm off him and shoved him back a few feet. The startled look he got from Ford morphed from anger to lust in seconds and Dana got nervous and excited just as fast.

Ford stepped back into Dana's space and didn't stop until he had him pinned against the door. He clasped Dana's wrists and slammed them over his head, holding him there. "I'm not saying you're not good enough. I'm asking: am I enough?"

They were both breathing hard in each other's face, their eyes dancing over their blushed skin. It was hard to think with all those muscles pressing into him, but he'd heard what Ford said.

"Yes, Ford. You always were enough."

As if in slow motion, Dana saw when Ford made his final decision. Releasing the tight grip on his wrists, Ford's hands eased down Dana's long, tattooed arms to his shoulders. Thick fingers rested on his neck as Ford leaned in, his beard scraping against Dana's sensitive skin, until he finally felt firm, smooth lips touch his. He fought to stay upright while Ford tentatively brushed kisses over his mouth and chin.

"I haven't kissed in over twenty years," Ford said into Dana's parted mouth.

Dana had a death grip on Ford's waist, to one, help him stay vertical, and two: because he needed to know the man was there in reality and he wasn't dreaming. "You're good at it."

"Bullshit," Ford whispered so gravelly while still nipping at Dana's bottom lip that he made the expletive sound seductive.

Dana began to kiss Ford back. The light touches weren't enough. Ford groaned into his mouth when Dana slid his tongue inside and got his first real taste of Bradford King. After the initial split second of surprise wore off, Ford kissed him back with just as much passion and need as Dana was giving him. He really was a good kisser. He liked how Ford clasped his neck and moved Dana's head into whatever position he wanted it to invade his mouth and Dana remained pliant to let him. Loved the eager little sounds that he had no clue he was making.

"Can I... I want to taste you, Ford. Please." Dana was practically groveling. But he was so famished for more, and he wasn't afraid to beg.

"I wouldn't last two minutes," Ford owned up. He pulled back to stare at him and Dana let him take in his fill.

PROMISES PART 3

CHAPTER TWENTY

Ford

Taste me. Ford was pretty sure that meant that Dana wanted to put his sexy, wet mouth somewhere on his body besides his lips and Ford thought he'd come simply from the thought of it, so he knew he'd been honest when he'd admitted that he wouldn't last long. He didn't even last two minutes when he beat off just thinking about Dana. Now he had the man here in the flesh. *Oh my god.* Three minutes was definitely not happening.

Dana drove his hands back under Ford's t-shirt, going for his hard nipples.

"Ahh. Jesus." Ford tilted his head back at the amazing sensations as Dana chewed at his throat.

"I'm not trying to pressure you. We can slow this down," Dana said with a hint of disappointment in his tone.

Ford wasn't disappointing Dana ever again. "No… I mean, yes. I want you to. More than you think." Ford took Dana's hand and led him to his bedroom. He looked around at the average space and tried to see it through Dana's eyes. He had no clue what his partner's house looked like, but he was sure it looked better than his, and felt homier, too. When he turned back to look at Dana, the man wasn't looking at his room, he was looking directly at him.

Feeling a little more confident the more Dana watched him. Ford grasped the hem of his shirt and pulled it over his head letting it drop to the floor.

"Jesus Christ," Dana whispered. "I've always had to steal looks at you. Never was able to just stare and appreciate."

PROMISES PART 3

Ford couldn't help the needy moan that escaped when Dana's hands were back on his chest, gently guiding him backwards to the bed. When the back of his knees hit the edge, Ford sat down, spreading his legs wide. His eyes almost rolled back when Dana dropped to his knees and nestled in close between his thighs. Ford thought it'd be weird to see Dana there, but it wasn't. He looked like he belonged there. He looked fucking gorgeous.

Dana took his own shirt off, and before it could even hit the floor, Ford wrenched forward and clamped his mouth down on Dana's thick collarbone. That scent was driving him mad. He smelled so damn good. His mouth watered as he realized he wanted to taste Dana, too. Bury his nose in his crotch and see if he found the same clean and sexy smell there too.

They kissed for a long time, learning what the other liked. Dana on his knees, alternating between Ford's mouth, his neck, his chest and his stomach. Ford's body hair seemed to be a highlight for Dana instead of a nuisance. His partner was doing a great job of easing him into this. Ford wasn't as nervous as he was when they first started touching. But those nerves ramped back up when he felt Dana pulling at his pants. Still breathing heavily, he let Dana remove them and his boxers at the same time. The cool air hit his throbbing dick, making him grunt and thrust up at nothing. Dana's hands gripped his pelvis, holding him down to the bed.

"Sit still." Dana winked, skating his strong hands up Ford's torso and pushing until he laid back on the bed. "I'm going to show you just how long I've wanted you, SEAL."

"Unnnh," Ford cried out unexpectedly. Dana calling him that brought his orgasm so close to the surface he was scared he'd shoot his nut right then.

"It's okay, babe. I know what to do," Dana murmured against his tight sack.

"Yes, do it," Ford gasped when Dana blew his hot breath on him.

He could feel Dana's trembling body, fighting with himself to go slow. That made two of them battling their strong urges, because Ford wanted nothing more than to bury his cock in Dana's mouth and down his throat until he gagged on it. But he controlled himself as Dana rubbed his face all over his groin, deeply breathing in the robust scent entrenched there.

It felt like forever before he finally felt Dana's slick tongue lapping at his balls, sucking one into his mouth while he held the base of Ford's dick. He was so gentle and methodical it was painful. His orgasm wanted out. The inevitable climax that was hovering on the edge of a feeble cliff.

"Dana. Fuck, that feels so… Ohh." Ford boldly spread his legs wider, encouraging Dana to suck harder, deeper. He ached so much.

"I knew you'd like that," Dana moaned, sucking the other side of his sack next.

Ford did, he loved it. The moment Dana took the head into his mouth, Ford knew it was about to be over. His partner's mouth was so warm and silky, he couldn't fight it no matter how hard he tried. "Dana," he growled in warning.

Dana didn't stop. Going down as far as he could, Ford felt him breathing rapidly through his nose as he picked up the pace. He tried to count in his head to distract himself, to prolong the incredible sensations overtaking him, but he only made it to four one-thousand. Ford arched his back and called out again. "Fuck. I'm coming, Dana… Augh! Fuck!" Ford stopped holding back and let the sensations consume him. He'd completely forgotten what it was like when your orgasm wasn't self-inflicted. It was a hundred times better.

Ford held Dana's head in place while he emptied inside his mouth, feeling him swallow hungrily around him. He was still grunting and shooting when Dana's mouth clamped down harder around his sensitive cock and a sharp grumble followed by a long moan cut over his own, sending a delicious vibration down his shaft to his balls. Dana didn't stop his suction until Ford was milked dry.

Dana

Dana knew Ford's natural aroma would blow his mind. He lay there with his forehead resting in the crook of Ford's thigh and groin while he recovered from his own powerful orgasm. He'd come so hard he thought he'd explode from the inside out. It took him a minute to compose himself, but when he did, a cocky grin appeared as he surveyed his work. Ford was stretched out on his back, arms splayed out to his sides, legs gaped open, his limp cock lying against his hairy thigh and a serene look of satiation replaced his usual hard expression. Dana had put that look there.

He climbed up Ford's body like he was a jungle gym. "Was it good?"

Ford slowly pried his eyes open and the sweetest, most beautiful smile spread his lips. "Kiss me again."

He did.

When they finally stopped, Dana ran his fingers through Ford's beard. "I knew this would be as soft as I thought it was."

Though Dana was the one issuing compliments, he didn't miss the admiration on Ford's face as he stared back at him.

"Past your bedtime, old man?" Dana taunted, when Ford yawned.

"Brat," Ford whispered in response, running his hand down Dana's back. He stopped at the top of his ass, like he wasn't sure if he should continue down there or not. After a few seconds, Ford's hand persisted until his entire, rough palm was resting on Dana's ass. He moaned to let Ford know he liked it.

It was getting late and they had to get right back on the grind in the morning. Since he hadn't been invited to stay, it was about time for him to go. "I better head out and let you rest." Dana looked at his watch. Shit. It was almost two. "Only got a few hours left to sleep."

Ford got up and cracked his neck. "You could've stayed, Dana. Next time bring a bag with you."

Dana jumped up with newfound energy. There was his invite. "Be right back."

Ford watched, confused as Dana flung his shirt and pants back on, commando, and ran to the front door. He didn't even bother with his tennis shoes. He grabbed his bag out of the trunk and darted back inside and down the hall. Ford was leaning back, resting on his elbows when Dana hefted his bag for him to see then dropped it on the floor beside the bed. "Done."

Ford laughed. He really laughed for him and damn if that didn't make the whole night worth it. Ford eyed him affectionately. "I got myself a fuckin' Boy Scout."

… PROMISES PART 3

CHAPTER TWENTY-ONE

Brian

This was his life. Being disregarded and dismissed. He was voiceless. He sat there in his chair watching a rerun of *America Ninja Warrior*, trying not to think of the hot little number that'd slipped through his fingers tonight. It wasn't the first time and it damn sure wouldn't be the last. He grunted and flexed his throat, pissed at the minimal sound he produced. He'd been doing the therapy sessions and the exercises, but nothing was freaking working. He was still making the same small whimpers and hisses he'd been producing for the past year. Admittedly, that was progress from two years ago.

After he'd finished helping Duke, he still hadn't wanted to come home. He probably would've gone to his brother's, but he wasn't blind to what was happening between him and Dana. It was a good thing and a long time coming. He'd never want to cock-block his brother, not when he needed some good cock in his life. As creepy as that sounded in his own head, the reality was, he wanted his big brother to finally get something that was just for him. Dana was an amazing man. If Brian was into alpha types, he may have made a play for Dana in the beginning while Ford dragged his big ass feet. But he and Dana fit better as brothers. The man was a good guy, a good friend. Even his sign language was getting better. His favorite thing about Dana was the man never pressured him about talking. Never pushed him to try harder in therapy, or hurry up and see another specialist. Or travel to the other side of the world and see if this or that expert could help him. Dana didn't see Brian as broken or defective.

Ford didn't either, but it was obvious he wanted Brian to talk to him again.

He wouldn't talk. Not now... maybe not ever. He was learning to accept that. It'd been beaten and tortured into his head to never speak again. That programming wasn't something he could snap his fingers and magically turn off. He'd learned to survive as a prisoner of war. It was either keep his mouth shut and live, or talk and die a quick death after betraying his country and his brothers. In his mind he associated silence with self-preservation.

Brian's phone buzzed beside him with a text notification. He almost ignored it, figuring it was Ford being his usual over-protective self and checking in on him. He was feeling some type of way about the cute guy blowing him off earlier, but Brian wasn't falling into a state of depression from it. Releasing a gust of breath, Brian picked up the phone and clicked on the messages icon. It was Rod, a buddy he'd met on Tinder last year. They'd become friends after a ridiculously horrible attempt at two tops trying to hook up. They ended up calling it quits and just having a drink. Rod didn't care that Brian didn't talk because the man was fine with doing all the talking. Rod had tons of stories, and a big mouth to tell them all with. He currently had a lot of time on his hands since he'd quit his last job at a local barbershop. Brian didn't mind listening to him. He considered Rod one of his best friends.

Rod: *I'm not going to the club tonight. My son wants me to have breakfast at his school tomorrow. You interested in using my pass to get in? Starts at midnight. The action is smoking in there Brian.*

Brian thought about it. Rod had been telling him about some secretive club that changed its location each week. It was by invite only or you had to come with someone who was already a member. It was basically a place to go when you wanted to get laid. If Grindr or Tinder were actual locations, then this underground club would be one of them. Rod told Brian the last time he went he joined in on an orgy and the time before that he'd been taken to a room and fucked by not one, but two twinks. A night of mindless sex didn't sound half bad since he was still worked up from the action of the bust and the action with Sascha. Now he sat in his home with a severe case of blue balls and no desire whatsoever to take care of it himself.

His size, his look, even his attitude was often misread. Brian wasn't an introvert. He didn't loathe friendship or getting to know a man a little deeper than how far his hole went. He wouldn't mind a date outside of the bedroom. Guys did love to be taken by him. He was a big top with a big cock and he knew how to use it, but he also had a mind. He wouldn't shy away from the idea of some light conversation before he rocked a man's world. Only one minor problem. Since he couldn't voice his conversation, no one wanted to have one with him. Who wanted to listen to a computerized voice? No one did. Hell, sometimes his hookups didn't even know he couldn't talk. They didn't bother to learn anything about him except how long it took for him to get his pants down and a condom on. So for now, he'd do what he usually did. He'd leave his heart at home and go out and fuck. Brian hit reply.

Brian: *Yep. Send me the address.*

The club was not what Brian had expected. He'd had the Uber drop him off about two blocks down from the empty warehouse. When he approached, there were two men standing outside, dressed in all black… so was Brian. They gave him a quick appraisal, one of the men looked like he appreciated what he saw, the other looked cautious. When Brian made it to the door, he slowly reached into his pocket and retrieved his phone. He showed a screenshot of his pass and without a word, the taller, more receptive of the two, opened the door and ushered Brian inside. A man dressed in a bowtie and G-string hurried to him, presenting a tray of shot glasses, half full of a light amber liquid. Brian took a glass and downed it with one gulp. Tequila. The good kind, too. Brian set it down and graciously accepted another, the young man watching intently as Brian swallowed down the second.

"Anything more I can get you, sir? Anything at all?" The server asked, his tone and body language implying he wasn't only offering up premium liquor, if Brian was interested. He wasn't. The guy looked to be in his twenties. Brian liked them pretty, but mature.

Brian shook his head and placed a folded bill on the guy's tray, not sure where he was storing his tips. With a courteous smile, the young man flittered away to some men standing at the end of a long, winding stairwell. There was also an elevator, but Brian choose to take the scenic route. When he passed the guys at the stairs, one of them reached out and hooked Brian's elbow, stopping him with a simple raise of his brow. The man was handsome as hell with an air of distinguished authority lingering around him. He wore a navy-blue power suit and a welcoming smile, but he screamed top. Brian wasn't interested in a contest. He wanted a sweet, tight, willing body to plow into. He didn't see anyone on the first floor that fit that description. Most people milling about seemed to be networking and making business contacts, not looking to get laid. Brian was going to kill Rod if he'd wasted his time.

He retracted his elbow as non-aggressively as he could, rejecting his second offer of the night. The business tycoon looked unaffected as he turned back to the men he'd been conversing with. Before Brian reached the top of the stairs, he could already hear the suggestive moans and smell the scent of sex lingering just outside the red velvet curtain blocking the entrance.

Brian dipped inside and the sudden darkness kept him from moving any further. He waited for his eyes to adjust. There were purple and red lights high up on the ceiling, giving the room sexy splashes of erotic lighting here and there. Most areas in the gutted-out warehouse were extremely dark and private. The windows were all either panted black or covered with curtains. Brian took another couple steps inside, his eyes finally adjusting enough for him to see what was going on around him. Jesus. Bodies were everywhere. There were couches, beds, swings, huge pillows, and blankets covered every available area of the floor. Some parties had as many as ten people, writhing and touching all over each other, and some couches had only a couple. No one was concerned about who could see whom. As he moved through the crowd, he was again propositioned, touched, and asked to join in. He wasn't into the group thing. Nothing he saw interested him. The sounds and moans coming from every direction had his dick hard and ready to play, but no one caught his eye.

Brian posted up against the wall all the way in the back, concealed by darkness. He'd noticed a quiet, secluded spot behind the stairwell that led to the private rooms along the perimeter. If he happened to see anyone he was interested in, he'd have a spot to take them where they wouldn't be seen, could have some privacy. Brian let the two shots course through his body, warming him deep inside while he kept up his hunt. He should've grabbed another from the bar before he came up, but nonetheless. He didn't want whisky dick. If he got lucky, he wanted to give the man a good time.

PROMISES PART 3

CHAPTER TWENTY-TWO

Brian

He'd been standing there for over an hour and was about to call it quits when he saw a timid face peek though the curtains on the other side of the room, followed by a compact body stepping through. From the distance, Brian couldn't see the man's facial expression clearly, but as he moved through the packed room, flashes of red and purple would hit his face and Brian caught glimpses of his slightly uncomfortable look. Brian could also see he was all man. Shorter than six foot, maybe five six or five seven. Longish hair that curled at the ends and pale skin. Brian gasped and swallowed when the guy turned around like he was going to run but instead steeled his spine and turned back to walk farther into the room. Eyes wide with shock, the man moved through the space, fighting off twice as many advances as Brian had. What did he expect? Brian needed a more in depth look. He appreciated the mood-setting ambiance, but the lack of lighting kept him from really seeing those beautiful features. But Brian *could* see a strong, tight little body was visible underneath those casual clothes.

By mannerisms alone, he was easily the most gorgeous creature there. He looked so wholesome and innocent. Hunters were attracted to that look… especially him. Brian saw the blue power suit and his two buddies come through the curtains, their eyes moving all over before they landed on the same object of desire as him. Brian was moving before them. He wanted that man, pure and simple.

PROMISES PART 3

The nervous man's fingers fidgeted in front of him and every few seconds Brian would notice him pulling at the material in the front of his tight jeans. Jeans that were getting tighter as he moved. Brian wondered if the guy knew that he was being stalked from two different directions. When the guy stopped to watch two men fucking one of the servers – still in his bowtie and G-string – Brian saw Power Suit approach the man from behind and pull him back against him. Moving faster through the crowd and fending off groping hands, Brian was close enough that he could hear his attraction's deep voice, which surprised him. He'd thought the man would be timid, but he was wrong. He may have been smaller and looked delicate, but the way he was frowning and jerking out of Power Suit's tight hold told Brian he wasn't a pushover, regardless of his stature.

"No, thank you. I'm not interested."

Brian heard him trying to be polite, but the suit was having a challenging time accepting rejection. Before Brian could reach them, a guy about the same build as him jumped in front of him, his bright blue eyes dancing over Brian's face and chest. "You looking for me, sexy?" The man asked seductively while boldly reaching for Brian's dick.

Brian frowned angrily. He had no choice but to grip the man's hand in a punishing hold, making him wince and cry out before jerking his arm back. "Alright, easy, man. I can take a hint."

"Hey! Back off, creep. I said not interested."

Brian looked up just as Power Suit started to pull his desire away from the crowd, looking to take him to a more private setting. Very few people turned their attention from what they were doing, not at all concerned. Some probably thought this was part of their game. The suit wasn't flat out abducting the smaller man but he still had his hands on him when gorgeous had been more than clear that he wasn't interested.

Brian finally got to them, his large body casting a shadow over all of them. He extracted the struggling man from the suit's grasp and tucked him behind his back. Brian glared down at the three of them, daring them to make a move. His eyes pointed, ready to attack if he had to. He was more than willing to fight for what he wanted. Brian felt lean, strong fingers grip his bicep and pull him back. The longer Brian stood there frowning, the angrier he was getting that those assholes had the audacity to try to take what didn't belong to them. When the suit put up his hands in surrender, the others retreated as well, turning away in defeat.

Brian watched until they were back outside the curtain and posed no further threat. He turned around and looked down at the man, still holding on to him. His touch was warm and strong. Brian clasped his hand in his – taking his date for the night – and began the trek back to the dark corner he'd been standing in. They were almost there when his hand was tugged, halting his movements.

"Um. Look. Thank you for back there. Those guys had some serious issues. But I think I'm going to head out. This isn't exactly what I thought it would be."

That makes two of us. Brian still held the small hand in his and brought his other around the small of the guy's back to bring him closer to him. He couldn't tell him "No," or "Please, just five minutes." Instead, he tenderly hugged him to his body, trying to show he wasn't a threat or a bully. Brian's actions, his touch, were his words. He rubbed his big hands up and down that frail spine until the man began to curve into the touch. When he pulled back, he stared into deep brown eyes that were full of lust and need. Brian nodded in the direction they'd been walking and to his surprise, the guy smiled warmly and followed closely behind. Like he'd understood what Brian had reflected. No one bothered either one of them as they made their way back to the other side of the warehouse where it was quieter, darker.

PROMISES PART 3

Brian walked behind the stairwell and, after a cautious, cursory glance to make sure that Brian didn't have anyone else back there with him, he followed him farther into the darkness. Brian leaned against the wall, giving the suspicious man some space, but when he walked right into Brian's arms, he molded that fit body to him and dipped his head down to capture the supple lips with his own. A long, sultry moan was emptied into Brian's starving mouth, making him hold on tighter, wanting to hear more. God, the guy could kiss so good. His tongue was sweet and warm, dancing with his own. And he was so verbal. Brian didn't usually kiss his hookups but there was no way he could refuse that hot mouth.

"I can't believe I'm doing this." The man breathed, his mouth open and gusting warm breath over Brian's heated face. "I don't usually... I don't."

Brian wanted to agree. Wanted to let the man know it was his first time here, too. After a few more kisses and nuzzling into the soft, curls tucked behind one of the guy's ears, Brian stroked one thumb down his cheek. He couldn't see his face in the blackness but he could feel the smile curving his lips while he peppered kisses along Brian's jaw.

"Did you know those guys? Do you come here a lot?"

Brian refused to pull out his phone and speak through a digital voice and ruin the mood. Instead he leaned down and bit the man on his neck hard enough for it to sting and then pulled back. He'd answered the only way he knew how.

The guy yelped against Brian's cheek, startled, then kissed him again. "Jesus. Was that a no? I'd love to know what yes would've felt like."

Brian slanted back in and dragged the flat of his tongue across the tight tendons down the side of his date's throat until he got to his collarbone, where he placed a gentle, wet kiss. A soft sigh reached him over the background noise.

"That felt nice." The man ran his thin fingers delicately over Brian's mouth and whispered, "You don't talk?"

Brian slowly dipped back down and bit the man again, the sting not as powerful, but enough for him to understand the answer. He was scared to lift his head up and see pity, disappointment, revulsion. When he did look, he couldn't see what the man was thinking but he could feel him. There were no disgusted feelings. Brian could only feel the man's craving for him.

"It's too dark for you to read my lips. You can obviously hear me, so you're not deaf. It's okay. You don't have to talk to me." The man whispered caringly.

Brian didn't want him to think he'd chosen not to speak to him. If there was anyone he wanted to speak to it was the man standing close to him. He had to let him know that this was who he was. A mute. Brian took the man's right hand and pressed it firmly against his chest. Although he couldn't see the beautiful face staring back at him in the darkness, he could feel the intense gaze on him, the warmth of accelerated breaths as Brian eased his date's hand up his chest to his neck. He meticulously positioned the man's fingers over the jagged scars on his throat. He swallowed thickly at the feeling of someone else touching him there. No one was permitted to. But Brian had to help this guy understand. Understand what his needs were.

His fingers were soft and cool on Brian's flushed skin. The tentative touches went from exploratory to comforting in seconds. Brian tried to control his breathing, struggling to keep his composure while a stranger – a gorgeous, compassionate stranger – touched his most untouchable place. Then, raising up on his tip toes, soft kisses were placed along the ugly scars, mixing soothing touches with sweet licks of his tongue over the raised flesh. Made the wounds feel precious and important, not shameful.

PROMISES PART 3

"Thank you for showing me." His guy said in a hushed, deep tone as he slowly began to pull his shirt over his head, then went for the button on his jeans, all while he spoke in a soothing but masculine tone, "I can feel… it's almost like I can feel what you have to say."

Brian's eyes widened. No one had ever said anything like that to him. Not even close.

"You need this." The sexy man spoke up again, his breathing labored, as a hard, slim erection bumped against Brian's thigh. "I can feel it. So do I. I need, too. I've never come to a place like this. But… I feel like I can do this with you… only you."

What in hell was it about this man? He was amazing. He was brave, beautiful, strong-willed. He was here for the same reason Brian was, but this guy wasn't just an ordinary lay. Brian leaned down and simultaneously tilted the small chin, which fit perfectly in his palm, up to meet him. The kisses were unique, unhurried… magical. Brian slid his thick tongue inside and bathed the sexy man's mouth with his, tasting and feasting in case this was their one and only time. He kept going until they were both moaning and gasping for air.

Brian took the small packet of lube and a condom from his pocket. Before he could fumble with his pants, his date began to undo them for him, then reached for the condom and lube. The guy slid down his body like a sultry dancer, making Brian's exposed cock bump his chin. He held his breath as the man licked and kneaded at his tight sack, then the base of his shaft. Brian blew out a hard breath when his dick was swallowed down as if by a professional. If this guy was out of practice, then Brian couldn't tell. He drove his fingers through the loose curls, closing his eyes at the softness juxtaposed with the hard suction on the head of his dick. Fuck! *Oh my god, that's so good, baby.*

His date didn't stay down there long, but the little bit of time he did spend there had Brian trembling and panting. He sheathed Brian's wet cock and lathered him up. Brian heard a satisfied groan and concluded his date was probably pushing some of that slickness into his own hole, getting ready for him. When he stood, Brian clamped the wall for balance, needing to calm down before he humiliated himself. He liked to think he was a good bed partner, but this man had him so out of sorts, he wasn't sure how he'd perform.

"It's okay, big man. You don't have to talk. I can do the talking for us." The man was practically naked, his chest bare and his pants around his ankles. He turned around and leaned over, bracing both hands against the wall. "Your fingers are big. I want to feel them inside me first."

Brian hissed, moving his fingers up and down the man's slick crease. He wanted to ask him so bad what his name was, but again, he didn't want to pull out his phone. Instead, he probed at the tight hole. Brian grunted and thrust his hips against that smooth ass. So tight. Brian bit his bottom lip while he concentrated on stretching one of the tightest holes he'd felt in a long time.

"It's been a while." His guy whined, his head turned back, lips dancing across Brian's throat as he leaned over him. "I trust you'll be gentle. I don't know how I know, but I think you will."

Brian kissed him again. Just as softly and warmly as before. Letting his date know he was a huge man but he had a tender touch. Brian caressed the skin over the man's Adam's apple then kissed him there. *Yes. I will be as gentle as you need me to be.* He slowly pushed two fingers in and out, his eyes closed while he absorbed every cry and moan his date had to offer. *You feel so good. I wish I could tell you how beautiful I think you are.* Brian pushed his fingers in deeper, his date cursing and arching his back as he did. Oh yes, and he had a filthy mouth. Brian loved that the man wasn't afraid to voice their pleasure for both of them.

"I'm ready. Now. Need your big cock right now."

PROMISES PART 3

Brian gently removed his fingers. If this guy only wanted his dick, he'd give it to him. He'd make it so good it'd be hard for him to walk away. With his mission set, Brian took his wrapped dick and pressed it to that slippery hole and thrust until his swollen head pushed past the tight muscle. His date let out a startled hiss, then quickly relaxed to let Brian ease his length the rest of the way inside.

"Oh god, you're big. Oh my god." His date moaned, one hand still on the wall, the other on Brian's thigh, letting him know he was still okay. "Keep going."

Brian clamped his teeth tight, not wanting his ghostly whimpers to be the first sounds this man heard from him. He was buried so deep the beautiful man felt bottomless, searing and endless. He put his massive arm around that lithe chest, holding his date in place and the other hand he tightened on his narrow hip for leverage. Brian leaned down and licked the soft skin again, picking up intensity as he got closer to that satiny throat. He moved in and out at an easy pace, letting his date get used to his girth. Brian was ready to pound that tight ass, to make him scream for more, to make him dig his blunt nails into his arms while he hung on.

"Yes. I'm ready. Do it. Nice and hard." The man begged, taking his hand away from Brian's thigh and putting it on the wall with the other in preparation for a thorough fucking.

Brian would do anything he was asked. He bent his date over farther, cupped his heavy hands over his shoulders, dipped his knees and started slamming his cock in and out of all that heaven. *So good.* Now the hard, passionate sounds of their love – skin slapping violently against skin – was mixing with everyone else's, but still Brian heard nothing but the sound of his pounding heart.

"Yes. Harder. Harder, fuck. Fuck me good."

His date was hollering exactly what Brian was crying out in his head. He was already ready to explode. Usually, he had a good several minutes in him, but for some reason he wasn't going to be able to hold it in. The man in his arms was different. Not like his usual hookups. The man could hear him. And he behaved as if he actually cared about Brian. No one cared about him except for his brother and his team. He'd be crazy not to at least entertain the possibility of getting to know the man driving him wild.

"Damnit. You're so fuckin' big. Do I feel good?" he moaned, tilting his head to the side waiting to feel Brian's answer.

Brian's groan wasn't as loud as his date's – nothing more than a manipulation of his breath – but it was something. Just in case it wasn't clearly interpreted, Brian lent down and used the flat of his tongue and his lips to answer in the affirmative. Squeezing, holding, and touching the man all over to let him know that everywhere his wonderful body touched Brian felt amazing to him. *Yes, you feel better than anything I've felt in a long time.*

"I can hear you. You said yes."

He said he heard me. Brian wanted to cry out with joy but instead jolted and bucked hard, his come shooting from him like a geyser. It was so powerful and unexpected it almost made his knees buckle, but he managed to hold on and keep pumping. He could hear his date begging for more over the ringing in his own ears.

"Ohhhh. Don't stop, don't stop, don't stop." The man chanted over and over, his fist flying with purpose around his erection. Then Brian felt the moment he came, his dick squeezed in an unforgiving grip as his date shouted then groaned a long curse. "Uggggh, fuuuuck."

Squeezing me so damn good. Brian could feel his dick still pulsing inside that snug channel while they both leaned there clutching each other, coming down from their earth-shattering orgasms. Still confined in the darkness of their little nook, Brian pulled his date back up to his full height, his cock slipping out while he kissed the top of his spine, the back of his neck and behind his ear. It was the first time in a long time that Brian wished he could whisper sweet nothings. And it was the first time that a man in his arms seemed content in Brian's silence.

Brian didn't know how long they stood there holding each other, perspiration leaking down their bodies, but Brian wasn't ready to let go. He closed his eyes and dropped his head into the crook of the man's neck and breathed him in for as long as he could with long, deep whiffs. If this was the last time he'd see him, then he wanted everything committed to memory. His scent, the way his tight body felt against him, the sound of his melodic voice, the feel of his gentle touches, and the way he came undone in Brian's arms when he sprayed his come all over the wall. The only thing that would've made it more perfect was if they'd been in Brian's bed and he'd heard his name cried out during the man's release instead of the word fuck.

Brian needed to get a name. He understood that everyone was at this club with the purpose of getting their rocks off with no strings attached and going on about their business. But god help him. Brian had a feeling he shouldn't let this one get away so easily.

Pulling up his briefs and pants, Brian knew he needed to have a conversation. Ready to ask this guy if he wanted to grab a really, really early breakfast, or go somewhere less crowded and get to know each other. Shit. If he said no, Brian would be confused… and hurt. *Don't worry. He'll say yes. He has to.* There was no way this tender soul could be a prick. Brian could feel something different in this man, even though he'd known him less than an hour, he felt they'd connected in a much deeper level than most of the moaning bodies in that building. Brian took the condom off and balled it up in a couple napkins then tucked it in his back pocket.

With a resigned sigh, his date pulled his pants up too, still leaning back against Brian's bulk. "I love your size." He turned around and nuzzled against the thickness of Brian's chest. "You're so big and warm. I could hang on to you forever." The words were said almost contemplatively, like Brian wasn't meant to hear them, but he did.

He heard the word forever.

Then it happened. Brian could feel the moment the man in his arms panicked. He'd said too much too soon, and now he was about to run. If Brian could only tell him he'd said the exact thing Brian had been thinking but couldn't say. Brian pulled out his cell phone to open his text to voice app. He had to tell him.

"I'm gonna go to the bathroom and wipe the jizz off my hand and thighs. I'll… I'll be right back." He spoke hurriedly and took off into the sea of bodies and strobe lights.

Brian finished righting his clothes. His guy was running, and Brian was going to run after him. As soon as he left his corner and his eyes adjusted to the confusing lighting within the still-packed warehouse, Brian saw the flashlights first before he heard the harsh commands of authoritative voices. Great. The police. He hurried in the direction he was sure his date had gone. He was glad he was tall, he'd be able see over most of the frantic heads that were flittering about in various stages of undress as they went for any exit not blocked by police in raid gear.

He wasn't concerned about the police. Even if he was arrested, Vaughan would get him out, before they could process him all the way. The man was a brilliant lawyer. Brian found the door marked Men's Room and burst inside to warn his guy that they had to get out of there, but to his surprise, no one was there. He was gone.

Commotion and chaos went on just outside the door, but he was oblivious. Brian stood there staring at the empty stalls, his mind refusing to believe that he'd given his all for nothing. He'd taken a risk and opened up to a stranger. Let him touch his

PROMISES PART 3

ailment, his weakness. Refused to hide. Why wasn't his angel there like he said he'd be? Brian walked past each open stall just to be sure. When he got to the last door, he knew he wouldn't find him in there but his heart still sank when he pushed the door open to find the stall empty. Wincing, Brian realized he was squeezing the hell out of his phone. He looked at the screen, the app still up and waiting for him to type what he needed to say. Too late. There was no one there for him to talk to. Not now, maybe not ever. He'd run away from Brian... like they all did. They were scared of him. Scared of his silence... and so was he.

CHAPTER TWENTY-THREE

Dana

Dana had hoped Ford would want to shower with him, but when he'd mentioned cleaning up, Ford had simply nodded his okay and let him go in the bathroom alone. It was fine. It was also very early. If that was Ford's first real intimacy with a man, then he'd take it easy and not let little things offend him. Jessica's constant berating had left him slightly insecure, but he was working on that. Ford didn't like anything except one hundred percent confidence.

Dana looked at his watch. It was almost three in the morning. They were going to be dead to the world when they made it into the office today. That's also something they were used to: operating on little sleep. Dana brushed his teeth with the spare he had in his bag, but he couldn't resist washing with Ford's soap. He was one of the few men that still used a bar instead of body wash and a poof. It smelled so good, Dana wondered if it was something as simple as Dial or Men's Dove, mixed with Ford's natural scent.

Dana stepped out of the bathroom as quietly as possible. He heard Ford's deep breathing before the soft snores reached him. He smiled. It'd been a while since he'd heard the arousing, yet soothing, sound of a man's slumber. Dana took his handgun from his bag and tucked it under the pillow on the left side since Ford seemed to prefer the right. He removed the towel from around his waist and thought about throwing caution to the wind and sliding under those soft covers completely naked and sealing his body around the man he'd lusted after so many nights. He watched Ford sleep for a couple minutes before he shook away the daring thoughts, slid on his clean pair of boxer briefs and eased under the covers.

Ford shifted and turned to look at him after Dana got comfortable. "I was wondering if you were going to watch me sleep the whole time or if you were gonna join me."

"It's taking a minute for all this to sink in," Dana answered, turning so that they lay on their sides facing each other. Dana couldn't resist scooting closer until they were circulating the same air between them. "I've wanted you for a long time."

"Wanted?" Ford stressed.

Dana rolled his eyes. "Triviality. Stop dissecting everything I say. Yes, I wanted you… and still do *want* you, Ford."

Ford snaked his arm under Dana's ribs and pulled until he was sprawled on top of him. Ford's strength never ceased to amaze Dana. With only one arm, he'd moved Dana's entire body and positioned it on top of his much larger one with barely an ounce of effort. It was enough to make him want to come again.

Dana repositioned himself, spreading his legs until his revived hardness rubbed against Ford's. Dana closed his eyes, his head reeling at the amazing sensations. "Damn. Your body is so hard. I knew it would be. In my dreams you were solid. Able to restrain me with one hand." He wasn't really speaking to Ford, more like murmuring to himself in disbelief.

Ford's hands were all over him when Dana came out of his trance. He was on top of Ford. It was all so surreal. He'd been cheated on and dumped all in the same night, but this was by far the best night of his life. Dana lifted his ass higher when he felt calloused hands squeezing his cheeks roughly. It was blatantly inviting, and he hoped Ford would accept.

"You trying to tell me something?" Ford growled, rubbing his beard all over Dana's jaw and neck.

He couldn't think, this was too much. Carnal overload. Was he trying to say something to Ford? Hell yes, he was. He wanted the man to take him rough and fast right there in his bed. Wanted to hear him call out his name when he came deep inside him.

"Just that it's yours, if you want it."

Ford watched Dana with an intensity he'd never seen before. It was a mix of caution and longing. Ford wanted him, he could see it, hell, he could feel it digging into his pelvis, but Ford was reserved. Careful of his heart, and Dana couldn't blame him. To anyone on the outside looking in, this looked like Dana on the rebound. Only hours ago, he'd caught his girl in the act... with another man, in an establishment he couldn't afford to take her to. Money and status had been their undoing. If only he'd solved this problem months ago – and explained their relationship was over – then everything wouldn't've been so screwed up tonight. Now there was cheating in the mix. It was a can of worms that he'd never wanted opened. But since it was... he might as well use those worms to catch him a bigger fish.

Ford gripped the back of Dana's neck and brought him down to his mouth. "If it's mine, then I can have it when I want it."

"Yes," Dana moaned, his hips beginning to thrust all on their own. It was the rich, throaty sound of Ford's voice that made him act without thinking.

Ford smacked the hell out of his ass, making Dana wail, jerk, and hiss in succession. "Stay still," Ford ordered, squeezing Dana's cheek where he'd assaulted it. "I can't think when you're doing that."

Dana smiled in triumph. Finally, he got some kind of confirmation that he was having the same effect on Ford that he was having on him. It was all he wanted... for now. "Don't think. We got plenty of time. Sleep, Ford."

Dana didn't know how, but he knew that Ford wasn't ready to consummate their relationship yet. Ford may not be ready to admit it, but Dana was. They belonged together. It'd always made sense, they'd merely ignored it. Dana made a huge show of sliding off Ford's torso, making sure to lazily rub his entire upper body along Ford's groin as he did.

Ford chuckled seductively. "Brat," he whispered in Dana's ear, wrapping his arms around him from behind and burying his nose in Dana's messy hair. Like it came naturally. In seconds, they were asleep.

Ford

Ford woke to the feeling of warm skin pressed against his chest and the smell of clean virility clinging to his sheets. It wasn't the first night Ford had spent huddled close to a man as he slept, but that had been for survival in freezing temperatures. This... this wasn't for survival. This was all pleasure. Without jostling him, Ford kissed the back of Dana's neck and carefully climbed from the bed without a sound. He went into the bathroom to take care of his needs, stopping briefly to stare at his reflection. He looked rested despite the lack of hours he'd gotten. When he came out, he stopped short at the sight Dana made. He'd rolled onto his back with one arm lying across his naked abs and the other tucked underneath his pillow. If his partner was anything like him, it meant he slept better with his hand close to his weapon. Ford adjusted his dick that'd yet to go fully down. His mouth watered at the one tan, muscular leg sticking out from under the white covers, the thin layer of dark hair in the middle of that thick chest that tapered down to narrow hips. Dana looked young and serene lying there in his bed. *My bed. Jesus. Dana's in my bed.* He looked striking there.

Ford rubbed his creased forehead. This man could be the end of him. He'd managed to fight and win every battle ever thrown his way, but if Dana captured his heart and hurt him... he'd lose that fight. He'd lose everything. His heart and his soul. He needed to clear his head. Ford put on his jogging pants and shoes and grabbed his truck keys. He'd drive to the park to save time. It wasn't even seven yet. He could get in a few miles before Dana woke up.

He'd been gone longer than he'd intended, but he also had a lot to sort out. Ford checked his watch. Shit. It'd been an hour and a half. He still had to drive back, shower, eat, and kiss on Dana for a while before they'd need to get to work. He liked the sound of all that. As he jogged back to the street his truck was parked on, he couldn't help but wonder if his life could really be like this. Someone home, waiting for him in his bed. Someone who wanted him, who cared about him… loved him. He thought of Duke and Vaughan and Quick and Dr. Chauncey. The way they shared their lives together. It was foreign to him, but it didn't have to be. Honestly, his biggest hang-up wasn't Dana's enjoyment of playing the field, but his age. The young man had a long life ahead of him, what would Ford do but hold him back with his irritable ways. Ford shook his head at his own disheartening thoughts. He wasn't exactly filing for Social Security himself. He'd never considered himself old because he didn't feel old. Ford had to go with his gut, and everything was telling him that he could trust Dana. Ford didn't know he was smiling until he entered the bakery around the corner from the park and the woman behind the counter lit up at the sight of him.

"That sure is a big smile you have on today. What a surprise. You wear happiness well. What can I get you?" she asked, her hands moving dramatically over the large display of fresh goodies. "You're in such a good mood this morning I almost wanna recommend my special. Pumpkin scones?"

Ford wasn't sure if his smile dimmed. It didn't feel like it. After all that running, he'd still only had one word to indicate what he was feeling and his neighborhood baker had nailed it at first sight. Happy. Everything was so new and provocative. He was picking up breakfast for him and his overnight guest, his partner, his beau… his something. Dana was more than all those things, but Ford didn't have a name yet. Boyfriend seemed too juvenile.

"Pumpkin sounds good." Ford grinned. He just realized that he didn't know what Dana liked. He knew he liked sweets but he didn't know what his choice of breakfast was. He smiled again. He had so much he was looking forward to learning. "And give me a dozen assorted breakfast pastries."

Ford hurried back to his truck, taking the back streets in his hurry to get home. His heart was hammering in his chest, but not from his exercise. He couldn't wait to eat breakfast with Dana. With the window slightly cracked, Ford enjoyed the cool air on his damp skin. But when he turned the corner onto his street, his temperature spiked and his skin heated all over despite the chill in the air. Ford's mouth dropped open and his head ached with disappointment.

Dana was gone.

CHAPTER TWENTY-FOUR

Dana

Dana paced back and forth, wearing a hole into the small space between Ford's bathroom door and the one window in his bedroom. *He wouldn't just leave. No way.* Dana dug his hands in his hair and walked back to the other side, keeping up the long, discouraging conversation with himself.

He didn't change his mind.
Not after last night.
Not after this morning.
Ford was happy. He wanted me… he'd wanted everything… didn't he?

"Ughh. Damnit." Dana couldn't believe he'd woken up alone. Had Ford changed his mind? He'd laid in bed as long as he could, but he didn't particularly like the idea of lying in Ford's bed without Ford. He got up and took his time getting dressed, checking his watch every ten minutes. It'd been an hour already and Dana was slowly, depressingly coming to the conclusion that Ford wasn't coming back, at least not until Dana was gone. He guessed that was the shitty thing about inviting someone over to your place, you had to run and hide until they left. Well Ford didn't have to stay away from his home any longer. He was leaving.

Dana aggressively threw his belongings into his duffle bag. His mind was doing a real number on him, constantly replaying everything they'd said and done last night. Sure, it'd started off a little rough, but he felt they'd come to an understanding. They were going to give this thing a try. Ford had let him touch him,

PROMISES PART 3

caress him... kiss him. Then he... *fuck*. Dana had blown him. His first guy in ten years. Only for Ford to get up before the sun and weasel out of bed and out the door. *Son of a-* Dana felt so stupid. There was no way he could go into the office and work beside Ford like nothing had ever happened.

So he didn't.

"We're a real couple of idiots, huh?" Dana grumbled, wishing he had some vodka or gin to add to his orange juice, but unfortunately, it was too early for that.

"I sure as hell am. I don't think you are, though." Sway shrugged. "You ran before you got any information, D. What if he had an emergency?"

"Then we all would've been notified, Sway. We all have on the same watches. We all get the same alerts."

"It could've been a personal emergency. You said you don't know him as well as you want to. Maybe he has some early morning ritual."

"Yeah. Making me feel like a tramp."

Sway laughed. "Come on, D. I think you're overreacting. You woke up expecting to find him... what if he came back home expecting to find you. From what you described – what happened last night – I don't think he left you like you think. Even after meeting him one time, he doesn't seem like a coward. A tad rough around the edges, but not a punk, man. He doesn't seem like a runner."

Dana opened his mouth to argue, then thought twice. "Why didn't he leave a note, then?"

Sway choked on his juice then looked at Dana like he'd lost his mind. "Because he's a man! What the hell you mean 'leave a note'? Should he have written it on the bathroom mirror in lipstick? Dude, you've been on the other side of the fence too long. You might wanna make sure all your gay licenses and registrations are still valid."

Dana sucked his teeth. He looked at his watch. It was after ten, he was supposed to be at work by nine. "Then he could've called."

"You could've called, too." Sway got up and poured them some more to drink. "I'm sure he's at work wondering where his partner is."

"Or not." Dana pulled out his cell. He had a text from Duke telling him he had until noon, then he better get his ass back to work. "Anyway, enough about my craziness. So, what happened with you last night? You look like something the cat dragged in."

Sway didn't say anything, instead choosing to fiddle with the tattered holes in his night shirt. His friend couldn't even make eye contact with him. As realization finally set in, Dana put his glass down and really stared at his best friend. Dana had been so wrapped up in his own shit he'd forgotten what 'I just got some' looked like, and currently his best friend was wearing that look with pride. "No damn way, Sway. Did you really… not at that club. You hooked up with someone at that club, didn't you?"

Sway covered his face and groaned embarrassedly.

"Come on, bro. Spill it." Now this was something Dana *wanted* to talk about. "What superhero ended your ten year drought?"

Sway laughed then looked at Dana with the dreamiest expression he'd ever seen. "Someone I could only make up in my dreams. The tallest, biggest, most refreshing drink of water I've ever encountered. He was amazing, Dana." Sway dropped his chin to his chest. "And I was an idiot. I ran… ran before I even got his damn name. By the time I came to my freakin' senses, cops were raiding the place and he was nowhere to be found. What's even more spectacular about him, D… is he blew my mind… and he never uttered a single word."

PROMISES PART 3

CHAPTER TWENTY-FIVE

Ford

"It's almost one o'clock, Ford. Where the hell is your partner?! We're losing time," Quick barked angrily while Ford stood at the counter with his back to him, making his fourth cup of extremely strong coffee of the day. Maybe the caffeine would be too much, overstimulate him and make him pass out. Anything was better than the constant argument in his head.

"I don't know, Quick. You've asked me that five goddamn times and the answer is still the same. I. Don't. Know," Ford snapped, moving past his stunned boss and back to his desk.

He hadn't told anyone about what happened last night. Obviously. Too humiliated to confess to being an old fool. Not just a fool, but an old fool. How could Dana do that to him? He'd let Dana put his mouth on him, sleep with him, he thought those things meant something. But that was just Ford showing his age again.

"Well, if he's not here in an hour, we go." Quick scowled and dropped down at his own desk, his long braid flying over his shoulder.

Ford kept his back to his boss as he checked his cell phone again. No messages, no emails, nothing. Dana had dropped him faster than a heathen dropping bible school. Quick got up again, stomping across the room to look out the front windows. Jesus. He didn't know what was irritating him most, his boss acting like Dana calling off for a few hours was the end of the world, or his partner dismissing him like a piece of shit.

"I'm gonna go to the courthouse and get a couple copies of the Harrison warrant and disposition. Duke's been wanting that in the file so we can officially close it. Then," Quick pointed at him, "If Dana isn't here and ready to go by the time I get back, both of you will be on my shit list. Believe that."

Ford didn't react to Quick's threats, just watched him walk out of the office. Ford tossed the file he'd been pretending to review on his desk and reared back tiredly, his mind going right back to last night. Dana's smile. His touch, his taste, the way he smelled when he'd showered with his soap. How was he to go back to being nothing but work partners now? Maybe he should find a new job. Fuck! This was why he'd avoided getting involved… especially with someone he had to work with. He knew better.

Ford looked at his brother's empty desk. He'd heard that Brian came in early and rode with Duke to do a bond for a drunk driver arrested late last night. Ford closed his eyes and sighed. He was about to get up and pace for a while when the front door to their office was pushed open and Dana barreled through the door, looking angry. Ford was confused. He was the one that should be mad here. Not Dana.

"Can I have a word with you?" Dana seethed.

Ford got up and slowly followed Dana into the break room. There was no one there but the two of them, so he had no clue why Dana felt he needed the extra privacy. Maybe this was the part where he told Ford he'd realized this morning that he'd made a big mistake and that's why he left. Well, Dana could save it. He didn't care. Ford came into the room, almost walking right to the coffee pot, but changed his mind. He'd had enough caffeine, he already could hardly sit still. He wanted nothing more than to charge Dana, wrap his arms around his body, and shake him until he understood how badly he was frustrating him.

"I can't believe you, Ford." Dana whirled around, his teeth clenched together, his words hissing between them. "I trusted you, man. I put myself out there and you… you hustled me. I can't believe you talked all that shit about Jessica, and look what you turn around and do. I deserve better, huh? You ain't treating me no better, Bradford. That bullshit you—"

He'd heard enough. Ford pushed off the chair so hard it flipped over. Dana's eyes widened a split second before Ford reached out and yanked him by his collar, pulling him into his chest. Their angry, scowling faces on a couple inches apart. "How dare you compare me to her? And I've never fuckin' hustled anyone in my life."

"Why, then?" Dana's boldness deflated so fast, Ford wondered if it was ever there to begin with. Dana looked so beaten and tired, Ford had an overwhelming urge to take it all on himself and make him smile again. He didn't know how Dana had ended up the one hurt by all this, but there had obviously been some major miscommunication. "Why'd you do that? That was messed up. I woke up and you'd left."

Ford realized he was still holding onto Dana but his grip was no longer as aggressive. Instead, his fingers were lightly caressing Dana's throat. Ford eased in closer. "Yes, Dana. I left you in my bed. Warm. Relaxed. Resting. I didn't do anything to hurt you. I watched you sleep. There was so much going on in my head, so much I wanted to say to you."

"Then why'd you leave?" Dana snapped.

"Are you that impatient, brat?" Ford held Dana's face in his big hands. His mouth was just barely brushing Dana's pursed lips. "I went for a run, goddamnit. I drove to the park. Ran to clear my head. I stopped and got us breakfast. When I came back… you were gone. I came back for this, and you were fuckin' gone." Ford crashed his mouth over his partner's, pulling Dana into him to show he was back in control.

When Ford let Dana go, he wavered on his feet, finally opening his eyes. Dana licked his swollen mouth, eyeing Ford with confusion and a little embarrassment. "I thought you. I thought you left."

Ford ran his hand over his short strands, looking away to hide his own frustration. He didn't have time for this. He couldn't help but think of how shitty his morning was, all because Dana had misunderstood his actions. And instead of talking with him about it, the man flew off half-cocked.

"Jesus. Okay. I'm sorry. I really am, Ford." Dana put his hand on Ford's shoulder and he shrugged it off without a second thought.

He was mad.

"I thought that… fuck… come on, Ford. You can see my point of view, right? I mean, come on."

"I don't have the time or the patience for Mickey Mouse shit, Dana," Ford argued.

"Excuse me?" Dana glowered.

"You heard me. If I say something, Dana, you should know I mean it. I've never told you one thing and done the opposite." Ford didn't pull away again when Dana approached cautiously. He wanted his touch and didn't have the strength to pull away from it again. "You can't run every time you're unsure of something. I've chased people all of my adult life, Dana. I love doing it. And I'm far from done. But I won't chase you. I shouldn't have to. If you want me like you say, then I'm standing right here. Why are you going in the opposite direction?"

Dana

Dana had never felt so damn young and inferior in all his life. He liked to brag about his maturity but honestly, he couldn't be sure he had any claim left to it after the ridiculousness he'd just pulled. For a long time, he'd been trying to win Ford's approval and affection, and as soon as he thought he had it, he'd managed to annihilate both sentiments in a matter of hours.

He stood there looking at Ford after what he'd just said. Dana wasn't sure how many times he needed to apologize… again. He wasn't even sure at this point if they were still giving this a try. "I'm not running."

"If you say so," Ford grumbled, leaning against the other wall, a table between them.

How had he gotten so far away?

Dana walked around the table and stood in front of Ford, looking up the couple inches of height difference into Ford's smoky eyes. He hoped what he was getting ready to say would be the right thing this time, because Dana couldn't stand the annoyed expression on Ford's face any longer. "Look. I'm gonna level with you. I admit I was still feeling a bit insecure about us. It kinda feels like I've been begging for a shot with you – or at minimum, a decent work partnership – for months, and when I finally got it, I guess I was still hesitant to believe you meant it."

Ford bent down until their foreheads were touching and Dana was able to take a much-needed breath of relief. Because he had been sure he'd blown it. Dana tangled his fingers in Ford's dense beard and pulled him down the last couple inches until their lips touched. Gently at first and then more forcefully, until they were moaning into each other's mouths and gripping one another tightly. When they finally pulled apart, Dana was gasping for air. Ford's touch literally took his breath away.

"Does this mean you forgive me?" Dana asked, widening his stance so he was low enough to bury his nose in Ford's soft beard. Damn. He even smells good here.

Ford growled, still holding Dana against his thick body while he laid down the law. "It means that if I leave you in my bed, Dana, that's where you better be when I return."

"I shouldn't've have doubted or assumed. That's my bad, okay. Next time," please let there be a next time, "I won't leave.

Even if you don't come back for days, I'll still be there waiting for you, Bradford."

"Good," Ford bit out.

Dana smiled. He took it for what it was. Ford keeping a tight grip on his control. It was probably to guard himself more than anything, because as sensitive as Dana was about his heart, he knew Ford was even more sensitive and overprotective about his own.

Dana flicked his tongue out and slowly ran it across Ford's bottom lip, tasting coffee and sweet pastries. "You taste too sweet to talk so hard."

Ford held back his full-on smile, only giving Dana a quick lift of one side of his mouth. It was enough, and sexy as hell. "What you taste is your breakfast."

Dana leaned back, looking a little confused until he realized that Ford had mentioned getting breakfast for them. "If it makes you feel any better… I'm still hungry."

Ford gripped the back of Dana's neck. "It doesn't."

Neither of them said anything for a moment. Not needing to fill the silence with more apologies or explanations. Simply standing close was good enough. The front door burst open and Dana heard his bosses' strong voices carry to the back of the building.

"Guess it's time to get to it. We only got a few hours on the streets now. Duke said he wants us to rein it in about nine tonight," Ford informed them.

They looked at their watches.

"Yeah. Let's go." Ford was slow to release him. Dana noticed it because he didn't want to stop touching Ford either.

Dana was nervous to ask the question and he probably should wait a bit longer until he was sure Ford had cooled completely, but he wanted to make it up to Ford. Wanted to be in his bed all morning. He wanted another chance. "Do you want me to come over after work?" Dana felt like ducking his head in the crook of Ford's neck but he was too much of a man to do that. He looked Ford in his eyes, waiting for his answer. Waiting for Ford to make up his mind.

"Yes," Ford finally replied.

PROMISES PART 3

CHAPTER TWENTY-SIX

Ford

After Duke and Quick finished chewing their asses out for causing them all to miss practically an entire day on the streets, they'd only been able to work a few hours and to no avail. They both knew how important this case was, so Ford had sat there beside his partner – silently supporting him – while he took his lashings. It was okay to take a personal day when the caseload was light, but not when they were hunting. Duke didn't play that. And Dana knew personal shit had to be kept out of the office. They couldn't call off because they were mad and having a bad morning. *His little brat.* Ford knew the real reason Dana had avoided the office this morning and most of the early afternoon. He'd been mad and afraid of seeing Ford. But he kept his mouth closed.

Ford finished showering and grooming his beard that Dana seemed to like so much. Who knew the man was so into hair? He'd dated women so much, Ford thought his rough features and hairy body would've been a turnoff to him. Ford couldn't've been more wrong. He'd just finished throwing on a pair of blue US NAVY sweats and a white tank top when his doorbell rang. He may not look as gorgeous as Dana, but he was smelling clean and had even dabbed on a little aftershave. It was as much primping as he could manage.

Ford opened the door, and sure enough, there he was, smelling and looking just as fine as always. Dana had obviously showered too, because his hair was still wet and combed back, making it look jet-black. He had on loose jeans with a simple black and gray retro Jimi Hendrix t-shirt with dark leather boots. His body filled out everything beautifully. While Dana wasn't as big as Ford, he wasn't small. He had strong arms and legs, which he used to his advantage on the streets. But Ford's eyes were glued to Dana's hard abs and solid chest under the snug shirt.

"You can keep staring, but can you do it with me inside? These bags are heavy, babe." Dana's voice, even his eyes, were full of edge and amusement.

Fuck. Ford closed his mouth, not sure if he'd drooled on his shirt or not, and stepped aside to let a still-smiling Dana into his home.

"Well, thank you." Dana kissed him quickly on the mouth on his way past. Not enough. He went into Ford's kitchen, dropping the three full grocery bags on the counter. Ford looked bewildered. What was his brat up to now? He never told Dana he had to bring his own food.

"What are you doing?" Ford asked, leaning against the counter while he watched Dana maneuver around his kitchen, washing his hands before he began to unload the bags.

"I'm going to make us dinner." Dana winked. "I'm starving. Did you eat already?"

"No." Ford pulled out two beers and popped the tops on them. "I was gonna order Chinese or something."

"Well, no need."

"You're going to cook?" Ford said skeptically, still looking oddly around at the scattered ingredients.

"Yes, Ford. I'm going to cook. It's not that complicated."

"You're cooking nachos?"

Dana looked in his cabinets until he found a small pan and put it on the range, dropping a small hunk of ground chuck in before turning back to Ford. "Good grief. I didn't say I was attempting a leg of lamb with mint jelly. It's only cheap ground beef with a bunch of crap on top. I'm not making a five-course meal, man."

Ford shrugged. "I'm a little surprised but, by all means. Go right ahead. I'll be in here watching TV."

Dana grabbed Ford's arm. "Um. What the hell you think this is? *All In the Family*? You're not gonna sit on your ass while I cook and call you when dinner's ready. Get your fine ass in here and help."

"I don't cook." Ford smirked.

"I don't need you to." Dana picked up the tomatoes and tossed one at Ford. "Start cutting. You can't fuck up a tomato. Any way you cut it, we'll put it on the pile. Same for the lettuce and avocado."

Ford was still looking baffled when Dana rolled his eyes and moved him to the edge of the counter, put the knife in his hand and started to show him how to dice. It was cute and silly at the same time. Ford knew he could cut up a tomato and shred some lettuce, but Dana's arms around him while he manipulated Ford's big hand around the knife were too endearing to put a stop to.

"See. Easy. Just keep cutting like that," Dana said softly, leaving his arms around Ford's waist while he did his menial job. Next thing he knew, he felt soft lips against the back of his neck, moving gently across his heated skin. Then Dana's hands were massaging his chest and abs as they moved lower and lower.

"You're gonna make me cut my thumb off." Ford put the knife down and turned in Dana's arms.

"Sorry. Got distracted," Dana whispered, tilting his head up higher. Ford leaned down, answering Dana's request for a kiss by slanting his mouth over his and taking a deep taste. A taste he'd missed while they'd been working this evening. There was no fooling around when they were on the streets. Dana had been focused. Watching all their backs while they canvassed some of the most dangerous neighborhoods in Atlanta. Ford had wanted to reach out and pull Dana close to him so many times, especially after a guy got aggressive when Dana kept

PROMISES PART 3

questioning him. Even Duke saw that Ford wanted to intervene but Duke caught him, telling him that he had to trust Dana now just as he had before they became more than work partners. He didn't like Duke's perception or observation, but his boss was right. Dana was the same badass he'd always been. He didn't need Ford coming to his rescue.

Ford wondered how his feelings had changed so much so fast. Ford kept kissing and licking and savoring until he started to smell something. "Burning," Ford grumbled.

"I'm hot too, babe."

Ford chuckled in Dana's mouth, scrambling to latch back on to his. "I mean your cheap beef. Smells like it's burning."

"Shit!" Dana jumped out of Ford's arms and turned back to the smoking stove. The meat sizzled and popped as Dana flipped and pushed it around the pan. "Phew. Okay, it's not burned."

Ford went back to his duties, his chest feeling light, his heart feeling wonderful.

"So, what do you think?" Dana asked, shoving a huge chip loaded with meat, cheese, sour cream and a lot of other ingredients in his mouth.

"It's good," Ford finally answered when he'd swallowed his own mouthful. "Keep it up, a man can get used to this."

"Me too." Dana looked serious when he said it.

They finished eating, Ford joined in to help Dana clean up his kitchen. They worked effortlessly, moving around each other in the cramped space without much thought. The conversation came just as easily. Ford found himself wanting to know so much more about his partner. Wanting to know everything. Dana talked about his childhood, about Sway and his deceased twin, talked about his drunk dad, his marksman training, while Ford listened with interest.

Dana

It was comical the way Ford got ready for bed. It was obvious he was used to his evening ritual and his space being his own. Dana would've liked for them to have gotten into bed together, but Ford had a different idea. He told Dana to go ahead and get relaxed while he checked and locked up his house. Dana would've done it with him, but instead, he got in Ford's bed and waited for him like he'd asked. He missed it if he was being honest, and had been nervous he wasn't going to be invited back in it. Lying there in nothing but his black boxer briefs, he answered a quick text to Sway, then put his phone down when he heard Ford's front door close and the locks engage.

Ford took a moment to stand in the bedroom doorway when he saw Dana sprawled across his big bed, then continued inside. Dana watched, engrossed, as Ford went about his regular routine. Placing his watch on the nightstand, a black Glock under his pillow, his boots in the corner. Then finally, the outerwear. Dana's mouth watered with every stitch of clothes that Ford removed. It was his own personal sexy bear strip show and he couldn't have pried his eyes away even if a purple alien had walked by. Neither took their eyes off each other until Ford was on top of him.

They both let out a sharp hiss when their hard bodies aligned and their solid cocks brushed against each other.

"Jesus," Dana moaned, wrapping his hands around all that mass, relishing the feeling of muscles pressing him into the mattress. "I can't believe you feel this good, Ford, fuck."

Ford was breathing heavily against Dana's neck, and every second or so, he felt Ford's tongue grazing over his skin. "You… You do too."

Dana pushed his hips up, rubbing eagerly against Ford's slick cock. He was leaking so much, both of them were, it wasn't long before they were sticky and wetly gliding over each other, letting nature take over. Thrusting and crushing together with a ferociousness Dana had never felt. Ford's goddamn hips were so thick and powerful, the combination so hypnotic, Dana was sure he was going to blow any second.

"You keep doing that and I'm gonna be done, babe," Dana breathed, squeezing Ford's broad shoulders, touching him everywhere his hands could reach.

He felt Ford take a couple deep breaths against his throat – which did nothing to calm his arousal – then his hips gradually slowed to a torturous grind. Ford was so sensual and stimulating, his cock hungry but not greedy. A testament to the man's maturity. Ford relaxed himself and set a completely different pace.

"Oh damn. This is... too slow. I'm gonna come, Ford."

Ford growled, nipping Dana's ear. "Not yet."

Dana threw his arms out to the sides. He had to take them off Ford's huge body. The flavor, the feeling, the sheer scent of Ford sent Dana's mind into a frenzy. He was frustrated, trapped between wanting to release the pent-up need in his balls and wanting Ford to make it last forever. He was debating what he *had* to have right at that moment when he felt Ford's body moving down farther and farther until Dana felt that thick beard brushing over the smooth hairs on his abdomen. *Is he about to...?* Dana was so still, not wanting to cause Ford to detour off course.

Calloused hands rubbed all over his thighs, spreading them even wider as Ford's bulk fit obscenely between them. Ford made eye contact with him, still taking his time as he moved over Dana's form. Looking like he appreciated every groove and ridge he saw. Ford's breathing was labored, his body pulsating right along with Dana's as he began to tremble with anticipation. Ford's mouth was way too close to his hard cock that was curved up to his belly, a thin line of clear liquid connecting to his stomach. Would that gross Ford out? He wasn't sure. God, he hoped not. His dick hadn't been sucked in....

"Augh, god!" Dana arched his back and shouted when Ford took the flat of his tongue and licked the precome from the head of his cock and then the little that had pooled on his stomach. Dana groaned, "Ford, please."

"Had to see if I liked it first," Ford answered huskily from between Dana's thighs. It looked like he was satisfied with Dana's response and the taste. He wanted Ford to do what he'd just done again… and again, about twenty more times and that would be all it took.

But Dana was too intoxicated to tell if his partner enjoyed his essence. Ford's slow, edging rhythm had him dazed and sizzling with desire. He could only stare in awe as Ford rolled Dana's flavor around on his tongue. Oh, he hoped Ford liked it, or at least could tolerate it. *For the love of all that is holy, please, say you like it.* It'd been months since he'd had a warm mouth on him. So long since he'd been with someone who cared about what he wanted in bed, too.

"You want my mouth on you. I can feel it. You're shaking," Ford murmured in the sensitive crease between Dana's thigh and groin.

"Yeah. I do. God, yes, please, Ford."

"I won't make you beg, Dana. I don't understand, but I want this more than I've wanted anything in a long time. Want my mouth all over you, my hands, everything." Ford squeezed both of Dana's ass cheeks hard enough to make him curse. Ford's big biceps flexed as he pushed Dana's hips upwards and opened his mouth, taking in the purplish head and sucking it harder than Dana was ready for.

"Shit!" Dana eyes flew open. He looked down at his partner, his lover. Shocked at the intense concentration in Ford's eyes. Shocked at the look of lust, showing beautifully over his masculine face. "Unnnnnh." The suction was so strong, Ford's cheeks caved in from the effort.

He didn't want to shoot in Ford's mouth – that might be overkill. His muddled brain was just coherent enough for that courteous thought. Dana breathed through his nose and tried to let it out of his mouth but it only ended up choking him. The pleasure was consuming. "It's s'good. Oh my god. I can't last, babe."

With each suck, Ford would go down a little more. Testing his own limits. He didn't ask for instruction, or even if he was doing it right. Ford let this act come instinctively. And oh hell, was he a natural. Even Ford's jaws were unforgiving, relentless. Dana's body shook while he fought for control. He was gonna come faster than a virgin on prom night. He clenched his hands in the covers as Ford continued to use his hands, his arms to regulate the tempo. Lifting and lowering Dana to however deep or shallow he wanted his cock in his mouth. Alternating between thirstily tonguing the beads of precome that kept accumulating at the tip of his cock and eagerly engulfing his length. Then, as if he'd forgotten about them and just remembered they were there, Ford cupped Dana's heavy balls and rolled them in his hand while he sucked him down deep enough that Dana felt Ford's soft beard against the base of his dick.

Dana's back bowed off the bed as he released a sound he'd never heard himself make before. One that would've been embarrassing if he weren't so far gone. He wanted to make this last so much longer but it was useless. He didn't think anything would tamp down his orgasm. It was going to be like nothing he'd ever felt. His *mind* and body were both being dominated by Bradford King.

He couldn't believe he'd gone so long without this kind of special attention. He considered himself a generous lover. Always wanting his partner to receive just as much – if not more – satisfaction as he did. But lately, that hadn't been the case. Dana was practically starved for affection at this point. Just because Jessica would jump on him and ride him until she came, didn't mean *he* was sexually satisfied at all. He was barely touched, hugged or kissed. There was always preparation he had to perform if he was going to put his hands on Jessica and vice-versa.

With Ford... with this man... he could be himself. He could just be Dana the marksman, the bounty hunter, and Ford would be happy with that. Proud of that. Proud of him.

The thought of this amazing man – a decorated SEAL – being proud of him was all he needed to tilt him over the ledge and send him falling hard. Dana was just able to clutch Ford's shoulder and shout his name before his release exploded from him, blinding him for the first couple seconds, then wracking his body with violent tremors and jolts as Ford sucked every drop Dana had to give. Ford never hesitated like he wasn't sure if he wanted that part of Dana or not. He took all of him, licked him clean, and from the look of fire in Ford's black eyes when he finally pulled off, Dana knew the feeling had been mutual. Ford had wanted to do that to him and had enjoyed it just as much.

Dana wanted to jump up and flip Ford over and return the gesture ten-fold, but he was boneless, completely shattered. Ford had done something to him. *Jesus*. His arms didn't want to work. His eyes would barely open, not to mention focus on something. With his legs gaped open because he couldn't summon the energy to close them, Dana laid there like a sexed-out ragdoll.

"Damn. Look at you." Ford climbed up Dana's body like a top predator and straddled him just below his hips. He reached down and gripped the back of Dana's neck and pulled him up to him, putting him in the perfect position to latch on to one of Ford's dark nipples. Dana was glad for the assistance because he wasn't sure he'd stay sitting up if Ford wasn't holding him.

"Mmm. Yeah, suck on it, brat. Suck it good," Ford whispered, his hand leisurely moving over his thick shaft. The veins were dark and red, looking ready to pop. But Ford kept the pace even. Dana was amazed how the man could be so turned on and so composed at the same time. He had to be aching to come by now, the dark burgundy head that was weeping and spilling onto Dana's belly was evidence of that. But Ford's fist wasn't flying over his thick dick, forcing his orgasm from him. Dana sat there mesmerized by Ford's lazy movements. The head reappearing every couple seconds from within Ford's big fist. He was able to keep this up for a minute or so before Dana felt Ford's body jerk on top of him and go rigid. Every muscle flexing hard for him. *Gorgeous motherfucker.*

"I'm gonna come." Ford's voice was so gravelly and dark it made Dana's chest vibrate and his cock attempt to twitch back to life.

"I want you to come in my mouth," Dana whispered in awe while he kept his eyes trained on the beautiful act.

"I'm gonna come exactly where I want to," Ford growled, grabbing a handful of Dana's wild, black hair and yanking his head back, exposing his long throat.

Oh, fuck yeah. This was what Dana missed. The animalistic act of letting a man completely wreck and own him.

Dana swallowed hard, his protruding Adam's apple bobbing eagerly. Ford's eyes narrowed when he caught it, his hand slowing even more, his muscles pulled so tight Dana's hands burned where they touched them. *So damn amazing.* Dana saw the moment his partner's orgasm rushed over him. Ford jerked within his hold, slowly pulled the satiny skin around his shaft almost completely over his slit, yelled, and shot against Dana's throat. Ford's scent filled the room, making Dana high all over again. While Ford towered over him, his body taut with pleasure, the first spurt of come hit Dana's Adam's apple so hard it made him jolt in surprise. Then the next one coated the skin just above his sternum before it finally started to lessen and run over Ford's fist. He didn't hesitate to take that and rub it over the rest of Dana's throat and upper chest.

Now Ford looked just a sated as him. Dana fell back, coated in Ford's come, content to stay that way the rest of the night. Ford dropped down next to him, groaning and still panting.

"Damn, Dana." Was all Ford seemed to be able to achieve between breaths.

Dana smiled, absently running his hand along the side of Ford's thigh that was against his. "Damn, Bradford."

Dana didn't know how long they laid there, satisfied with light touches and silence, but Ford was the first one to break the quiet.

"I'm'a get a washcloth and wipe you off."

Dana almost blurted out "No," but maybe Ford didn't want to sleep with Dana while he was covered in semen. Dana had no qualms at all about it, but different strokes and all that. He was even more surprised when Ford sat on the edge of the bed and began to slowly, appreciatively run the warm rag over Dana's throat. It was damn near a sponge bath, especially when Ford returned to the bathroom, rinsed the rag, warmed it up again and came back to resume his important job, focusing now on Dana's chest. He could only watch in amazement and complete admiration.

"I don't know what to think when you look at me like that, Dana." Ford's deep, husky voice permeated the dim room.

"Don't think," Dana whispered. "Just feel."

Because this was it for Dana. Nothing could feel better than Bradford King. Nothing.

PROMISES PART 3

CHAPTER TWENTY-SEVEN

Ford

Ford's alarm went off at seven. He'd wanted to get a run in before work, but just like most mornings, it was hard to get out of bed. Too much temptation. He turned over and looked at the warm, sexy man sleeping next to him. His tanned skin, so gorgeous against the cream-colored sheets. In the past two weeks, Dana had slept at his house every night except three, and only because his best friend had needed him one night and the other two, they'd both been too exhausted from work.

Their days on streets had been tiring and unproductive. Duke was getting antsy, thinking their bounty had skipped town. But something kept telling Ford that the man wouldn't leave his baby brother to rot in jail alone. The Grossmans were too close for that. Ford and Brian understood this better than any of the other guys and kept telling Duke that John was going to avenge his baby brother, one way or another. Because that was exactly what Ford would do. He didn't like to compare himself to a criminal. He was a sailor, a Special Warfare sailor. He didn't break the law, had defended his country in times of war. But sometimes war and crime went hand in hand. Ford had been considered an honorable man until *he* broke the law, too. Military law. Tossed his career and almost lost his freedom... for his brother.

"Hey. Why you look so serious so early?" Dana's sleepy voice filtered through his unpleasant memories. Ford looked down at his man. Yes, Dana Cadby was his guy. He wished he'd known months ago that Dana could make him feel as good as he did, because he would've pulled his head out of his ass a long time ago. And he didn't only mean making him feel good physically, because Ford's chest seemed to expand anytime Dana was around. Anytime Dana sought out his touch. Anytime Dana showed him attention. Anytime Dana showed his skills in the field. It was official. Ford had it bad.

"Nothing," Ford murmured, leaning down into Dana's hot skin, burying his face in the crook of his neck and breathing in his sleepy scent. Dana always smelled and felt so good to him, like the warm sunshine on his runs. Ford rumbled when Dana's hands found his chest and started fingering the coarse hairs across his pecs. "Keep it up and I'm canceling our run this morning."

Dana smiled up at him, looking like a young sex god. "That's what I was hoping you'd say."

Ford let Dana pull him back down, he didn't hesitate to go willingly. He never did.

Ford and Dana had explored each other's bodies most nights for a few weeks now, and each time it got better and more intense, but he'd yet to penetrate Dana. There was no particular reason, except Ford knew it'd been a long time since Dana had done it. And never for him, so he wanted things to be right... he wanted to be ready... meaning, he needed a little guidance.

That's where Brian came in.

Ford debated for a while on who he would confide in to help with the basic questions he had. Duke was one of the first that came to mind, but the man joked too much. No doubt his boss would've turned his questions into a ridiculous after-school-family-life-special. Duke was all fear and revered on the streets, but behind closed doors and away from the office, he was an annoying goofball. The man was head over heels in love with his partner, so of course he was giddy ninety percent of the time. Ford wasn't hating. He was finally starting to understand the excitement of having someone.

Having chosen his brother, they'd met up at Brian's place a couple nights ago to have beers and relax while he helped Brian work on his boat, which he kept in his backyard. It was a small pontoon, just like the one they'd had when they were kids. Brian found it online when it was nothing but a shell and scrap, but after a year, it was starting to resemble what Brian had envisioned for it.

Ford enjoyed his time with his brother, just the two of them. It'd been a while. He'd been wanting to get up with Brian a lot sooner, but he seemed distracted lately. Anytime he or Dana asked Brian to come over, he came up with some excuse for why he couldn't. And the excuses kept getting weaker until Ford knew Brian was flat-out lying and avoiding them. He appreciated his brother giving him and Dana space to grow their fresh relationship but *no one* could push Brian out his life. His brother had something on his mind too, but until he was ready to talk about it Ford wouldn't push him.

Instead, Ford asked all the usual questions. The ones that made him feel like an over-protective brother, but oh well. He asked how Brian was doing with therapy. Did he feel he was progressing? Had he been doing his vocal cord exercises as instructed? Yep. Basically, all the questions that made his baby brother roll his eyes and give Ford the one-finger sign that everybody understood. No interpretation needed.

After a few beers and a sore back from hauling the materials to construct the new seats on the boat, they'd finally sat down and gotten to the nitty gritty. Ford was surprised how seriously his brother took his questions. He'd barely refrained from covering his face in mortification when he admitted to Brian that he wanted to make Dana fly in bed, wanted to make it the best he'd ever had. Brian had simply nodded and started advising. Even when it seemed to get a little uncomfortable for Ford, Brian kept him focused. Ford didn't want to imagine his little brother doing some of the things he'd mentioned. Rimming, stretching, prostate massaging... it was a lot to take in. And a lot of images to try to erase from his head. Meaning, there were just some things a man didn't need to know about a family member. Like their sexual preferences. But Brian kept it relatively painless. From what he understood, his brother didn't want him to be a mediocre lover and insisted he tell him things in detail, even show him a short video. When Ford got back to his place, he went straight to the bedroom. He was used to seeing Dana laid across his bed or on his couch watching TV and Ford didn't wait to show what he'd learned about the art of proper fingering.

"Mmm. Yeah, right there," Dana moaned. "Deeper."

Speaking of fingering. Ford had two already inside Dana, crooking and searching out that magic place that made Dana whine and moan his name. Ford didn't think he'd ever tire of it. He stared down at the look of bliss on Dana's face. His brow creased, his lips parted, Dana's beautiful skin was flushed, a fine sheen of sweat forming on his nose. Ford fought to keep from pouncing on top of Dana and burying his throbbing cock as deep as it would go. From what his partner told him, Dana'd already had more than one inconsiderate lover. He'd be damned if he'd add himself to that count. *Goddamn.* "So damn hot inside."

"You want inside this heat, babe," Dana told him, not asked him, lifting his ass higher in an erotic invitation. It was so firm, tight, with just enough muscle. And Ford loved nothing more than to slick down the soft brown hairs that sparsely covered those enticing mounds with the flat of his tongue.

Yes, he wanted in badly.

Dana's smile was soft, sensual. His warm mocha bedroom eyes were gazing at Ford's face, like he was the reason the sun rose this morning. He never thought anyone would look at him so reverently, so adoringly. Especially someone like Dana. Strong and gorgeous to a fault. Ford was damn proud to have a man like him and he'd be sure to not only show Dana, but tell him regularly. So when they'd gone on their first actual date to dinner and bowling, Ford wasn't afraid to show Dana some public affection. Let everyone know that the beautiful, deadly man on his arm was his partner in every way.

Feeling his chest expand and heat with… with… Ford gasped. Feeling his chest warm from the realization that he was in love. Ford swallowed his emotions and really looked at the man in his bed, the man that'd captured his heart, the man who owned him.

"Ford," Dana whispered, gently running his fingers through his beard.

Ford hadn't noticed he'd stopped moving his fingers until Dana clenched tightly around them.

"God, I need you. I want you to fuck me, Ford." Dana dragged his nose through Ford's beard. His toned arms were pulling Ford down on him, wanting him to cover him.

Dana loved Ford on top, said he liked the feeling of Ford's strength. Ford straddled Dana's thighs and pushed his fingers in deeper, earning him another sexy-ass groan that went all the way to the bottom of Ford's balls. He reached over to the nightstand and pulled out the small pack of condoms he'd put in there last week. Dana's eyes widened then dropped back to narrow slits, his mouth falling open as he breathed heavily with want.

Ford was so serious, the way he was focusing on Dana. Towering over him, dark eyes boring down into sexy brown ones. Ford rolled the condom down his cock, lined himself up with Dana's pulsing hole, and dropped all his weight down, putting both forearms on either side of Dana's face. Dana stared up at him. Ford stared right back. This was a pinnacle moment in his life. He could feel it down deep inside him – love – with extreme arousal and craving mixed in. Ford was feeling so damn much at once, he worked overtime to control himself. He'd make this wonderful for Dana, that was his mission, and he'd never failed one of those.

PROMISES PART 3

Dana

Dana couldn't take his eyes off of Ford's penetrating gaze. Those smoke-black eyes held a level of knowledge and maturity that turned Dana on to no end. Even as Ford's thick cock pressed into him, stretching him beyond what he thought possible, he couldn't bring himself to look away, to look down and watch it disappearing inside his body. Ford had him riveted. On the man, not his cock. Though he felt every inch, every vein, every maddening throb as it slid inside his walls. What he was receiving was *all* of Ford, everything that he had.

Love. Dana saw it, saw it when Ford stopped fingering him and stared at him. Dana knew the look, because he was looking at Ford the exact same way. He'd hoped Ford would tell him, would say it out loud, but instead, he chose to show it. And, oh, god when he finally felt full, low-hanging balls against his ass, Dana released a shuddering breath and opened his legs wider to let Ford put on the best damn show that he could.

"Are you okay?" Ford gritted through his teeth, like his restraint was on the verge of snapping.

Dana ran his hands down Ford's broad back to his furry ass and squeezed him tightly, pulling him in even deeper. "Unnnnh," Dana moaned loudly, feeling Ford drop his weight even more, pressing his face into the hair behind his ear. "Everything about you is heavy… even your damn cock. Fuck me, Ford. Now."

"Impatient brat," Ford murmured in Dana's ear and licked the shell before pulling out just a bit and easing back inside.

"Holy shit," Dana breathed.

Ford repeated that move, pressing deep inside Dana, going so slow and making him feel every inch of him. *Oh, hell. Not this slow shit.* It was always Dana's undoing. It seemed Ford loved to bring Dana to the edge and keep him suspended there until he was ready for Dana to fall for him. Ford paused, pulsing inside, before easing out again. He drove back in even slower, not stopping until he was groaning huskily in Dana's ear, pressing his groin tightly against his with every down stroke. Ford stayed there, rubbing Dana's thighs that were cinched tightly around him.

"It's so hot, baby. You're so damn hot inside." Ford's voice was so coarse and husky, Dana had to strain to hear him, and strain harder to hear him over his own cries.

"It's yours. I'm yours, Bradford." Dana turned his head, searching out Ford's mouth then taking a bruising kiss, pushing his tongue in and out, fucking him with it, hoping the carnal act would get Ford revved up and make him go crazy, fuck him into the mattress.

"You *are* mine, Dana," Ford said, wrenching his mouth away from Dana's hungry kisses. He reached under Dana's back and brought his strong hands up to cup his shoulders, using them to drive Dana's body back into his. Pulling Dana to him, not only physically, but mentally.

Ford drove back inside, faster than before, but the pace still unhurried and maddeningly overwhelming. Dana could feel the storm brewing inside him every time Ford's hips rolled salaciously between his thighs. The thunder he felt low in his sack, the stirring of his cloudy seed, ready to be shot from him. The streaks of lightning that shot up his spine when Ford's thick head brushed his spot, making his toes curl and his back bend.

"Love it when you fuckin' do that," Ford rumbled against his mouth.

Dana's hole clenched at the sound of Ford's voice. He wanted to be ravaged. "Please fuck me. Fuck me harder, faster. Please go faster, Ford," Dana begged. He was too hot and horny to care how smutty he sounded. He just needed to come. He couldn't think, couldn't function. Orgasms brought clarity. He had to end the madness.

PROMISES PART 3

Ford chuckled, licking and kissing away the disappointed tilt on Dana's lips. "You want more." Ford thrust back inside with power and stamina, making Dana cry out in ecstasy. "My greedy brat," Ford whispered affectionately and ran his hand through Dana's crazy hair, his fist clenching around the wayward strands, like his control was shattering. "I want you always feening for my cock like this." Ford slammed inside Dana again.

"Yes! Yes, like that!" Dana yelled, his orgasm so close it scared him, because he knew it was going to destroy him. Ford had edged him long enough.

Ford reared up, walked his knees forward so Dana's ass was up even higher, in prime position. Ford grasped Dana's right leg and pulled it up on his shoulder, leaving one hand on his thigh to keep it in place. Ford put the other hand over Dana's throat and began to pound into him with the relentlessness of a man possessed… of a man on a mission.

Dana pressed his head back into the pillow, clenched his teeth to keep from screaming like a banshee, and held on for dear life, letting his body be dominated by this fascinating beast. He clawed for purchase on Ford's biceps. Needed anchoring, because he was flying. Ford nailed his prostate with each commanding thrust, sending Dana over. He hadn't even thought of touching his cock, neither had Ford. It wasn't necessary. His body strung tighter than a bow, Dana shot like a cannon between their bellies. Ford fucked him all the way to paradise. Had so many moves, changed so many gears, Dana had no choice but to surrender.

"Ford," Dana whined pathetically as Ford continued to drive his stiffness in and out of him, not stopping the torment of his sensitive ass.

"Still want me to fuck you hard, baby?" Ford growled.

Oh my god.

Ford leaned back in, gripped Dana's hair and pulled, dragging his nose up Dana's throat to his ear. Flicking his tongue out to lick at the small beads of sweat. Ford bit his earlobe, then sucked it between his teeth. "Liked being fucked hard didn't you, brat."

"S'good, babe," Dana slurred like he was smashed. He was.

They sucked mouths, sucked tongues, sucked fingers. Once the passion had been ignited in Ford, he'd added his personal combustion that gave their sex a life of its own.

"You ready for me?" Ford huffed. His breathing hot and branding on Dana's neck.

"Yes, Ford. Come, babe. I'm ready. I'm yours."

Ford let Dana's leg go, took both arms and hugged Dana to him. His hips moved with purpose, but he kept that slow, sensual rhythm. Transporting them to a faraway place. "I'm'a come. It's coming, baby. Say it again," Ford groaned.

"I'm yours," Dana whispered tenderly.

Ford's body went rigid as he chanted in Dana's ear. Into his mind. Accenting every word with a determined thrust. "Yeah. You're. Mine. Love it when you say that. Love it. Love it… love you. Auuuugh, Dana!"

Dana eyes widened. He'd heard it. Heard it the exact same time he felt Ford's cock thicken and pulse inside him. Ford shook and trembled with his release, stroking Dana's damp hair and nuzzling behind his ear, still murmuring and promising Dana forever.

He closed his eyes and believed every word.

Ford loved him. He hadn't thought he'd *hear* it anytime soon and he especially hadn't thought he'd hear it now. While they were… But Dana wasn't mistaken and it wasn't a hoax. Some may be turned off by or skeptical of a man confessing his love – for the *first* time – during a mind-blowing orgasm, but Dana wasn't one of them. He knew Ford meant it. He never said anything he didn't mean. Ford told him and showed him this morning that he loved him. And damn, what a show it was. Encore.

PROMISES PART 3

Chapter Twenty-Eight

Ford

"Baby. Babe. Dana!" Ford called louder from the bathroom door. "We gotta go."

Dana rose tiredly from his nap and peeked one bloodshot eye open. They'd been working day and night all week. All of them looked like warmed up shit.

"No," Dana groaned sadly. "I just went to sleep."

"Come on," Ford said, pulling up his leather pants. "Duke just got an anonymous tip that two of John Grossman's top guys were seen driving a black Infinity SUV in Grove Park."

Dana was up and moving, throwing his gear back on. He looked ready to work but he also looked beat. Ford had to admit, he was feeling the fatigue too, but he was trained to fight through it. He could rest when he died. It was harsh, but the motto he lived by. He was just as ready as the rest of his team to get this bounty closed out. He and Dana had only made love again once, and while it was wonderful, Ford wanted to have the energy to make it explosive. Right now, he pushed himself to put one foot in front of the other. It was dangerous to work under these conditions. Ford knew it in his gut. Their reflexes weren't as sharp when they were so sleep-deprived.

They'd had a total of five hours of sleep in two days. To say they'd beefed up their surveillance was a gross understatement. They were right on John Grossman's ass. He had to know his freedom and his reign as meth king on the streets of Atlanta, were soon coming to an end. Not only was Duke's crew looking for Grossman, but the APD had a warrant for his arrest in connection with a drug deal gone terribly bad last month that'd ended in casualties, one of them being an innocent bystander. They believed John Grossman had something – everything – to do with it. A final hit, a big payoff before he was to jump town. Now it was a race to the finish. If Duke lost Grossman to the APD, he'd lose the bounty. Therefore, all the work they'd done for weeks would be for nothing... not one dime.

When they were set to go, Ford waited for Dana to finish checking his rifle bag. He always had it ready, but he still double-checked it before he walked out the door. Brian was on his way to ride with them. When they got to Grove Park, they'd split up into teams.

Dana dropped his bag by the door and leaned heavily against it, pinching the creases between his brows. Ford walked up to him and pressed him into the hard surface.

"You okay?"

"I'm good, babe. Don't worry about me. Stay focused." Dana opened his eyes and answered. He put his arms around Ford's waist and held him close, resting his forehead on his shoulder.

It was as if Ford's touch brought Dana comfort. He put his hand on Dana's unshaven jaw, waiting for him to turn into it and kiss his palm like always. When Dana didn't, still standing motionless with his eyes unfocused, Ford's nerves ramped up. His partner looked too tired to even remain upright.

"Baby. You look dead on your feet. I think...."

"No." Dana cut him off, trying to open his eyes wider. "I'm good."

Fuck. Ford didn't like this. He wanted to intervene on Dana's behalf, but he knew his partner wouldn't appreciate that at all. He couldn't go behind Dana's back. Ford wasn't the boss, but he wasn't afraid to tell Duke that he was pushing his guys too hard. They were true beasts. But even beasts rest sometimes.

Ford tilted Dana's head up, looking down into eyes surrounded by dark circles and bags. "When this is over I'm taking you somewhere. Away."

Dana's weary smile made Ford want to whisk him away right then. "You mean like a vacation? Where would we go?"

"I have some place in mind. It's a surprise." Ford stroked Dana's chin and leaned in for a chaste kiss. Neither of them was up for more. Still, Dana's smile was what he'd been looking for. He'd missed it dearly this week. He needed that smile in his life. That smile was what started his day. Desperate to see it, Ford remembered Dana's best friend, Sway, had told him that Dana loved surprises. So he went with it.

"Really? When can we go? Is it sunny and warm?" Dana pleaded quietly against Ford's throat.

"Yes. Really warm," Ford answered huskily, imaging Dana laid out on gorgeous white sand in tight trunks under the warm Cancún sun. He'd always wanted to go there, but it never seemed to be the right time. Or he made excuses that it wasn't the right time. Ford had served with a lieutenant who was from Mexico and all he did was brag about it being the best place in the world to visit when one needed a reprieve… needed to get away. He and Dana needed that, like yesterday.

They had been together for two solid months now, they were practically living together in Ford's home. Working together, coming home together, it wasn't anything like Ford thought it'd be. He remembered thinking relationships were too hard, too time-consuming, too stressful, and although the start of their connection had been all those things and more, Ford wouldn't change it. Not ever. Dana was everything to him, and each day that feeling got stronger.

Ford felt bad not telling Dana sooner that he'd looked into this trip, but he really had wanted it to be a surprise. Wanted to show Dana they could have a life. A real life together as a couple, just like Dana always wanted. He also wanted to show

Dana he could keep up with him. While the age difference was not a bother to Dana, Ford still thought about it. He just wanted to reassure his younger lover that he wouldn't be a drag on their relationship. Quite the opposite. Ford felt like a whole new chapter in his life had begun. He wanted to vacation, adventure, and see the world through new – in love – eyes.

The knowledge of a trip to paradise coming right after was what kept Ford going these past few days. It was only fair for Dana to have a little gleam of light at the end of this long, dangerous tunnel, too. And Ford told him just enough to get him excited but still make it a surprise.

"I love you, Ford." Dana pulled Ford's mouth down to his, this time making the kiss longer, wetter.

"I love you, too, babe," Ford confessed, his voice abrasive, a look of utter seriousness crossing his hard features. He didn't know why Dana trembled in his arms sometimes when he spoke, but he simply squeezed him tighter and kissed him longer.

Ford could hear Brian's car pull up in his driveway. It was time. He knew this was it. They were going to encounter Grossman, and Ford had a horrible, sinking feeling that the man wasn't giving up his freedom without a fight. Wasn't going to let what happened with his brother go unpunished. Someone would pay before this man went down. Ford had two of the most important people in his life with him. The duty, the job, his responsibility to protect them weighed heavily on his shoulders. How would he keep them both in his sights, keep them both safe?

"Stop it. You have to trust me. I know I may not look it, but I'm ready. I got your back out there, you know that. I'm not taking my eyes off any of you. I promise." Dana straightened his back and steeled his spine.

That was his man. Yes, somehow, Dana kept all of them under his watchful eye.

"I do trust you. *You* know that." Ford tugged on the straps of Dana's bulletproof vest, slamming their padded chests together.

"Then let's go get this fucker so you can take me to my surprise."

Ford nodded proudly as Dana hefted his bag and walked out the door.

Dana

It was cold and overcast, the day as dreary as Dana felt. The drive to one of the most dangerous neighborhoods in Atlanta was quiet and tense. All of them getting on their game faces. It wasn't the time to fill the cab with unnecessary chatter. It was distracting and annoying to all of them. Dana was in the zone and needed to stay that way. After being in the car for twenty minutes, he was finally feeling his Red Bull kick in. He'd hidden his stash of energy drinks from Ford, since he thought they were a ploy of the devil. Dana didn't know how the man did it. His partner was like a machine. He was sure it was from Ford's years of service. Hunting and trekking in conditions far worse than this and with even less sleep. Dana only wished he had half of the determination and bravery his SEAL possessed.

Dana rode in the passenger seat while Ford drove. Brian was in the back, and every so often Dana would catch his somber face in the side mirror. His thick lips in a persistent downward slope. Brian's look wasn't only from weariness, but something entirely different. He and Ford had talked about it on multiple occasions, but Ford insisted his brother was good. Dana considered Brian a very close friend. He didn't like the way he'd been acting lately. Depressed, almost. Was Brian upset about him and Ford being together? It didn't really make sense, especially since Brian gave Dana helpful tips. Maybe he missed time alone with Ford. Which, again, wasn't logical, because Ford was always asking Brian to hang out and he kept declining.

Dana turned in the seat and looked at Brian. He was just as fierce-looking as his brother and every bit as handsome. Protected in black leather from head to toe, his dark eyes hidden behind black shades. Dana signed to him.

"I'll need therapy after this."

Brian scoffed. The noise just loud enough to be heard over the engine. He shook his head unbelievably and answered Dana. *"You can join me."*

Dana grinned and turned back around in his seat. He was getting better at signing. He and Brian hadn't hung out in a while, but he still kept watching and learning from the ASL videos Sway gave him. When he didn't understand something, Sway was able to clarify it. If he was going to be in Ford's life for the long haul, that included Brian. He'd gained a lover and another brother. He needed to be able to communicate with him. Ford wasn't ready to accept it, but the fact of the matter was, Brian might never speak again.

The portable radio in Ford's truck crackled to life. Quick's gravelly voice was the next sound they heard. "Stay on Donald Lee Parkway, Ford. Our contact works at a club off there, just past Peyton Ave. We're parked in the back lot."

Dana heard Brian cock his 9mm in the back seat, readying his own fire power. Dana kept his eyes forward, using his wide peripheral as Ford navigated them through the neighborhood. It didn't look like one of the city's highest crime areas, but it certainly was. And Dana wasn't taking any chances. The club looked abandoned from the outside, not a single car in the front. Ford slowly drove around the back of the building to an area that wasn't designated for parking, hopped the curb and drove over the desolate field and pulled up beside Duke's truck, which faced the opposite direction.

Damn, looking at his bosses, it was clear they'd gotten even less rest than they had.

"Alright, fellas. Let's do this."

"Do you have a solid visual this time?" Ford asked irritably.

Duke frowned, but he answered Ford's question. "I do."

"Where's your contact?" Dana asked.

"He's inside. He's the manager here. This is also his neighborhood. He's had his ear to the ground for me. He said his guy last saw the SUV at a BP just past the overpass. He confirmed that big Grossman was inside," Quick answered.

"How you want to do this, Duke?" Ford grumbled.

"Leave your truck here, Ford. Dana, you find a perch and stay there. Try to make it a good location. Quick and I will be a mile and a half up, just before the BP. I'm sure they're no longer there, but someone saw which way they went. Brand new tricked-out Infinity trucks are hard to ignore. You see anything Dana, you know the drill. Use the comms." Duke angled his head at Ford. "You and Brian split the parkway on this end and work your way back towards us. You on one side, Brian on the other. Scour the stores, shops, everything. Ask questions to whoever you run past but keep it moving. We only got one shot. When he hears we're here, he's gonna run."

"No, he's not," Ford said drily. "It's why he's here. For us."

Duke and Ford shared a look that Dana easily interpreted. This was a set up?

"How well do you know this contact, Quick?" Brian signed. Dana surprised himself by translating it for him instead of Ford.

"I admit. I was surprised he called," Quick answered honestly.

That was all any of them needed to hear. It wasn't far-fetched that big Grossman could've flipped this guy. This could all be a double-cross. John Grossman's final departure in a blaze of glory. Right here where the cops knew gunfire was as common as fireworks on the Fourth. No one would come running. Their team was on their own.

"Then let's be unpredictable." Duke nodded and drove away.

CHAPTER TWENTY-NINE

Ford

He was ready to go but he couldn't seem to make his right knee stop bouncing. Something was about to go wrong. He could feel it so deep. Unlike anything he'd felt during all his years enlisted. He watched painfully as Dana took off around the backs of buildings, staying hidden from the main street, looking for the right rooftop to watch from.

Brian tapped him on his shoulder to get his attention. When Ford pried his eyes away from Dana's back and looked at his brother, he signed to him quickly. *"It's because you love him. It's why you feel antsy. Restless. Dana's got this. I need your head with me, Ford."*

His brother was right. Ford didn't deny a single word. Dana was his partner when doing surveillance and intel. But on the streets, Duke and Quick were fast to put Dana's superior marksmanship to use as their sniper and pair Brian and Ford together. Dana was a crack shot. He'd saved Duke's life more than once. Saved Brian's, too. Dana's eyes were as sharp as an eagle's and he didn't miss his mark. But Ford needed him safe with him. Damn, he had to somehow get past this. He couldn't work this way.

"Come on, bro." Brian got out the truck, popping his back as he straightened his huge body. He pulled his mugshot of John Grossman from his back pocket and put it in the inside, front pocket of his thigh-length coat. Brian couldn't ask questions on the streets, but showing bounties' pictures had gotten him a few leads in the past. Or maybe it was his look that got him results.

PROMISES PART 3

Ford walked out from behind a building a couple minutes after Brian. When his brother was on the other side of the four-lane parkway, Ford began to walk up the street, his eyes taking in everything as he did. Everyone was a suspect to him. Any one of these innocent-looking people could be on Grossman's payroll. Ford trusted no one. Not the old lady pushing her cart of god-knows-what up the cracked sidewalk. Not the mechanic putting a new tire on a late model Corolla in the bay of his small shop. Not even the homeless man sitting on the ground outside the Crazy Cutz. Maybe the guy was hoping to panhandle enough money to cut off the matted mop on top of his head. Ford approached him, money already in hand.

"God bless you, brother." The man said thankfully, with a decayed smile, when he saw Ford holding out the money.

"How long you been out here?" Ford asked, pushing several dollars into the man's filthy hand.

The guy had the audacity to count the bills before he answered. "Seven years."

Ford refrained from cursing, but barely. "You seen a black Infinity cruising through here today?"

"Maybe... maybe not." The guy said, looking at the bills now like they suddenly weren't enough.

Ford snarled and pulled out a twenty-dollar bill. "Your sign says Will Work for Cash." Ford slammed the money in the cup so hard he knocked from the man's hand. "Fuckin' work! Do something good for this neighborhood. Have you seen this man?!" Ford's voice was thunderous. He pulled out his own copy of Grossman's mugshot and held it right in front of the conman's face.

"Okay, okay." The guy reared back and looked at the photo. It took barely two seconds. He tucked his money in the front of his grimy pants, which may have been khakis at one point in time, looked up at Ford and grinned evilly. "Nope. Have no clue who John is. No trucks, either. Matter of fact, I don't think I've ever seen a black SUV in my life." The man sniggered.

Ford's patience broke. He grabbed the man by the collar, which quickly ripped under his assault, and shoved him hard against the cement wall. He would've taken his money back, but there was no way his hand was going down the front of that man's shorts. Ford was usually more collected, but this guy picked the wrong day to toy with him. Ford bared his teeth, sneering. "You piece of shit. Where is he? Where's Grossman?"

"Hey! Hey, let him go!" A guy came out the barber shop with a long black stick in his hand, one that looked similar to a police baton, but without the handle. Three more men came out of the barber shop behind him, two black and the other biracial, or maybe Hispanic. They all wore blue and black work smocks except for the light-skinned one.

"Maybe you should pick on someone your own size, man." One of the young barbers barked. He was more muscular than the others, but still not as big as Ford. The man had large fists, balls of steel, he even had the heart to defend a homeless man. But none of those things was enough to stop Ford.

Ford dropped the homeless man and let him scamper off. Still reeling, he turned to face his newest problem. He pulled out his bounty hunter's star and flashed his identification.

"That means shit to us. It's not a police badge, so why don't you get the hell out of here." Baton Holder was moving closer with Balls of Steel, but Ford wasn't backing up. A stick... really. If a grenade didn't scare Ford, a goddamn baton sure wouldn't. "Leave, man."

"I will. As soon as I get what I came for."

"All you're gonna get is a beat down if you don't get your ass out this neighborhood."

"I don't wanna hurt any of you. I'm here for one man. Grossman." Ford watched their expressions go from angry to shocked to defensive. "I can tell you know him. Where is he?"

PROMISES PART 3

"Leave, dude." The light-skinned one said, turning and walking back to the shop. One coward down. Was Grossman scarier than Ford?

"You must have a death wish." The baton holder said. "I wouldn't rat on big John. No one on this street will. So, get the hell…."

Ford advanced faster than any of them could move. He had his arm up, cocked, ready to throw a haymaker. Ready to make someone go to sleep, but the crook in his elbow was hooked and held by a leather-clad forearm. Ford roared and whirled on his brother. Brian's look of confusion and fury was like a bucket of freezing water on Ford's hot head. Brian didn't have to sign anything, his dark, expressive eyes said exactly what he was thinking.

What the fuck is wrong with you, brother?

"Y'all trying to jump us?!" Balls of Steel yelled.

This made more men come pouring from the barber shop and the Rockwood Ink tattoo shop next door. Each guy looking more menacing than the last. The tattoo owner was a white man, big, bald, without a single un-inked inch of skin. He had a bat leaning on one shoulder. "You two men lost?"

Fuck. He and Brian were good. But Ford counted nine men now. He'd at least take one or two hits. Something he wasn't really in the mood for. He needed to save his energy for Grossman. Besides, his brother was giving him an infuriated look, though he stayed close to Ford's side.

Popping his neck, he and Brian both tucked their suspended badges away – no one could use the chains to choke them – and got into a fighting stance, standing back to back.

Baton and Balls were the first to approach, looking a lot more confident now that they had more back up. Scowl in place and fists up, Balls hadn't even made it within five feet of Ford when the sound of rapid gunfire from a Remington rifle pierced the air. Most of the men ran for cover, not recognizing the difference between gun-powder filled bullets and empty shells. Three-inch gold empty bullets were sprayed skillfully at the men's feet, only inches away from them. The brass hit the ground, forming a perfect arch. When the shooting stopped, it looked like a bullet barrier surrounded him and his brother.

Dana.

Magnificent.

Ford didn't need to turn around to know his guy was there. Somewhere out there on a rooftop, weapons all around him, watching, assessing, then finally acting. Ford's grin was threatening. "That's a warning. The next round won't be empties."

Firing live ammunition was a huge no-no for them, so Dana often used that tactic as a warning. He used the Remington only to fire duds. They didn't want to hear the sound of his A5 special, which was no doubt already in his expert hands.

Brian held up the picture, looking at each man. Silent. Deadly.

Everyone was quiet. The tattoo shop owner took his bat and pointed up the street. "If I'd known that's why you were out here, I would've shut this shit down a long time ago."

"Stay out of this, Chuck."

"Fuck you," he said to Balls. "This is my neighborhood, too. And Grossman's meth addicts have robbed both our shops. Can't believe you'd defend them, Mac." Tattoo turned back to Brian, still using his bat to point north. "They were at Han's restaurant an hour ago. I don't know what's up. I can't tell you the last time I seen John or Ray in this neighborhood. But if you're here to get them the hell out, I'm happy to help."

Now, why couldn't everyone be model citizens like that? The Grossmans were a disease in their community. Stringing out men, women, and kids with their duped-up meth. Ray and John didn't care as long as the money continued to flow. Ford nodded in thanks to tattoo guy and began to move away from the dispersing mob. He needed to contact Duke, but Ford didn't dare turn his back until he was sure no one would sneak attack them.

When they were back on the main road, Brian's hands start moving fast, angrily. *"What the hell were you thinking?! You want to get into a street fight... NOW! Ford, you got to get yourself under—"* Brian's cell rang, cutting off his berating.

Ford frowned. It was Dana using the CB technology on his cell. Why wasn't he using the earpiece or the watch to communicate? Ford thought again. Dana hadn't communicated with him at all during the whole ordeal. None of them had.

Brian pressed the button and Ford could hear Dana's tight voice. It was choppy and broken but there was no mistaking it. Dana was suspicious. Something was wrong. Goddamnit! Ford knew it.

Dana

"There's a signal killer somewhere. Our earpieces, cells, all useless. Even the watch. I can't talk through the mic. I can still see your locations, but I have no audio from it. I was trying to reach you the whole time, Ford." Dana was watching Ford and Brian through his scope. He could see Ford was listening.

Ford took Brian's phone. "I know. I'm... I'm sor—"

"Stop. We'll talk where it's warm." Dana hoped Ford caught what he was saying. They had a trip to go on. They needed to stay focused right now. They'd gone from being the hunters to the hunted. Otherwise, why was there signal jammers in the area?

Dana heard it the same time as Ford and Brian, the sound of tires screeching in the distance. Then the sound of gunfire followed by return gunfire. *Shit, shit, shit.* Dana dropped his cell and hurried back to the other side of the roof. He turned his rifle towards where he'd last seen Duke and Quick.

A black Infinity SUV barreled out of a side street between a Western Union and a pawn shop. They were almost a half mile up the street. Quick and Duke were running on foot. Dana could see Duke's wrist up to his mouth but he couldn't hear anything. There was no damn audio. The jammers were screwing with all their tech. Part of the reason they were so successful as a team was because of their superior communications. John Grossman knew exactly what he was doing. He had to split them up, eliminate their ability to coordinate. It was the only way to take them out.

Ford and Brian were running full speed, every now and then one of them having to dodge a pedestrian. Dana was glad the weather had driven most people off the streets, because he wasn't going to hesitate to shoot Grossman dead in the middle of Donald Lee Parkway. Lethal force was always their last resort, but this bounty wasn't going to let them arrest him. He was already using his own deadly force against them, they had a right to defend themselves, even defend the innocent people that were going about their day with no clue they were in the middle of a war.

Dana took aim at the tires, ready to flip that big bastard over when the driver cut in front of an oncoming minivan and turned down the side street just before he got to Dana's block. *Shit.* If they looped all the way around and came back up, that'd put them in perfect position to shoot and probably hit Brian or Ford. He needed his guys to go the other way. Dana put his wrist to his mouth and yelled but, of course, he didn't get a response. He looked for his cell. Couldn't find it. *Fuck!*

Dana left his bag, his Remington, and his SALT. With nothing but his Sig and his Glock tucked in the small of his back, he took off for the fire escape. He had seconds, maybe. Grossman would be back and Dana's guys would be vulnerable. They hadn't seen which street Grossman cut down and wouldn't know which street he'd use to sneak up on their sixes. No wonder he'd chosen Grove Park to lure them to. With all the side streets, fields, brush, trees, it was vast enough to give Grossman room to play and turn Duke's team around in circles.

Dana jumped down the last few rungs of the ladder and took off at a sprint. He heard tires and the revving of an engine. He had one block to run. Brian and Ford were at least a quarter of a mile away. It looked like Brian was about to break off from his brother and Dana wanted to yell at him not to leave Ford.

He saw the nose of the SUV ease out from Peek Road. Not even fifty feet from his heart. Still running at a breakneck speed, Dana pumped his legs harder and faster than he'd ever had to. *Go faster, goddamnit.* Dana grunted, his thighs burning from the energy he was exerting. His team needed him. He wouldn't fail Ford. Dana could see the glint of metal in the lowered passenger window. It was him. Grossman. With his eyes set on the love of his life. Eyes that were murderous with intent to kill. *No, no, no.* Tires peeled and screeched. Dana fired twice into the air, warning them. Ford – hearing Dana's alarm – was just able to dive out of the way when the SUV jolted out of its hiding place.

Grossman pointed his chrome handgun out his window, aiming at Duke as he and Quick ran towards them. Dana stopped, took aim and fired, hitting the passenger side door. He saw Grossman jerk his hand back inside and duck down. The driver spun the truck and headed back in Dana's direction. Two women were coming out of a seafood restaurant, Dana waved his gun for them to go back inside, but still had to run out in the middle of the street to dodge them when they stood there like deer in headlights.

Now it was just him facing off with a fifty-eight hundred-pound, rapidly approaching vehicle. He stood in the middle of the parkway with his feet braced apart, pointing his death-maker at the driver.

"Dana, MOVE!"

He could hear Ford yelling, but he ignored him and kept his gun aimed. This was going to be over, right now. He was tired of this. Tired of the restless nights and the constant looking over their shoulders. Tired of Grossman. The SUV was close enough that Dana could see the frustration, the anger, the rage all over his ugly face through the windshield. Dana fired twice and hit the driver dead center in his chest. Blood splattered the windshield, blinding him. Grossman's panicked face was a small consolation. Dana changed his trajectory, pointed his SIG at Grossman. But before he could get the shot, Grossman lurched over, grabbed the wheel and jerked, sending that huge grill right for him. Dana only got one shot off, hitting their bounty in the shoulder, before he had to dive out of the way.

Unfortunately, he didn't dive fast enough.

PROMISES PART 3

CHAPTER THIRTY

Ford

The sight of Dana in the middle of the road with Grossman headed straight for him was enough to give Ford a heart attack, but when Dana didn't move fast enough and that big truck clipped his man, sending him flying ten feet in the air before he dropped to hit the asphalt so hard he bounced, Ford was sure his heart had completely stopped beating. Ford clutched at his chest but he kept running. Dana was motionless on the ground. His body twisted in an awkward angle.

God, please. Don't take him from me. Ford hadn't prayed that prayer since he'd heard of his brother's capture by insurgents in Afghanistan. He kept going, had to get to him. Dana had only been a block away from him and look what happened. Ford kept running. He didn't know how he was putting one foot in front of the other when his body ached all over like he was the one who'd just been hit. It felt like his soul was shattering, his heart breaking.

The SUV crashed into a light pole about a hundred feet away. Brian was already there when Grossman fell out the passenger door onto the ground, crawling, gripping his left shoulder. Brian didn't bother to be gentle. He kicked Grossman over, putting him face down on the sidewalk and zip tied his wrists.

"Dana!" Ford yelled hoarsely. Cars honked and slowed, trying to move around him, since he was running in the middle of the street. Sirens could be heard, but they weren't close enough to provide Ford any comfort. Dana needed help, fast. He hadn't moved at all. Was he… was he? *God*. Although the truck only clipped him, the way Dana fell back to the ground, his head making devastating contact with the asphalt was what had Ford so damn terrified.

He got to Dana, dropping down hard on his knees by his side. "Baby. Baby can you hear me?" Ford knew his voice sounded like he'd been chain smoking for forty years but he didn't know how to clear the emotion. Quick and Duke had sat Ford and Dana down when they admitted to their relationship and what it would mean for the team. Quick simply told them to stay professional and they'd have no problems. Duke told Ford to treat Dana as his partner not his boyfriend on the streets. To leave his heart at home. Ford looked down at Dana, a bruise already forming on his cheek, a gash at his hairline that was bleeding way too much. Ford put his hand to Dana's forehead and applied pressure. He couldn't leave his heart at home, when his heart was with Dana.

"Come on, Dana. Open your eyes." Ford was crouched down at Dana's ear, hoping he was whispering. "Baby, please."

Duke and Quick were there next, huffing and looking just as concerned. Ford could hear them talking, he could hear Quick's raspy voice barking commands at people standing around and creeping past in their cars.

Dana hadn't moved an inch, Ford couldn't even see his chest rising. More blood seeped through Ford's fingers and Dana had yet to open his eyes. Ford was petrified, but he did it anyway. He put two fingers to Dana's neck, feeling for a pulse. Ford's hands shook so badly, it took him a while to pick up the faint beat. But it was there. Ford turned and roared at Duke. "Where's the goddamn ambulance!"

"Two more minutes," Duke answered, squatting next to Ford, looking over Dana's prone form. "Hang in there buddy, they're coming."

Two minutes! "Maybe we should take him ourselves?" Ford didn't want to wait another second to get Dana some help, but he knew before he even said those words that it was the absolute worst thing to do.

"He could have internal injuries, Ford. Don't move him," Quick said as gently as he could. "I sent Cayson a text. As soon as we clear the jammers he'll get it. He'll be waiting for him to arrive."

Maybe Ford looked like he was about to lose it, because all of them were giving him a little space. Hearing that Quick's partner, Dr. Chauncey would be overseeing Dana's medical care was a relief. The man was an amazing doctor and surgeon. Ford trusted him. When the ambulance finally got there, it took Brian and Quick to keep Ford from breaking into the ambulance to ride with Dana. Damn their rules. He didn't want him out of his sight.

"Get him in the truck and get him to the hospital," ordered Duke. "I'll go make sure Grossman is handled and deal with the police. Quick will follow you. Go! Now!" Ford didn't know who his boss was talking to. He felt like he was drifting from reality. When the ambulance disappeared, the red lights and siren no longer distracting Ford, he looked around like he had no clue where he was. What was wrong with him? He could hardly catch his breath, his heart felt like it was beating hard enough to be seen through the Kevlar. God, he was so confused, light-headed. His legs felt like they were battling quicksand. Ford felt himself being dragged and practically tossed into a vehicle. It had to be his brother. No one else could move him like that.

"Can you handle him? He's in non-med shock."

Ford's head rolled on the headrest. Quick was there talking to Brian through the driver window, but it sounded like they were talking in a tunnel, even their faces looked distorted and fuzzy. Ford closed his eyes, he didn't want to look anymore, but as soon as his lids shut he saw a vision of Dana falling to the ground. Ford was jostled hard, then harder. He cracked his eyes open, Brian's face was there, his gaze worried and stern. He had his big hand on Ford's shoulder, shaking him. Brian started to sign something but Ford couldn't keep up. Couldn't make out the images Brian formed with his hands.

"Just go. I'm right behind ya." Quick hit the roof of the cab with his fist and was gone.

Dana

This was the strangest pain Dana had ever felt. He hurt a lot, but he also felt numb. Everything was dark and quiet. He wasn't in his bed, or Ford's. *Ford*. Dana groaned and tried to shift his position, but that made matters worse. What the hell was going on?

"Dana. Sit still, buddy."

Dana recognized that smooth, comforting voice. It was Cayson.

"You got an IV in this arm, so keep it down, Dana."

Dana didn't know he'd moved it. His other arm felt heavy and restricted. As his mind struggled to the surface and back to full consciousness, he began to remember what happened. Who told him it was a clever idea to go toe-to-toe with an Infinity? *Shit*. Ford was gonna strangle him. Where was he?

"Ford," Dana rumbled, coughing a little at the scratchiness in his throat. Then the pain in his head registered. *Good god.*

Cayson chuckled softly, while lifting Dana's eyelids and shining a bright light in them. "You two are meant for each other. He's just outside, Dana. I unfortunately had to have him removed from the room when I was resetting your wrist. No matter how many times I told him you couldn't feel anything, he insisted I was hurting you."

Dana smiled on the inside, his cheek ached when he attempted it on the outside. He needed Ford more than he needed morphine. He just wanted to go someplace warm and sleep. "So, what's the verdict, doc? When can I get out of here? I'm fine, really. Nothing a couple days' rest won't fix."

Cayson laughed a little louder. "You big tough bounty hunters. You're always fine. Get shot… you're fine. Get stabbed…. you're fine. Get run over by an SUV… you're fine. Fall twelve feet to the concrete on your head… juuuust fine," Cayson sing-songed.

"Doc," Dana moaned miserably. "I think my head might be trying to split open." Each word he spoke felt like a spike to the back of his head.

Cayson went around the bed to the IV pole and pushed a couple buttons on the flat screen that regulated the medicine. "Gonna up this a little now that you're awake. You been out for a few hours. You sustained a grade three concussion, Dana. I was debating putting you in a barb-coma."

"What?" Dana frowned, but the pain that caused made him want to vomit.

"A medically induced coma. Your vitals were stabilized but you wouldn't wake up. We did all the necessary scans and one of the best neurosurgeons in Atlanta reviewed your CT for brain function. He saw no swelling, masses, or ruptures, so I held off on the coma. But just the mention of it made Ford very difficult to deal with."

Dana's heart warmed.

"I want to finish telling you about the rest of your chart before Ford breaks in." Cayson looked up at the computer monitor mounted on the wall next to Dana's bed then back down at his metal clipboard, flipping a couple pages back and forth before he started to speak again. "Besides quite a few bumps and bruises, you came out of this pretty good and pretty damn lucky. No major concerns except for your wrist and your head. Your concussion is severe, but now that you woke up on your own and you seem to be coherent – you asked for your man first and you recognize me. I still want to ask you a couple more questions."

Uggh. I just want to go home with Ford. Dana was perfectly, psychologically fine. Feeling annoyed, but unable to be rude to his boss's partner, Dana just squinted his eyes at the cute man. He was just able to see Dr. Chauncey's attractive face. He was classically handsome. He didn't stop traffic, but if you were lucky enough to get to know him in any of his capacities, he became increasingly gorgeous. A brilliant doctor and friend to all of them, Dr. Chauncey was used to patching them up, whether in the hospital or the office... the man was solid, and Dana respected him. He was glad to be in his care because he knew he was being treated by the best and would only get the best.

"What day of the week is it, Dana?"

"Thursday."

"What do you do?"

"I'm a bounty hunter."

"What's my man's name?" Cayson winked.

Dana almost rolled his eyes, but that would've probably hurt, instead he sighed softly and closed them, answering the question. "Quick."

"What year will next year be?" Cayson asked, wording the questions slowly in that soft, soothing doctor tone, mindful of Dana's headache.

"2018."

"And who will the president be?"

"Oh god, don't make me say it."

"Alright. Your brain's intact." Cayson scribbled down a few things on his clipboard, then set it to the side to type on the computer imbedded in the wall. "I'm going to get the supplies to do your cast in here when your pain meds kick in more."

"Cast?" Dana forced his eyes open again and flinched. His brain must've been pissed at receiving another command because a sharp pain began to pound furiously behind his right eye. *Jesus, take me now.*

"You broke your left wrist. You put that arm out to break your fall. Which I believe is what really stopped you from having more serious, internal injuries," Cayson told him, watching him carefully.

Dana had been so still to avoid additional hurt he hadn't realized why his arm felt so heavy and restricted. There was a huge splint on it, keeping it stabilized. "I… I." It still hurt too much to talk. He could feel the fuzzy feeling of the narcotic spreading through him, but he needed it to hurry up and get to his head.

"Don't try to talk. Just relax for a while. I got a cocktail going for you. I'm gonna try to get your headache to something you can tolerate, but you're going to feel it for a while, I'm afraid. You got six stitches on your brow. That cut bled something wicked, too. You'll have a scar, but I'm sure you don't mind. It only adds to your appeal, Dana." Cayson smiled sweetly, trying to make Dana feel better. He squeezed his shoulder in support. "Best news. Quick told me that's not your primary shooting hand. Although, I know you're badass enough to shoot with both."

"You stroking my ego to make me feel better, Doc?" Dana's mouth twitched.

"Nobody better be stroking anything in here," Quick said, coming through the door with Ford right behind him, practically pushing him to the side.

Cayson shook his head, still looking at Dana's chart, an adoring smile and soft blush creeping up his ivory cheeks. He didn't bother to turn around, even when Quick came up behind him and put his arms around the doc's narrow waist, Quick's long, dark hair falling over his shoulder onto Cayson's clipboard. "Roman, go on. Get. I'm working, here." Cayson used his elbow to push at Quick's chest.

It was funny to see him shove and boss Quick around when the doc was so much shorter and a lot less muscular than the huge bounty hunter towering over his back.

"Later," Quick rumbled, not caring who heard, before he finally let Cayson go.

Dana tracked the movements of the man stalking farther into his room and around the foot of his bed, his hot, coal eyes so forceful, Dana gasped and fought not to close his eyes in fear. He not only saw but he felt everything Ford was feeling. It was all there in those damn eyes. Anguish, panic, fear, yearning… boundless love. The kind of all-consuming love that could drive you insane. And that's exactly how Ford looked right now. Still in head to boot black on black. Those leather pants creaking with each step, making a frightening song, like the soundtrack to a horror movie as death drew nearer.

When Ford was finally standing over him, Dana held his gaze. Tried to tell him he was okay without having to speak it. He was feeling more lethargic, groggy, the medicine moving rapidly through his bloodstream now, but he couldn't drift away. Not until he knew Ford was okay. Not until he reassured Ford that *he* was okay. Dana struggled to keep his eyes open. He wanted to reach out to him, but one hand was useless and the other one was wired up. He needed to touch. God, he just needed one touch.

Ford leaned down and pulled a lever on the side of Dana's bed and lowered the guard rail. He leaned in, slowly, careful of where he touched. With both arms on either side of Dana's head, their faces so close Dana could smell the sweat that clung to Ford's skin, Ford turned and snarled at everyone else in the room.

"Get. Out."

For a moment, no one moved. Then Brian walked backwards a few steps and pulled the door open, looking at everyone expectantly. Dana hadn't even noticed Brian come in, he'd been so engrossed by Ford. When everyone was out of the room, Ford turned his attention back to Dana.

What could he say? With Ford overwhelming him like this, he had absolutely no words. Dana had scared him. He knew that. But he'd also done his job. Ford couldn't expect him to do anything less. Was it a tad reckless and extremely dangerous? Yes. But that was a given in their line of work. He'd never deliberately hurt Ford. He was showing him he'd put his life on line for him. That's how much he loved him. His strong feelings for Ford started a lot longer than two months ago.

"Baby," Ford croaked.

Dana's world tilted. He felt a tear slide down his temple. Ford took his thumb and shakily wiped it away. "I'm sorry. Please don't be mad."

"Shhh." Ford tenderly stroked the side of his face that wasn't bruised. His voice just a garbled whisper. "I was so scared. Jesus Christ, I was scared. But I'm not mad at you, brat."

Dana felt another tear. To hear Ford call him that was the only medicine he needed. He'd come close to never hearing Ford say anything so loving ever again. He had so much to live for, he needed to be more careful. No wonder Duke and Quick were always so cautious. Dana finally got it. He wanted years with Ford… not months.

"I swear, I'm not mad. You saved us, you saved my brother again." Ford squeezed his eyes closed, fighting the moisture building inside them. "You were amazing out there today. Fearless. I'm so damn proud of you."

Dana wished he could hug Ford so badly. Ford buried his face behind Dana's ear, careful to keep his weight off him – and just breathed with him. Breathed in the realization that they were okay. They were together.

"Love you so fuckin' much."

PROMISES PART 3

Dana whimpered, there was no other word to describe the relieved sound his soul made when it splayed open. "I love you too, Ford."

CHAPTER THIRTY-ONE

Ford

"Babe, we might as well stay here. There's no need for you to get up and disturb yourself when you're already comfortable here and go to my place... for what?"

Dana had just been released from the hospital, a quarter to noon, after being kept another day for observation. Cayson didn't take any chances. He'd made Dana go through another CT SCAN *and* sent those files to a published physician in England that Cayson was acquaintances with for a third expert opinion. When his doc and good friend was satisfied – and not a moment sooner – Cayson released him. They'd planned to just stop by and check on Dana's place before they continued to Ford's, but when Dana went inside and sat down, his sore body quickly got comfortable on the soft leather sofa.

Dana was sitting on the far end of his sectional with the recliner all the way back. Ford knelt down next to him and put his hand on Dana's whiskered jaw. "You good with that? Staying here? Because I am. Your place is great. We'll stay here so you can rest and recover in your own bed."

Dana smiled at him. That was enough confirmation. Ford stayed at Dana's side, kept stroking his cheek. Still thanking god two days later that this amazing man was still with him.

"Kiss me," Dana whispered, gazing right back at him.

Ford leaned over and pressed his mouth over Dana's, immediately moaning at the suppleness of that full bottom lip. He sucked it into his mouth, flicking and teasing it with his tongue. Dana reached his right hand up and stroked Ford's ungroomed beard, then began to tug him closer.

"Hey," Ford protested gruffly, pulling back. "Trying to get me going, brat. You need to be resting."

"I am resting. The parts that were injured. Nothing happened to my mouth... or my dick." Dana grinned sexily.

Dana had Ford's nose wide open and that fact no longer scared the shit out of him. He trusted Dana. Knew his heart was safe with him. "Don't even think about it. I'm gonna bring my bag in here. All our hunting gear is still in the truck."

Ford hadn't left Dana's side the entire forty-eight hours he'd been in the hospital.

"When I'm finished, you're going to take your meds and catch a nap, while I figure out what we're having for dinner."

"I don't need that medicine. I feel fine," Dana bitched. "Besides, it makes me feel crazy."

Ford sighed, tenderly running his hand over Dana's hair while he lay there with his eyes drifting shut, a cute pout on his lips. He was a crappy patient. Like most men, Ford assumed. Dana didn't like being doted on, and he didn't like being told what he could and couldn't do, but he already knew that about his brat.

"You'll be too sore to think if you don't take anything, babe."

"Some Tylenol will be enough." Dana waved at Ford dismissively.

"As long as you take the ones the doc gave you, that have codeine in them, I don't care." Ford got up and walked off.

Dana's cell phone rang and he smiled – that brotherly affectionate one when he looked at the caller ID, and Ford knew it was Sway. He went about doing what needed done while Dana told Sway of their plans to stay there and asked him what time he was heading that way.

"How's he doing, bro?" Brian signed, sitting across from him in the other recliner.

Ford took a long drink from his water bottle before he signed back. Usually he spoke to his brother out loud, but Dana was resting in the bedroom and he didn't want him disturbed. That's why they were watching sports highlights on mute.

Dana's den was dark, comfortable and had only his touch all over it. A leather sectional, draped with homemade crocheted throws Sway's mom had made for him. There was one brick wall with an actual wood-burning fireplace in the center. On the mantle were pictures of Dana with Sway and his family. He even had tall artificial plants in the corners and knickknacks on the end tables. If replica 1903 Colt WWII bullet shells could be considered knickknacks. The large television, complete with video gaming system and a sound bar connected to it was mounted on the shortest wall. The furniture was oversized and worn and the room smelled of leather with a faint hint of gun slick. Ford looked back over at Dana's gun cabinet. It was a work of art. Taking up the entire length of the longest wall – it looked custom made – the oak gleaming under recessed lighting. Not only were Dana's prize weapons inside – some rare, some antiques, some just expensive as hell – but also his awards. Multiple medals and plaques. Framed pictures of him at international competitions. Ford stared at them every time he was at Dana's. He liked it here. Still, looking around, it was certainly more lived-in than his place. With his bare walls and sparse furnishings. Dana had an eighty-by-fifty, knitted tapestry of a large bullseye on the wood-paneled wall. Ford was surrounded by Dana. He felt home. Ford turned to his brother.

"He's doing good. Strong as hell. Doesn't hardly want me to help him do anything. He hates the way the drugs make him

feel, but when he holds out on taking the pills, the pain is too much and he gets... cranky."

Brian smirked at him. *"You mean he turns into a bitching, unbearable asshole."*

Ford didn't agree with his brother but he didn't disagree, either. It was only seven in the evening and Dana had already bitten his head off twice. Ford was too happy for him to be alive to get upset by it. Dana could be as cranky as he wanted. The case was over and as soon as he was healed, he and Ford were out of there... out of the country.

"Ford."

Ford jumped up like his ass was on fire when he heard Dana's groggy voice call out from the back room and hurried down the hall. He heard his brother's low, breathy laugh but he didn't care.

Dana's bedroom was just as comfortable and homey as the den. Decorated with bold, masculine browns and blues. His bed was big, with a soft down comforter folded down at the foot. He had a flat screen mounted in there too, with at least four hundred DVDs arranged immaculately in the entertainment stand underneath. The halogen lamp in the corner was on its lowest wattage, casting an ethereal, toasted-honey glow on the ceiling, making the room appear warm and peaceful. And his lover was resting comfortably.

Dana's eyes shuttered before finally focusing on Ford. He'd only been asleep a couple hours but the meds were probably just peaking at their maximum strength. Ford came over to Dana's side of the bed and eased his big body up next to him. "Hey, Superman. You sleep well?"

"Shut up." Dana chuckled lightly.

"How you feeling? Still in a lot of pain?"

"Not too bad. Head still a little achy." Dana hissed in frustration.

Ford ran his palm over Dana's forehead. He was damp and clammy. Ford got up and went into the bathroom, grabbing the first washrag he saw and rinsed it thoroughly. He came back and started to pat Dana's face with the cool cloth.

"You hungry?"

"A little. I don't want anything heavy, though."

Ford kept stroking Dana's face while he spoke. "Perfect, because Sway is bringing some soup his mom made for you. She said you loved it as a kid."

Dana's eyes beamed with excitement. "Ginger chicken and rice soup. Oh, babe. It's a mother's love in a bowl. You'll have to try."

Ford leaned down and kissed Dana's forehead. "I will."

The doorbell rang, followed by a couple sharp raps on the door. "Sway's here," Ford murmured against Dana's lips. "I'll be up front with Brian. The doc's coming by to check the bandage on your head around eight. I'm sure Quick will be with him. But you let me know if you're not up for company."

"Stop worrying. I'm not a doll baby." Dana bit Ford's lip.

"Brat." Ford sucked Dana's tongue. He didn't want to let go, but he could hear Sway talking to Brian so he knew he'd better get out there. Ford regretfully pulled away. "I'll be up front."

"Love you," Dana said.

Ford kissed him again and left the room. He walked into the den, surprised to see his baby brother staring at Sway with the oddest expression, his mouth slack and his skin a little pale. Ford frowned and moved closer, turning his attention to Sway. He looked taken aback by Brian, but he kept talking.

"I grew up with Dana. So, you work with him too, you're Ford's bother, right? I'm Sway." Sway held out his hand, looking up at Brian, waiting.

When Brian didn't clasp his hand, still staring at the man like he had wings, Sway scoffed and took his hand back.

PROMISES PART 3

Ford stepped forward. "Um, my brother doesn't—"

Sway held his hand up, turning his back to Brian and speaking to Ford. "It's okay. No need to explain, Ford. Is Dana asleep? I just wanted to peek in on him on my way home. I'm kind of walking on fumes. I've been at the hospital since six this morning."

"No. He's awake. I'll take this and make him a bowl. He seemed eager for it." Ford took the still-warm Crock Pot Sway had set on Dana's breakfast bar and took it into the kitchen.

"Sure." Sway cut his eyes at Brian and darted them away just as fast and left, heading down the hall.

Ford walked over to Brian. "What was that all about?"

"I think I know him, Ford."

CHAPTER THIRTY-TWO

Brian

It couldn't be. Brian's heart was beating so hard he had to put a hand to his chest and brace his heavy body against the wall with the other. What were the odds that the man he'd been obsessing over for months walks right through the damn door? With this kind of luck, he needed to play the lottery. Brian nervously ran his hand over his rough stubble. How could he be sure it was him? Was he so desperate to have him again that he was hallucinating? He hadn't gotten a good look at the guy's face at the club. It'd been dark in the main area. Brian had only caught glimpses of those delicate features under the red and purple strobe lights. When they'd nestled into their love cave, everything had been pitch dark.

But damn if he wasn't the exact same height and build. Brian couldn't see all the definition because he was wearing scrubs, but he saw enough. Even his hair looked like it was a perfect fit. It was light brown, long, with soft, golden curls tucked behind his ears. Brian remembered those curls, remembered they'd smelled like vanilla and sandalwood. If Brian could somehow march back into Dana's bedroom and pull the smaller man to him and bury his nose in his hair, that would give him validation. But Dana and his brother would probably think he'd flipped his shit.

Brian had begun to pace back and forth. He wanted it to be the man from the club so much his body vibrated. *What did he say his name was again?* Brian had been struck stupid while the man was introducing himself.

PROMISES PART 3

Sway! Yeah, that's what he said. It sounded sassy and sexy. Brian liked it. It fit, from what he'd seen so far. Brian had answered the front door. The shock was all over Sway's pretty face when he saw him, but he swallowed noticeably and looked up Brian's full six foot three body and *told* him he was there to see Dana. What sparked the instant fire of recognition in Brian's gut was Sway's voice. That voice had plagued his dreams for weeks. The way Sway had whispered and moaned in Brian's ear when he was deep inside him. The way he unconsciously understood what Brian was feeling and spoke his words into existence in that sweet, harmonious voice. He couldn't mistake it. It was him. *It's him!*

Brian balled up his huge fists and pressed them into his eye sockets. Sway had to be his, he had to be. Brian didn't want to be alone anymore. He understood why people came to those clubs, but there was no denying they'd shared something deeper than a fuck. They'd shared a connection. Enough of a connection that it deserved exploring.

Only, Sway hadn't looked all that impressed when he looked at him just now. There was plenty of light in Dana's foyer. Brian had on a plain, white collared shirt and black jeans. Nothing fancy. Sway was gorgeous. No other word to describe him. Brian wanted those delicious lips back on him. He knew they were juicy to suck on, but he had no idea they were so pink. Brian wavered on his feet. Oh god. Sway's compact little body. Brian remembered, captivated by the memory of how the smaller man had climbed him and enjoyed him.

"Brian. Brian, I'm getting worried. Look at me."

Brian dropped his fists. His brother had stopped him mid-stride and was standing inches in front of him, squeezing his shoulders. He'd been so lost. Trying to desperately come up with a plan to communicate with Sway. Brian's eyes flew open in panic, his mouth working, but no sound coming out. He tried to shove past his brother. He hadn't missed Sway, had he? He hadn't left while Brian had zoned out?

"Brian," Ford snapped, restraining him. "What's wrong?"

Brian finally got his hands and brain back on one wavelength so he could speak to his brother and explain why he was acting like a nut. Brian stepped back and took a few deeps breaths. *"That guy... Dana's friend. I'm pretty sure I know him, Ford. I have to talk to—"*

A throat clearing made Brian jerk his hands down and turn towards the entrance to the den. Dana was in thin pajama pants and an old tank top. He had his arm around Sway – his eyes still glassy and unfocused – while his friend helped support his weight. Sway was giving Brian a quizzical look as he gently helped Dana settle down on one of the recliners. Sway adjusted the pillow at Dana's back, ignoring Dana's huffs and pleas to stop fussing over him. Sway took one of the throws and eased it over Dana's thighs.

"Ford, you might want to start a fire. It's gonna be pretty cold tonight," Sway told Ford, tucking the blanket around Dana's legs.

Ford walked over to the fireplace and began to load a few logs.

"I'm not an invalid, Squirt. It's just a headache and a broken wrist." Dana shook his head fondly.

"Shut up, you. I'm still mad at you," Sway hissed at Dana. If he was going for an angry expression, he'd failed miserably. There was nothing but brotherly love all over his kind face. "Scared me and mom half to death. You were all over the news, D."

Brian stood there, enraptured. Sway was a caring man, a nurturer. Brian's soul cried out. After Sway put Dana's bowl of hot soup in his lap, he turned to Brian and looked him up and down with attitude.

PROMISES PART 3

After a few seconds of them playing an interesting staring game, Sway put his pale hands up, his thin fingers zinging a reminder to Brian's foggy brain of what they felt like around his cock. Brian watched in total disbelief and fascination when Sway began to sign.

"So, how do you think you know me?"

Brian wasn't sure he believed it, until he heard Dana chuckling. Brian was frozen. Sway was indeed signing. He knew sign language. Brian's arms hung limp at his sides. He blinked when his brother slapped him in the center of his back on his way past. Brian hoped his hands weren't shaking when he started to answer.

"I'm Brian. Can we talk... privately?" Brian wouldn't dare embarrass Sway and admit in front of everyone that he knew Sway from a seedy sex club. That Sway was the one that'd blown his mind and then run away.

Sway tilted his head, still watching him carefully with alluring brown eyes. Brian almost smiled, remembering how cautious Sway had been before he'd let Brian lead him to their dark nook that night.

"Okay." Sway gestured and headed back towards Dana's bedroom.

Ford gave Brian a look of encouragement when he walked by.

"Wasn't trying to eavesdrop on your conversation, but I caught my name." Sway's hand gestures were majestic. His eyes joined in when he signed.

Brian closed the door and turned back to feast his eyes on his desire. He was so close to walking over and crowding Sway's amazing body back against the corner and grinding weeks' worth of frustration and loneliness out of his body. He'd almost resorted to breaking the law and hacking into street security cameras near the club to track down which direction Sway had gone that night. To maybe get a license plate if he'd driven. But that's not what he was supposed to use his skills for. Not to spy on love interests. That was called stalking. But god did he ache so much. Craved Sway, craved his body, his understanding. Now to add to the list of amazing qualities Brian already respected about Sway, he could also sign.

"How do you know how to sign?" Brian needed to start light, because he had to calm his raging libido before he got within five feet of Sway. He hoped Sway didn't look down, but he seemed to be concentrating on Brian's eyes, anyway.

"My aunt's hearing impaired. She pretty much helped raise me."

Brian nodded. He was moving closer to Sway, his body drawn to him. *"You don't have to sign back to me."* Although Sway spoke beautiful sign language. Long, graceful fingers. Brian preferred his voice. *"I can hear you... But I don't speak."* Brian waited for that to sink in. That should get the gears in Sway's head turning. He couldn't have met very many mute, six foot three men in his life.

Sway's eyes narrowed, he took a couple steps back like he didn't believe the conclusion his brain just came up with. Sway shook his head no, but Brian nodded his yes.

"Can't be."

Brian continued to advance as Sway backed himself into the wall. *"You didn't sign before."*

Sway coughed. His eyes still wide with doubt. His voice wasn't as steady when he replied, "You didn't either."

"If I'd known." Brian was standing right in front of Sway, he slowly brought his hand up and brushed the back of his hand against the feather-soft curls falling along Sway's creamy neck. *"I don't understand how I missed you so much. Why it hurt when I thought I'd never find you."*

"You're a bounty hunter? Jesus. You're so... so big. Your arms... and... oh my god." Sway's face was nestled against

Brian's throat. Every word he spoke was husky and filled with hunger.

Brian continued to run his hands over Sway's hair, along his long, smooth throat, reacquainting himself with all those compelling feelings that'd had him mesmerized from the start. Brian dipped his head and inhaled. *Ahh. Vanilla.* He wrapped his big arms around Sway's shoulders and hugged him to him, embracing him just tight enough to not hurt. Brian rejoiced when Sway melded to him like the perfect glove.

He didn't know how much time passed. Minutes. When Brian began to shake at the feeling of Sway's nimble fingers unbuttoning his collar, Brian squeezed tighter. His scars. Sway wanted to feel his scars again. Brian gulped, cringing at Sway being able to not only feel them but, see them, too. They were ugly, but Sway's words were not.

"I remember everything about that night. I dream about that night. The way you touched me. Like no one has before. I wanted… enjoyed it so much it scared me. I knew I couldn't have you. You were too much man to want me." Sway popped the last button and pressed his lips against the deepest scar, across Brian's Adams's apple. He whispered, his voice pain-filled, "It is you. God. I thought I'd never see you again. I left that night… but I came back. You were gone. I was too late."

He'd come back?

Brian couldn't do the "What if" game right now. All he knew was fate had kissed him tonight. He was taking in everything Sway was confessing. Glad to hear that Sway hadn't been able to dismiss Brian as easily as he thought he had. Brian took a handful of those golden curls at the back of Sway's head and squeezed, closing his eyes in ecstasy. He pulled his hair gently so Sway was forced to look at him.

"I don't know how I remember your eyes. It was so dark in there, but somehow I could still see them." Sway licked and nibbled along Brian's collarbone while he murmured dazedly.

Brian wanted to get his lower body involved. His cock was stretched down his thigh, throbbing against the rough material of his jeans, but he kept his hips still. Sway wasn't here for a one-off. Brian needed to show him he didn't let his dick lead him. Needed to show Sway he knew how to treat a man with respect.

Sway was clinging to Ford's collar, keeping it wide open while he rubbed his jaw along Brian's neck. That silky goatee grazing across his coarse one. How was Sway able to make Brian feel proud of his scars? The way Sway caressed them and tasted them, like he wasn't disgusted by them. What if he knew how he'd gotten those cuts? Would he still feel that way? Brian wouldn't go there with Sway in his arms. Not now. Not ever.

"We have to stop."

Brian leaned down and sank his teeth into the tender skin over Sway's jugular. He pressed harder to show his extreme dislike of that suggestion. Stopping was not happening.

Sway moaned loudly, his breathing became faster and heavier. "Oh my damn. Oh, Brian. I remember that, too. Jesus. Remind me if I like your no better or your yes."

Brian smiled against Sway's cheek. He kissed him gently there. Respectfully. Sway said his name. Brian had never heard a better sound. He wanted to get out of there, get Sway alone. *"Have dinner with me. Right now."*

Sway moaned again, this time it held a hint of anguish. "I can't. I have to get home. I've worked twelve hours today so I probably smell like a rank dog, and my mom's nurse leaves at nine."

You smell wonderful. "I understand." Brian did, but he hated it. He had an unrealistic sinking feeling that he'd have to wait another ten weeks before he saw Sway again.

Sway took his hands from Brian's throat. He looked like he was in a deep internal debate, but he finally stood up straighter and turned those hypnotizing eyes on him. "Dinner sounds nice. Dana has my number. Call me… soon."

PROMISES PART 3

I'm calling, alright. As soon as I get home and get in bed.

Brian walked Sway out the room, his hand held tightly in his. The front room was buzzing with activity. He didn't know how they'd ignored his team's loud, rowdy voices, but he swore he hadn't heard a word back there. Only the sounds of Sway's song-like voice. Brian disregarded everyone's curious looks and the way the conversation came to a dead halt when they walked by. He could see Vaughan sitting on Duke's lap out of the corner of his eye. Quick was rubbing Cayson's back while he redressed the bandage on Dana's head. Ford close by Dana's side. They all had someone.

Finally. This was what he'd chased Sway down for that night at the club. He just wanted a chance. A chance to be happy, too. To not be alone in his silence.

Outside, he opened Sway's car door, but before he let him get in, he had to have him against his body one more time. He wanted a kiss, wanted a deep, lasting taste. He'd managed to wait this long to have Sway, he'd grit his teeth and wait a little longer. The more the wine aged, the sweeter it tasted. He'd have those pretty lips soon enough. He nuzzled the side of Sway's face again, kissing his cheek, lingering there a long time. It was how he communicated. His touches were his words, his love letter. He was telling Sway he was so thankful for this magical night and he couldn't wait to see him again.

Sway leaned back like he'd understood. Crazy thing is, Brian believed Sway truly could hear him. Sway rose up on his tip toes and gently brushed his lips across Brian's. A tease of a kiss. "Soon," he said simply against his lips then ducked inside the car, closing the door.

Brian stepped back and let Sway drive off. Watching him disappear into the chilly night, Brian hated that he didn't know where Sway lived, and he suddenly had an overwhelming feeling to take off running after him. He'd see him again. He deserved this chance. He'd lived through hell. It was time for his slice of heaven. His throat made a clipped noise of longing. Frightened and surprised at the sound, he gripped his neck, swallowing hard at the weird vibrations he'd felt. Had he imagined the sound? He didn't know how long he stood there, his breath ghosting in front of him, stunned. Brian jerked his head up when his brother finally called for him to come back inside. He hadn't realized he'd been staring at where he'd last seen Sway's fading taillights.

Sway. Maybe he was the one. The one who held the key.

PROMISES PART 3

CHAPTER THIRTY-THREE

Dana

"Thanks Doc, I appreciate it. But, seriously. How long do I have to be on these funky pills?"

Cayson put the last of his supplies in his travel bag. "As long as you need them. Switch to over-the-counter when you're ready. Don't suffer though, Dana. You need to be able to rest comfortably to heal. Concussions are a serious matter. You still want to be careful moving around the house. Can't have any dizzy spells where you trip and fall."

"I know, Cayson, you explained all that at the hospital. But my head is doing better." Dana sank deeper into the couch and leaned into Ford's warm side. He made everything so much better. Dana could deal with the discomfort. He just needed Ford's touch. To be engulfed in his scent. Okay, it was time for everyone to leave. He appreciated the visit, but he was ready for bed. He'd gotten all his well wishes. His bosses congratulated him on a kick-ass job, Duke also chastising him for being a bit too overzealous. Duke's partner, Vaughan, brought him five new blu-rays to watch while he was on vacation.

These men gathered in his living room were his family. His team. He loved hunting beside such warriors. He loved all of them with all his heart, but no offense, he needed a break. His mind and his body burned for Ford. They needed time to work on their relationship. It was still so new and fresh, regardless that it'd been simmering for three years. They needed privacy.

PROMISES PART 3

Dana turned his head upwards, catching Ford's attention from his brother. Ford cupped his cheek, leaning down to quickly peck his lips. "You tired, baby?"

"Yes," Dana whispered against his jaw.

"Alright." Ford kissed Dana's temple then eased away from him. He stood up, his deep voice cutting off the chatter. "Thank you, good people, for coming over, but I think it's time for Dana to turn in."

"You just made me sound like I'm ten years old and you're my daddy." Dana frowned at Ford.

"I *am* your daddy," Ford growled right back at him.

The guys roared with laughter, especially when they saw how red Dana got. Everyone began to file out, giving Dana an easy fist-bump on their way by him. Cayson told him he'd be back to check on him tomorrow evening and followed Quick out the door. Ford talked quietly with his brother on the porch for a few minutes, Dana assumed about the crazy scene that had happened with Sway. Dana couldn't wait to hear what the hell that was all about. He'd call Sway, but a phone call would probably bring back his headache.

Dana rested on the couch until Ford finished cleaning up the few dishes that lingered on the table, locked up his house, and turned out all the lights.

"Bedtime, handsome." Ford's deep voice in the darkness made him shiver.

Ford helped him stand up. When he was sure Dana was steady, he let him go to walk on his own. Of course, he was less than an inch away from him. Dana pressed against Ford's side.

Ford rumbled against his mouth. "You're too damn much, you know that."

Dana ground his hard cock against Ford's thigh again. "Yeah, I know," Dana moaned, burrowing into Ford's throat. Damn, he smelled so good. Bold. He couldn't get enough. Even feeling like he did, his body still responded relentlessly to the impressive man. He took his right hand and ran it up Ford's chest until he got to his throat. He stroked him gently there before continuing to his beard where he dug his fingers in. Dana felt his cock leaking in the thin pants he wore. His voice quivered, "I want you, Ford."

An inferno of desire blazed in Ford's onyx eyes. Yet, with the tight control of a SEAL, Ford took Dana's hand away from his face and tucked it against his chest. He carefully turned them around and began to walk them towards the bedroom. Dana could feel Ford's thick erection bumping into him as they moved in unison. He wanted to at least jerk Ford off. His right hand was perfectly fine. But when they were inside the bedroom Ford kept his big hands in neutral zones on Dana's body as he tucked him into bed. He leaned down and kissed Dana chastely.

"Babe," Dana begged.

Ford sat on the edge of the bed.

"When you're healed, baby. I'm taking you away, just like I promised. Taking you someplace warm and bright. Where there are no police sirens, just peace." Ford brushed Dana's hair back and ran his thumb down his face to his cheek. "And when we get there, I'm going to make love to your body on every surface we come to. Inside and outside. Under the stars. Beneath a waterfall. On a beach. In a hammock on our hotel balcony. Everywhere. I'm going to love on you forever, Dana."

With his casted hand lying on his stomach, he took his right and clasped Ford's wrist. He held him while Ford continued to touch him. "That sounds perfect. Where are we going?"

"It's a surprise." Ford smiled a smile that was only for Dana.

"I already know, so you might as well tell me." Dana blinked harmlessly.

Ford shook his head, cupping Dana's cheek with his hand. "Such a damn brat."

PROMISES PART 3

Dana turned slightly and kissed Ford's palm, letting his eyes fall closed, Ford's ruggedly beautiful face fading from view. He was fighting sleep so hard. Doc had given him more pain medicine so his body was finally tolerably numb and his wrist no longer throbbed, but drowsiness was pulling him under fast. He didn't want to sleep. He wanted more of Ford. Wanted to stare at his face and listen to his voice all night. Wanted to feel his hands on him. Dana sighed and let Ford's touch do what it did. He could no longer fight it, he was exhausted, but he felt good. He felt whole on the inside. He dozed into a deep, peaceful slumber, reassured by the words Ford whispered in his ear – comforted that he'd been promised a lifetime with Bradford King.

The End

ALSO BY A.E. VIA

Blue Moon I: Too Good to be True

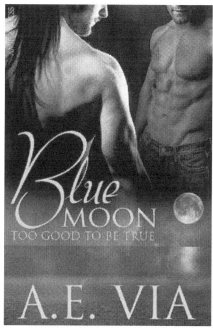

Blue Moon II: This is Reality

Blue Moon III: Call of the Alpha

PROMISES PART 3

You Can See Me

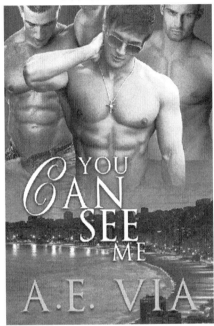

Nothing Special (Nothing Special Book 1)

Embracing His Syn (Nothing Special Book 2)

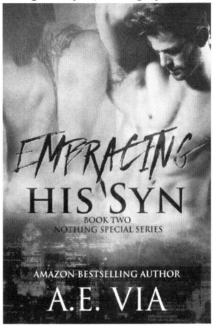

Here Comes Trouble (Nothing Special Book 3)

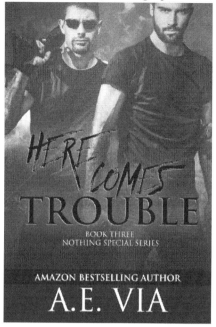

Don't Judge (Nothing Special Book 4)

Nothing Special V (Nothing Special Book 5)

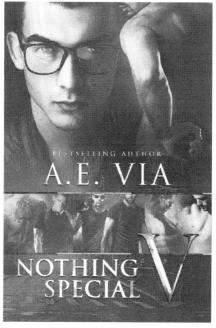

Promises Part 1

A.E. VIA

Promises Part 2

PROMISES PART 3

Defined By Deceit

The Secrets in My Scowl

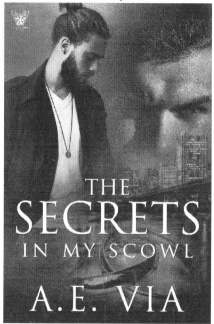

Printed in Poland
by Amazon Fulfillment
Poland Sp. z o.o., Wrocław